IF YOU'RE OUT THERE

IF YOU'RE OUT THERE

KATY LOUTZENHISER

BALZER + BRAY

An Imprint of HarperCollins*Publishers*

Balzer + Bray is an imprint of HarperCollins Publishers.

www.epicreads.com

ISBN 978-0-06-286568-7

Library of Congress Control Number: 2018014218

Typography by Michelle Taormina

20 21 22 23 24   PC/LSCH   10 9 8 7 6 5 4 3 2 1

❖

First paperback edition, 2020

to my bright spots

& to all the friends and fighters out there

IF YOU'RE OUT THERE

From: Zan Martini <martiniweenybikini12@gmail.com>

To: Priya Patel <priyawouldntwannabeya514@gmail.com>

Date: Fri, Jul 6, 11:32 pm

Subject: I'M DOING DRUGS! LOTS AND LOTS OF DRUGS!

Okay I'm not really doing drugs. Just thought this might help get your attention. Seriously, where the heck are you? Read my texts woman! And CALL ME!

From: Zan Martini <martiniweenybikini12@gmail.com>

To: Priya Patel <priyawouldntwannabeya514@gmail.com>

Date: Sat, Jul 7, 4:09 pm

Subject: I'M PREGNANT!!

Someone's gonna be an aunty. . . .

Okay I'm obviously not pregnant. But wtf? Do they not have wifi or phone service in California? We have so much to discuss! How are things with Nicholas Wallace Reid? How's the apartment? And how soon can I come swim in your pool??? You DO realize that this year's impending sucktitude is all your fault, don't you? The least you could do is hit me back!

From: Zan Martini <martiniweenybikini12@gmail.com>

To: Priya Patel <priyawouldntwannabeya514@gmail.com>

Date: Mon, Jul 9, 10:20 pm

Subject: PHEWF!!! SEX TAPE TAKEN DOWN!!!

Okay, really, I promise. That will be the last in this series of delightful announcements. Maybe you're busy unpacking and don't find this as funny as I do (I find it hilarious actually). I considered I'M COOKING METH! and ALL CLEAR GONORRHEA-WISE! But I decided to spare you the mental picture (well, until now). And the meth thing was too similar to the drugs one. And anyway let's be serious—you're the chemist in this relationship.

Since you're clearly DESPERATE for the details of my life, soccer camp was fun, though it did little to alleviate my chronic boylessness this time around (sorry if that's disappointing). Anyway, back to work tomorrow. Did I tell you Whit's moving in? We're going to Michigan next week. It won't be the same without you . . .

From: Zan Martini <martiniweenybikini12@gmail.com>

To: Priya Patel <priyawouldntwannabeya514@gmail.com>

Date: Sat, Aug 4, 11:30 pm

Subject: Hey . . .

Did I do something wrong?

ONE

Tuesday, September 4

I keep coming back to the same shot. A pair of sandy to-go cups, sort of leaning into each other—like a contented couple, looking out at the distant city lights against a watercolor sky. It was May, almost her birthday, and we'd spent the afternoon bundled in sweatshirts on one of Mom's ratty yoga blankets, blowing dollar store bubbles at the lake.

"You know what's weird, Zan?"

The ice in our Vietnamese coffees had nearly melted, the half-filled cups slick with condensation. Priya's eyes were closed, her face bathed in peachy light. She'd used my actual name, which meant she was thinking serious thoughts. Otherwise I'd be ZanaBanana, or Prescription Xanax, or Alexander Zamilton.

"What?" I said, dunking my wand into the suds.

She made a visor with her hands and looked at me. "Before my mom got married, she had your mom down as the person who would get me if something ever happened."

I unpursed my lips, just before the bubble broke. "I didn't know that." I staked the bottle into the sand and brushed my hands clean. "Would I have gone to you guys? If something happened to my parents?"

I felt terrible before she even said it.

"Doubt it. You have a whole family." She flipped onto her stomach. "It's so wild to think about. We would have been like . . . sisters."

I sprawled out beside her. "We are like sisters."

She hadn't quite been her chipper self all day. But I believed her when she smiled and said, "True." She bent down to take a sip without moving her cup. "I guess all roads lead to us."

"Alejandra?"

I'm still lost in the picture—in that day at the lake—when someone clears her throat.

"Alejandra."

I don't recognize my Spanish name at first. Then I glance down at the Sharpied name tag emblazoned across my chest. Señora O'Connell is standing over me, her eyes on the cell phone resting not so subtly against the frayed hem of my denim shorts.

2

I steal a final glance at those happy, sunlit to-go cups on the screen. "Sorry," I say, the word slow to arrive. I slip the phone into my backpack. "I mean, *lo siento*."

Señora O'Connell lets out a clipped breath, as if determined to stay positive. At the whiteboard, she begins scribbling in bright green loops, her ponytail bobbling along as she talks—each orange strand practically screaming, *We're Irish! And no, this is not our first language!* I can't say her accent is all that good—the vowels dull, consonants soggy.

I feel bad for her, though. She's new, and no one's really paying attention. Skye and Ying, fellow soccer girls, are whispering in front of me, while Eddy Hays, resident idiot, has formed a pillow with his hands at the next desk over, not even trying to hide his plans to nap. I guess this year I might as well be new myself. My older friends have graduated. And Priya, well . . . It's going to be a long year.

I'm still observing Eddy, mildly impressed by the boldness of his sleep, when he pops up. "Hey, Zan," he says, as if suddenly confused. "Where's your other half?"

The words sting. "She moved," I tell him under my breath.

Señora O'Connell turns around, the Spanish trailing off. She surveys the room and glances at the clock: still ten minutes before the bell. "Oh whatever." She sighs, her shoulders slumping with the sweet relief of English. She nods to a kid up front and holds out a stack of papers. "Pass these back, will you?"

"Uh. Hello?"

When I look up, a boy is standing in the doorway, all legs and sunken chest, his grown-out blond hair swept back into a short knot. He takes a step inside the room. "I think I'm supposed to be in this class. I was in AP by mistake and it was over my head." His eyes settle on Eddy, who has since resumed his nap. "This seems . . . more my speed."

La Señora tucks the flaps of her cardigan around herself. "I'm going to choose not to take that personally. But hey." She finds a sheet of labels on her desk. "*¡Bienvenido!*" she pronounces, a dry-erase marker flying from her hand as she slaps a name tag on his shirt pocket.

I find myself mirroring the boy's curling lips as amusement flits across his face. "*¿Gracias?*" He bends down to grab the marker from the floor and catches me watching him. I don't look away, and for a moment, he doesn't either. "I think you dropped this," he says, returning the marker to our teacher.

La Señora studies him a moment, through narrowed eyes. "You're one of the nice ones, aren't you? Please tell me you're one of the nice ones."

The boy smiles. "I'm one of the nice ones."

"Manny! Where are my buffalo wraps?"

It looks like a head of purple cabbage has exploded at the salad station.

"Manny?" I had to run to make my shift after school let out, shoving past hordes of Cubs fans as they spilled out from

4

the Red Line. It felt good to run, to think of nothing but the clock. Now I'm hacking away at veggies while my tables wait, enjoying a familiar rush of frazzled self-importance.

"*Hello?*" I crane my neck as I chop. "I need one seitan and one tofu. And table six wants more veg gravy for the meatless loaf."

Manny shakes his head and pulls a basket of zucchini from the deep fryer. "I don't understand these people."

"Just cook the food," says Arturo, entering the kitchen through the swinging double doors. Manny grumbles something in Spanish and reaches a tatted arm to raise the volume on his banda music, which, to my untrained gringa ears, sounds a little like polka and mariachi had a baby.

Arturo slides his messenger bag onto the counter by me. "Busy out there."

"Seriously," I say. "Who knew so many vegans liked baseball?"

He chuckles, wiping the grease from his glasses with the bottom of his checked shirt. "How was school?" he asks. "First day back, right?" My face must give me away. "Aw. Poor Zanny-poo."

"Stop," I say with a deadpan expression I hope will discourage any further sympathy. I scrape a mound of cabbage into a plastic bin and slot it into the salad bar. "I'm handling a serious salad shortage over here. Not to mention a major meatless loaf emergency. The lady at table six says it's dry."

"Wonder why that could be," mutters Manny.

Arturo yells over the trilling trumpets, *"You do know I could fire you, right?"*

"Your own uncle? Please. You don't have the *cojones.*"

Arturo sighs, resigned. "Never work with family, Zan."

I bend down to grab cucumbers from a box on the floor. "Well, related or not, you need to hire another person to do this prep work. This is well beyond a waiter's job description."

"I know," says Arturo. "I've been meaning to. I think I just got used to . . ." He grimaces.

"What?" I say.

"Priya was always doing prep in her downtime. Said she found it therapeutic."

"Yeah, well," I grunt, carrying an armful of cucumbers to the sink for a rinse. "I find it to be a pain in my ass."

Arturo laughs. "You're right. I'll post an ad." He clears his throat as I begin to chop. "Sorry. I know I shouldn't bring her up."

"It's fine."

He hesitates. "Well, I guess . . . While we're on the subject." He fishes through his messenger bag and pulls out an envelope. "Priya's last paycheck keeps bouncing back in the mail. She must have given me the wrong address for the new apartment. Or maybe I took it down wrong. I don't know. Do you have it?"

I swallow, my saliva thick, and wipe my hands on my apron

before pulling out my phone. After a quick search, a June email from Priya comes up.

I know I shouldn't, but I read it anyway.

> Your semi-weekly love letters may be sent to: 418 Bellevue in Santa Monica, Apartment C. Care packages welcome. Send cake. We have one week left, Zan. One week! Wait a minute. WHY AREN'T WE EATING CAKE RIGHT NOW? Okay fine, you convinced me, I'm coming over.

Over my shoulder, Arturo looks back and forth from the phone to the envelope. "It's the same address I have," he says. "I'll check with the post office. Maybe I need the extra zip code numbers or something." He frowns suddenly, looking me over. "Who'd you sit with today?"

For a minute I'm somewhere else, still hazy from her lingering words. "Hm?"

"For lunch. At school. Who'd you sit with?"

"Oh." I'm back to hacking at the cucumber again, just slowly enough to avoid mutilating myself. "I didn't . . . It was nice out. I sat under a tree."

When I glance up, Arturo maintains eye contact in that awful way he does. I think it's all the improv training. He and his teammates share a collective subconscious. They make up instantaneous scenes and say, *Yes, and!* to everything that comes their way. They also sing. In public. Arturo's life is essentially my worst nightmare.

"Can't you sit with the soccer girls?" he asks.

I stop chopping in a huff. "I was the only junior on varsity last year. Everyone I played with graduated. The other senior girls this year are . . ."

"Better than a tree?"

"They're fine is what they are. I'll get to know them when the season starts this spring. Happy?"

Arturo scratches at his stubble. "I think I'm gonna have to cut back your shifts."

"What?" My hand flies open.

"Jesus!" cries Arturo.

I look at my clenched fist, wrapped around the handle I caught midair. A second later and the blade would have pierced one of his canvas flats.

Arturo eyes me warily. "Nice reflexes, by the way."

"Thanks," I breathe. "Sorry."

"What were we talking about?"

"My shifts," I say, still a little dazed. "The ones you cannot take away from me." My heart pounds as I scoop cucumbers into a bin. This job has been my life raft all summer. It was a loophole, or a wormhole, or whatever kind of hole it is that lets your mind go blank.

It's not as if there aren't reminders here. Priya and I applied to this job together—got hired the same week Arturo came on as manager. There were countless shifts, helping each other through dinner rushes, trading stories of our most eccentric customers, collapsing in those sparkling booths at the end of a long night.

But Priya is at home, too. She's at school, at the beach, on every walk through the neighborhood. At least in a restaurant there's no time to think. Because in a restaurant, you've got zucchini and gazpacho and seitan wraps to attend to.

"You took every shift I offered you this summer," Arturo is saying. "You never had any plans! I can't be the enabler here. You're much too young to become a hermit."

"Look. Can we please . . ." I wipe my forehead with my wrist. "I'm drowning here."

Arturo slips on gloves and lets out a sigh. "You're right." He gestures to the knife. "Gimme. . . . Carefully."

"Thanks, boss," I say, the to-do list already buzzing through my mind as I hurry away. Through the crack in the double doors, I peek at my tables, right as Samantha barges in with a bucket of clanging dishes. "Ouch!" I stumble back, the area around my eyebrow beginning to throb.

"Shit! Sorry, Zan." She whips her head back toward the kitchen. "Manny! I need polenta fries and a quinoa burger. And so you all know, I was up studying until three a.m. last night, so nobody bug me!" After law school, Samantha Yun will surely go on to be a state prosecutor, a federal judge, or some kind of badass bajillionaire litigator. But for now we serve Veggie Joes together, and she's pretty much the greatest.

"Hey, you okay?" she asks, swiveling back to me as I cup my forehead.

"Yeah," I say, laughing though it definitely still hurts. Arturo walks up and she lets him kiss her cheek. I avert my eyes out of respect. Sam hates PDA.

"Have you been considering my proposal?" asks Arturo.

"Uh, no," says Samantha.

I perk up. "What proposal?"

"I'm trying to get her to introduce me to her mom," he says, turning to her. "It's not fair, you know. The entire Reyes family practically throws a parade whenever you come over."

I smile back and forth between my adorable bickering work-parents, but Sam just rolls her eyes and walks off to make a salad at the station. "You want to kill my mother?" she asks as Arturo follows, with me at his heels. "You want that on your head?"

"So, what?" he says. "I just have to be Korean?"

"Not necessarily." Sam pauses in contemplation above the shredded carrots. "But maybe like . . . Like a God-fearing anes-thesiologist. That'd be pretty good."

He groans. "At least let her give me a chance. You could take her to one of my shows!"

Samantha gives me a knowing look—the kind that makes me love her. "He really thinks that'll win her over. Watching a bunch of guys in plaid pretend to be a talking spaceship."

"That was one scene," says Arturo, possibly pouting.

Sam softens a little, smiling his way before looking around, as if to regain her train of thought. "Oh right. Some lady keeps whining about veggie gravy."

"Crap," I say. I rush to the back to ladle some out myself and bolt toward the double doors.

"There's a one-top for you, too," Sam calls after me. "Reggie. Table nine."

Out in the crowded dining room, I deliver several salads, even more apologies, and the long-awaited gravy before finding Officer Reginald Brooks at his usual booth. He's sipping ice water in full uniform, his radio crackling.

"Let me guess," I say, not even bothering with the notepad. "Zucchini fritters, extra sauce, vanilla-coconut milkshake. And a side salad so it's healthy."

"It's a common misconception," he says, slapping his stomach. "Vegan and low-cal are not the same thing. My wife finally figured this place out. If you see her, maybe don't tell her about the milkshake. Better yet, I was never here at all. We're on a diet."

I roll my eyes. Reggie is looking lean as ever, strong and clean-cut, his dark skin practically radiating good health. "Your secret's safe with me, Reg."

He nods up at me. "Hey, what's up with you? Something's off."

"Oh," I say. And here I thought my mood was lifting. "I

guess I haven't seen you in a while. It's . . . been a weird few months." I've known Reggie since long before he started coming here—since middle school, actually, when my nut-ball of a mother dragged me into the Lakeview Community Center after a self-defense class let out and asked Reggie—a cop and perfect stranger—if he could teach her eleven-year-old how to box. I was the product of a newly broken home then, and she felt I had some anger to unleash. "It's funny seeing you, actually," I say. "My mom keeps hinting I should pick up where we left off. You know her theories on catharsis." We share a smile.

"Well, I still teach self-defense every Thursday," he says. "However, boxing lessons remain exclusive to scrawny kids with persuasive moms."

"Good to know," I say, walking off. "I'll get your order in."

"Hey!" he calls after me, and I turn around. "How's your shovel hook these days?"

I laugh. "You know? I have no idea."

The air inside my house feels weightless after a walk through the muggy night. I lean back against the door and soak in the stillness. "Hello?" calls my little brother, Harrison.

I round the corner toward the darkened living room. He and Whit are lounging on the L-shaped couch, their legs fanned out in opposite directions, heads together over a shared pint of ice cream.

I smile. "Working hard, I see." They're gazing blankly at

some home improvement show I can't believe my brother likes. I hold my apron over the coffee table and release it, the bulging pocket of loose change landing with a thud. "You two look like you just went through battle."

Harrison sighs up at me like a haggard adult. "We unpacked eight more of Whit's boxes tonight. Eight!" Though disheveled, he's still rocking the bow tie we picked for school this morning.

"Hey," says Whit. "I got you ice cream, didn't I?"

My little brother finishes his bite and looks at her. "Our mom's right, you know. You do have an unhealthy attachment to your stuff."

Whit drops her jaw, somewhere between amused and offended. "Your mom said that?" She narrows her eyes. "Oooo, Alice, you're in trouble. . . ."

I balance against the wall and slip out of my sneakers, tiny foot bones compressed and aching from a long shift. "Where is she anyway?"

"Client meltdown," says Whit. "The woman can't say no." I shudder, in a good way, as a glorious draft from the AC tingles against my skin. "Well?" says Whit, her eyes on me. "How was the first day back?"

"About what I expected."

I settle in beside Harr, and Whit raises the pint. "Pistachio." She's out of scrubs tonight, wearing cutoff shorts and one of Mom's old Flaming Lips T-shirts tied up at the sides. "We made extra lasagna, too. For the workaholics."

"Like mother, like daughter," I say, stealing Harrison's spoon to dig in.

Whit raises an eyebrow as she toys with a shiny, stiff curl of black and brown and gold. "Uh, daughter doesn't have a mortgage."

"Or friends!" I say through an enormous creamy mouthful.

I sort of like how casual Whit is with me. She doesn't get all parental or try to cheer me up. Instead, she lets the comment hang in the air as she presses her lips together. A lot of the time it's like we're still feeling each other out.

Whit's eyes flit to my bare legs glowing in the TV light. "You really didn't leave the house much this summer, did you? I'm honestly worried about your vitamin D."

"Hey now, I left on occasion," I say. "And this is some primo frecklage over here." But she's not wrong. Next to her smooth, brown skin mine looks pretty much translucent. It's something I've come to accept. My dad's olive-toned Italian half must have been off duty when the genes were being divvied up.

"Was your day better than mine?" I ask.

Whit draws a long breath. "Let's see. I had to go in at four in the morning. It was after eleven when I finally got a chance to sit down and drink some coffee. . . ."

"Oof," I say. "That sounds bad. Waking up early is stupid."

"Zan," says Harr, bug-eyed. "S-word."

Whit smiles. "But I delivered a healthy baby. Cute little guy.

Well, big guy. Ten pounds. And the mom was tiny, you should have seen her. Weaker sex my—" She stops, a glint in her eye. "Butt. Weaker sex my butt."

I sink into my brother. "And you, Harr? How was your day? Is Matilda still your girlfriend?" He doesn't answer.

Whit gives a somber shake of the head. "We hate her now."

My brother guffaws, scandalized, and Whit seems confused.

"H-word," I explain with a smirk that says, *Duh.*

My brother burrows against me. It seems he's taking the breakup well. With my cheek resting on his head, I almost forget he's no longer that squishy toddler whose obsessions included tortoises, jelly beans, and Barack Obama.

Keys jingle and a door slams down the hall. *"Hellooo?"*

Mom peeks into the living room. "Oh. Look at that. All my favorite people on one couch." She kicks off her heels and pulls out a set of heavy dangly earrings with mini forks and spoons on them.

"We made extra lasagna," says Harrison. "For the workaholics."

Mom shoots Whit a playful glare, then looks at me. "So?"

"It sucked," I say. My brother gasps again and I slap my forehead. "Sorry! Other S-word!" Mom holds my gaze for a moment, her doe eyes sinking in as if to say, *Should we talk at length in the other room?* To which I respond, *Please, no.*

"And you, my son?" asks Mom. "How was second grade? I'm so sorry I couldn't pick you up."

"It's okay," says Harr. "And it was fine."

She pauses a moment. "What's the Matilda verdict?"

He shakes his head and Mom's bottom lip slides into a pout. "My poor babies." She plants a kiss on Whit before plopping down on the couch, and I get a waft of her coconutty smell. She leans forward to remove a fuzzy orange cardigan. "I thought you guys were going to unpack tonight."

"We did," says Harrison. "Eight boxes."

Mom gazes down the hallway toward Whit's looming towers of cardboard. "Lord help us."

The episode ends and Harr scrolls through the options, pulling up Meryl Streep mid–*Mamma Mia!* where we paused it the other night.

"Can we watch a little more?" he asks. "Now that you're home?"

Mom pulls him close. "You are the perfect son." They snuggle up, and Whit smiles, watching Mom more than the screen.

These two have hardly been able to hide their giddiness since Whit moved in. Their friends say they're like teenagers in love. It's a comparison to which I cannot relate.

Mom met Whit in the hospital cafeteria two years ago, waiting on X-rays for a broken foot. Priya's stepdad, Ben, was supposed to pick up Mom later that afternoon, but she texted that she'd found another ride. I don't know how people do that. Just meet and talk and fall head over heels. For the first few months, we were supposed to believe Whit was a friend. Then at a Cubs game all together one night, Harr leaned across the row to Mom, nodded at Whit, and said, "You love her, don't you?" Mom turned red, and Whit choked on her hot dog.

My phone buzzes and I jump to my feet. I find it buried beneath my apron and promptly deflate. I should know better by now. It's a text from Arturo.

> Okay fine, I'm an enabler. Can you work tmr in addition to your other shifts this week? I'm guessing yes since you've gone all Boo Radley on us? You're taking Thursday off so help me! Ps. For the love of Amy Poehler, talk to some humans at school tmr, k? Abrazos.

I text him back.

> No promises on the human front, but I'll be there. Love Boo.

I slip out into the kitchen to lop off a chunk of lukewarm lasagna, doubling back to swipe my apron from the table. "All right."

"Bed already?" Mom's eyes reveal a flicker of disappointment.

"Yeah. Sorry. . . ." I ruffle Harr's hair and bend down to let Mom squish my face for an exaggerated smooch. Whit just nods. We don't have a bedtime thing yet.

"Sweet dreams," calls my brother as I climb the stairs.

Even once I close the door, I can still hear the murmur of the TV between bursts of happy chatter. When I turn around, I'm not entirely surprised to see a relic of my past resting in the center of the room. It's my old freestanding punching bag, brought up from the basement. I haven't used it since the Reggie days—not since the year Dad moved out. There's a sticky note from Mom.

Kick this year's butt.

I half laugh and drop my apron to the floor, not even bothering to count my tips. Piles of shorts and rumpled T-shirts litter the floor, separated into vague categorical piles of Sort of Clean and I Guess I Should Wash This. It's the room of someone who's only half-awake.

Some photos are taped straight to the pale green paint. Others have been stabbed with tacks, layered over movie stubs and funny birthday cards. Me and Pri in Michigan picking apples in the fall. Pri on Mom's shoulders at the beach because even at age fourteen Priya was still freakishly light. Me and Priya filling water balloons at the park with Harr when he was only three. He called me An. He called her Pee.

I chew my lasagna standing up.

Needs salt, or cheese. But I don't feel like going back downstairs. It's not as if I taste much anyway. My senses have become duller lately. Like it's not quite me who's doing the seeing, the smelling, the tasting.

18

"Blech," I grumble to my plate. "That's enough of you."

A fit of laughter from Mom and Whit comes reverberating through the walls. Harr probably said something cute. I'd drown them out with music but I find that it's no help. Sometimes I think I'm a bad teenager. There's no band that knows my soul. Most of the time I just liked what Priya liked—a step up from "basic bitch" pop, but nothing obscure enough to say, "their old stuff was better."

I stand, slumped, scanning the room for something comfortable to sleep in. Every step seems to require a little too much of me. Wake up! Brush teeth! Speak to people! Do things! I spot the sleeve of an oversize T-shirt poking out from under my bed and, with superhuman strength, crouch down to retrieve it.

A sliver of lime green catches my eye, hidden by all the junk that's found a home down there, and I realize what I'm looking at.

The book feels strange in my hands as I stand. I can't remember the last time I rifled through its pages. I peel open the cover and out jumps the bubbly, gel-penned handwriting of my middle school self.

THE PRINCIPLES OF PRIYA

Even as a tween Priya was so full of grand statements about life—some astute, some downright weird—that at some point

I started writing them all down. The notebook has seen some wear and tear. I turn the page and smile.

#1

Pigs forgive you when it's bacon.

When Priya first spouted this one off, I shot chocolate milk straight through my nose. The way she saw it, pigs were intelligent enough creatures to accept sacrifice for the sake of greatness. In subsequent years, this principle remained the sole exception to her otherwise steadfast vegetarianism.

#2

Hug a lot. Even if it's weird.

We were divided on this issue. Priya lacked my regard for personal space. If she liked you, she hugged you. And some-times it *was* weird.

I skip ahead, to the middle—age fourteen or so.

#126

First the train, THEN champagne.

This was a lesson on the virtues of preparedness, and Priya never let her stepdad live it down. He'd taken us with him to a swanky dinner with some old colleagues who'd flown in from New York. At the end of the night, in a moment of enthusiasm, he paid for the whole table. But when it came time to buy our rides home from the Loop, his credit card was declined. Up on the platform, on the wrong side of the turnstiles, Priya looked disappointed. You would have thought Ben was the kid.

#127

Beware of inspirational bathroom plaques, and the people who put them there.

#128

... Also starfish-shaped soaps.

... Thematic soaps in general.

... Or anything nautical.

I laugh lightly. Priya drew inspiration from Ben's mother for this one. I only met the woman a few times, on her rare visits here and a lone day-trip to her home in Indiana, but she was referenced often—famous for the motivational throw pillows and posters she sent as gifts, each line of pseudo-Buddhist wisdom written out in varied whimsical fonts. Priya also took issue with whimsical fonts. (See *#129: Enough with the whimsical fonts!*)

I flip ahead.

#208
Ladies before mateys!

Priya didn't like calling friends hos (over bros). Or chicks (before dicks). So here she preached in ye old pirate English. To her credit, she lived by this one when she met Nicholas Wallace Reid. I think she didn't want me to feel like I was coming in second. I think she knew she was falling hard. My breath catches a little when I see a burst of Priya's handwriting scribbled beneath my own.

Especially if that lady is Zan.

I slam the notebook shut and chuck it across the room. It lands, uncathartically, with a little plop in a soft heap of dirty laundry. My laptop is already taunting me from the floor beside my bed. It's the same standoff we've been having every night.

And like always, I lose.

I climb under the covers with a familiar sense of dread. I settle back, tap the screen awake, and there they are. Two new photos. The first is painted toes in flip-flops. The caption?

California Dreamin. Maybe everything happens for a reason

Oh, rub it in, why don't you? With poor punctuation, no less. I move to the other—a blueberry tart at an ocean-view table. It's almost humiliating how much the words hurt.

I think I may never go back. . . .

I rush through the other ones—ones I've seen before. So elegantly filtered. Palm trees, and beaches, and California skies. I wish she could hear me as I whisper to myself, "What the fuck, Pri?"

Then I close the laptop and go to bed.

TWO

Thursday, September 6

My bag hits the ground and I plop down beneath my tree. Yes, I know. The loneliness tree. Arturo can suck it.

"Hey, Zan." Skye and Ying wave as they glide up the grassy slope by our school. I spot Lacey a ways behind them, jogging to catch up.

"Oh hey!" she says, stopping when she sees me.

"Hey, Lace."

She rests a moment with hands on knees, a long ponytail of dark brown hair falling forward. "Woo!" She stands abruptly, her head narrowly missing a low-hanging branch. "I need to get myself in better shape before spring. That or get ready to watch me do some serious benchwarming. It'll be nothing new. You always were the talent."

"I'm sure you'll be fine," I tell her. Lacey and I were in the same soccer league in elementary school. We bonded the way little kids do, over nothing important. I liked that her mom brought orange slices to practice. I liked her house. I jumped on her outdoor trampoline.

I squint up as light filters through leaves behind her. A crinkle forms between her eyebrows. It seems I'm being evaluated. "You know, you can sit with us," she says, nodding toward the hill's summit, where Skye is no doubt already peeling off layers to lie out in the sun. I'm sure Lacey's friends will be fine as teammates, but in our brief interactions, I've struggled to relate on any sort of meaningful level.

Skye DeMarco is a far cry from stimulating. I'm pretty sure the girl could talk about Kardashians all day. And then there's Ying Li, who pretends she doesn't know she's extremely pretty and uses words like "heinous" to describe herself. In this little game, I believe you're supposed to say, "What? No way. *I'm* heinous!" And then you and Ying compliment each other for the rest of your lives.

"It must suck with the rest of last year's team gone," says Lacey, scrunching her nose like a cute, concerned bunny. "And I heard Priya moved?" I tense at the mention of her, but Lacey doesn't seem to notice. Actually, her eyes are sort of gleaming now, the way they do when she's prowling for an inside scoop. Sometime around middle school, Lacey became the go-to girl for salacious intel. I do occasionally wonder where her allegiances would lie if the day's big story was ever about *me*. "So, are Priya and her boyfriend doing the whole long-distance thing? I've seen pictures. College guy, right? He's cute. Like, dork-sexy."

I laugh. "I guess you could say that. And yeah, I think that's the plan."

"I have to say, it's weird to see one of you without the other around here."

"Definitely weird." I sigh, miraculously impassive as I glance up the hill. "Anyway, thanks. That's really nice of you. But I've got some reading to do."

"Suit yourself," says Lacey with a shrug. "I'll see you in English?"

When she's gone, I rest against the tree and close my eyes, grateful for the return to silence. A heavenly breeze cuts through the thick, midwestern air and I feel my body start to settle. It's the warm months that remind you that Chicago is nothing more than a paved-over prairie—the flatland held up like an offering to the scorching sun. The hill by our school is the only one I know of. I guess that's why everyone likes it so much. I pull out a paper-topped tin of leftover mac 'n' peas from the restaurant and take a bite.

The truth is, it's pure relief to be alone. Who says solitude is a bad thing? Maybe it's a path toward clarity. Maybe I'm just . . . Thoreau-ing it for a while.

My phone dings, and I perk up like an idiot.

From: Anushka Jha <anushka.gretafund@gmail.com>

To: Yasmine Baker <yasmine.gretafund@gmail.com>,
Ben Grissom <ben.gretafund@gmail.com>, Priya
Patel <pripatel514@gmail.com>, Alexandra Martini
<alexandra.j.martini@gmail.com>, Caroline Sax <csax34@
yahoo.com> . . .

Date: Thu, Sep 6, 12:11 pm

Subject: Let the fundraising BEGIN!

Hey team!

We at Girls Reaching Equality Through Academics are thrilled
to kick off the countdown to our inaugural Teen Volunteer
Summer Term!

So without further ado . . . Let's talk INDIA! Nine months from
now may sound far away, but remember, we have to raise
enough funds to cover flights, housing, food, supplies, and
all additional expenses for six whole weeks! To supplement
your individual savings and crowdsourcing, we'll be holding
monthly meet-ups here in the office to plan events (think bake
sales, auctions, NON-DEGRADING car washes, etc.). And for all
you non–New Yorkers, we're happy to be a resource from afar.
To stay on task, let's get those fundraising proposals in by the
end of the month, shall we?

Also, not to be completely embarrassing, but Yasmine and I
want to send big props to our mini CEO in the making, Priya
Patel. Summer Term was her brainchild, and this year she'll be
taking what we hope will be one of many steps in carrying out

her beautiful mother's legacy alongside her stepfather, our prince and financial wizard, Ben Grissom. (Yasmine is leaning over my shoulder telling me to stop before I get overly emotional, so I will leave it at that. But we are so proud of you, kiddo!)

Welcome to the GRETA Fund family, ladies. You pumped? GET PUMPED!

XO, Anushka & Yasmine

I lean back against the rough bark. India was all Priya and I talked about last spring. But now . . . I shovel in a few bites. I should write them back and tell them I'm not going.

Then again.

The thought makes me stop chewing. Priya would have to face me if I went.

I set the tin aside. No. What if I scared her away? That would be going too far. Not that I think she'd give up so easily.

Sita brought Priya to India only once, when she was little. Years later, Priya still clung to the faded memory—walking with her older cousins along Juhu beach, snacking on chaat and trying to take it all in. There was a time when Priya was excited to show me India herself. She said I wouldn't believe the sweltering summers, the crowds, the colors. I know she was itching to go back.

Anyway, this trip is Priya's baby. She thought it up. Pitched it. Fought for it. Hell, I was there—literally, right beside her on the couch as she made her case via Skype at the monthly GRETA board meeting.

I remember thinking my best friend was kind of a badass that day.

Ben had been particularly skeptical, but I knew she'd wear him down. "Is this even what your mom would have wanted?" he asked from his own computer. We were maybe ten feet apart from him and Priya gave him a *WTF?* look from across the living room.

"What?" he said. "I'm just saying. Do-gooder volunteer trips abroad? I can see kids using it as a photo op. Or, I don't know, a quick résumé builder for college applications. Is that who we want to be?"

Yaz and Anushka frowned into their shared screen, and Priya sat up tall. "Look. I hear what you're saying, but I think we can make this a big enough commitment that people don't treat it that way. And why not let people use their privilege for good? We could be fostering the next generation of people like my mom." I could tell Yaz and Anushka were intrigued, judging by their growing smiles.

I gave Priya a nudge. She had this in the bag.

She shot me a smile and returned her focus to the screen. "From a practical standpoint, this would help us get grants from larger organizations that might not otherwise notice us. Suddenly we're not just a dwindling fund. We're a multifaceted nonprofit, creating opportunities for cultural exchange."

"Our girl has a point, Ben," said Yaz into the camera as Anushka nodded along. "We've been spreading ourselves thin—taking on more schools than ever before. Qualifying for new grants could certainly help."

When their conference ended, I stayed for dinner, and afterward we did homework in the attic. I rarely brought up Priya's mom. It was a kind of loss I couldn't possibly understand, and I never wanted to cause her pain. But that night I thought she should hear it. "Your mom would be really proud of you, Pri." I looked up from my page and she bumped me with her body—a silent *Thanks*. Then she went back to her textbook.

I find GRETA in my contacts and hit the button, ripping out grass as the phone rings and rings. Tempted as I am to stir up drama with a mass reply, it's clear she doesn't want me there. And this is hers. I'll tell them I can't go. It's not a good time. I can't raise the money. They might know I'm lying. The GRETA ladies are practically aunts to Priya. They probably know her side of things.

"Zan?" says a happy voice that must be Anushka's. "That you, sweetheart?"

"Oh," I stammer. "Anushka, hi."

"We've been sprucing up the office. The new phones have caller ID."

"Nice," I say. "How's, uh, how's everything?"

"Oh, you know us. The job never stops. Did you see my email? Got some fund-raising ideas already?"

"Oh, uh. No, not exactly."

She *tsks* into the phone. "How's life apart? Are you and Priya surviving?"

"Well . . ." So she doesn't know. "It's been . . . strange."

"I can imagine. You poor things. There's no one quite like a best friend. Yasmine here is giving me a look, but it's no secret I'm her everything." I hear murmuring in the background. "Watch your mouth, Yaz. We both know you don't mean that." Her chuckle turns to a listless sigh. "Tell Pri to give us a call, will you? We haven't talked since she had bacon cupcakes delivered to the office for my birthday. They were somehow both disgusting and delicious and she was incredibly pleased with herself."

I laugh under my breath. "Sounds about right."

"Listen, dear, we're actually about to jump on a call with Ben. Was there something you needed?"

I sniff and straighten up. "You know, it can wait."

When we say goodbye, I have to pull myself together. *Inhale, exhale* . . . More and more, the stinging eyes and heavy chest come uninvited, out of my control. I guess some part of me hoped Anushka might know. Might slip and tell me everything. Or at least give me a hint.

My phone vibrates with a text and I wipe my eyes with the sleeve of my hoodie. It's Samantha.

Out sick with cramps from HELL. Annnnnd I wasn't the only one to bail so we have no servers. AHHH! I know it's your day off but please say you can sub when you're out of school?

I start to reply when I notice the clock and look up. The hill has mostly cleared out, a few stragglers hurrying inside. "Crap," I mutter. I must have missed the bell. I grab my stuff, dust off my shorts, and bring my trash to the boxy bin by the school entrance. I check my schedule and groan. Even if I hoof it, there's no way I can get to the other end of the building in time.

I hear scuffling behind me and turn around. In the distance, a tall boy trails a much smaller woman on the gravel path. It appears she's straining to drag him by the arm with both hands, like a sack of potatoes over the shoulder.

"Jesus Christ, Bonnie. Would you let go of me? I'm not a little kid."

"Well, you act like one sometimes," says the woman.

"So I took a long lunch. Can we please talk for one second?"

"Nope." She harrumphs and resumes pulling, though it's clear he's letting her. "I didn't go to all this trouble getting you here so you could sit on my couch and watch *Judge Judy* all day."

As they draw closer, I realize that it's him—the lanky blond kid from Spanish class. He didn't come back yesterday. I was actually a little disappointed he'd switched out.

"Don't you have a job you should be at right now?" he asks. They stop a moment and he pulls himself gently from her grip. "Look," he says. "I can't figure out how, but people know."

"How could they . . ." After a pause, she says, "You know what, who cares what people think? Screw people!"

The woman reaches for his arm again, but he shrugs her off. "I'm going, all right?"

I can't seem to stop listening to them, but they're getting close, and before I can even explain it to myself, I'm wedged into the space between the wall and the garbage—which, unfortunately for me, is smelling pretty rank in the hot sun.

The walking has stopped.

"It's just . . . All this high school stuff . . . None of it matters," says the boy.

"Well, good thing you can graduate this year and be done with it forever, then."

They're only a few feet away, and it sounds like I'm right there with them. I hold my T-shirt above my nose to block the smell and try not to make a sound against the scratchy gravel. "You'll be fine," says the woman. "It's a brand-new year. I'm going to leave now."

"Super," says the boy.

"Will you at least try? Please?"

He sighs. "All right."

"That's my good boy. I'll see you at home."

"Yep." After a moment he calls after her, "Now go back to work, you stalker!"

"I will!" she calls out, her laughter trailing off. "But know that I have eyes everywhere."

I hear footsteps pass by, then the door to the school opens.

I wait for it to close, but it doesn't.

Instead I hear his voice overhead. "*Hola,* trash girl. You can come out now. You wouldn't want to be late."

Standing before Señora O'Connell's class, I find myself momentarily frozen—the second latecomer of the afternoon.

"*Ustedes llegan tarde,*" says our teacher: You're late. I cross my arms, uncross them. They're limp, and long. Where do I normally put these things?

Because life is excessively cruel, Lanky Blond Kid did *not,* in fact, switch out of my Spanish class, which means—FUNNY STORY—we were headed for the same place. After I sheepishly stepped out from my spy perch–slash–garbage can, he held the door for me. As I grazed by, I think I managed a quiet "Thank you" to the ground before bending down to tie my already-tied shoe. Once he was a safe distance ahead I walked slowly behind, waiting for him to peel off. But he never peeled. So I just sort of weirdly followed. Very weirdly.

Oh God so weirdly.

Señora O'Connell holds out stapled packets for us both. "You missed the lecture. Pluperfect. It's a hoot." In my utter humiliation I refuse to look at the boy. "There's an explanation at the top if you're lost," says la Señora. "And you can work in groups." I don't say a word. I just take my packet and scurry to the back of the room.

"We missed you in class yesterday," I hear as I slide into a desk. At the front of the room, Señora O'Connell has clamped down on the boy's packet to hold him there another moment. "But I was assured over the phone earlier this afternoon that it won't happen again."

"So you're the rat," he mutters.

"Excuse me?"

"Nothing. I'm sorry. I'll be here from now on. With bells on. *Yo te prometo.*"

"*Le,*" she corrects. "And you were supposed to be one of the good ones." At this, the boy smiles a little. He's pretty cute. Not that I'm looking. "Well, get to work," says la Señora, releasing him. "Seriously. *¡Ándale!*"

I focus on my worksheet as his footsteps approach. And then, to my horror, the chair beside mine screeches, and an outstretched hand comes into view. "I don't think we've properly met. I'm Logan."

After a pause, I peek up and say, "Zan," whilst dying a thousand miserable deaths on the inside. I can't stop picturing myself climbing out from behind that damned trash can. But his eyes are kind, if a little tired. And forgiving, I think. His palm is soft and cool when I take it, and perhaps a bit electric.

We break apart and he settles in at his desk. I tap a pencil against my page, inexplicably compelled to speak again. "Guess that was kind of weird of me back there, huh?"

"What do you mean?" He rubs his jaw as he scans his worksheet, and I realize he's having fun with this. "Ohhhh. Oh, right. The spying thing."

I feel my cheeks go red but push through it. "Was that your mom?"

"Aunt," he says with a flicker of fondness.

"You're new," I say, stating the obvious.

"I am."

"So." I clear my throat. (Why am I still talking???) "Did you guys just move here?"

I fill in a couple more blanks. Yo *había hablado*—I had talked. Tú *habías hablado*—You had talked.

"Me and my sister," he says. "We came here to live with my aunt. We were in Indiana before."

"Oh." I stop short, afraid to say more. I think of Priya and all the questions people used to ask her about Ben. No one could quite grasp how a single white guy wound up raising her. There was a standard line of questioning. Was she adopted? Half white? A foster kid, maybe? It was as if people felt she owed it to them to make herself easier to place. When the story came out, sympathy and praise inevitably followed. Priya was *so brave*. And Ben was a *such* a *stand-up guy*. She never asked for these opinions or for these reminders that her mother was dead. But people had no freaking sense.

"No one died, if you were wondering."

I laugh, a little startled. "You're very direct, aren't you?"

"Oh, that's nothing," he says, staring at his paper again. "Direct would be pointing out how absolutely adorable you find me."

I jolt upright. "Uh, correction. You are not direct. You are delusional."

"Says the girl who watched me from a trash can."

My mouth falls open in mock outrage. "Um, *excuse you*. I was only watching because you were getting *owned* by a woman half your size! Let's be clear about this. I was spying for personal amusement."

"Keep telling yourself that." He's grinning, and it strikes me that I am too.

I hear a grumble and look over to see Eddy Hays perking up from a nap on my other side. "Hey, keep it down over there," he says grouchily.

"Eduardo," calls la Señora from the front of the room. "So nice to see you conscious. Perhaps you can join Zan and Logan's group. Get yourself something other than a zero for the day."

"Sure, why not?" he says, turning to me. He wiggles his eyebrows. "What are we working on, hot stuff?"

"Pluperfect," I say. "Like, for example, *You had been asleep.*

And *I had preferred it that way.*"

The comment doesn't seem to register. "You know," he says, "I'm thinking of switching to your gym class. I hear we're doing ballroom dancing. Let me take you for a spin?"

"Not unless it's my lifeless corpse," I tell him.

"You can't walk away from history, Zan."

I turn to Logan. "Since he's obviously intent on bringing this up in front of you, I might as well get ahead of it. Eddy and I played a round of spin the bottle at a bar mitzvah party once. We were *children* and I puked after."

"You did not," says Eddy, a bit wounded.

Without warning, a wave of ache comes over me, but I try not to show it. I can still picture Priya so vividly—the horror rippling across her face as I winced and bravely accepted the kiss from Eddy, cross-legged in the circle among the discarded yarmulkes and shimmering disco lights.

Like the tweens we were, we'd spent a lot of time pondering what kissing would be like. Priya, especially. The girl was always ready to fall in love. But Eddy was *not* what either of us had in mind.

I can still see us at my house that night as I ferociously gargled mouthwash, Priya watching worriedly from the lip of the tub.

"We need a system moving forward," she said. "Like a code word for *Get me the heck out of this!*"

I spat the blue liquid into the sink. "That could work."

"I propose *blueberry*," she said. "I like blueberries."

"Well, isn't that kind of a problem?" I started to leave, then doubled back. "What if you really want to bring up blueberries? What if it's not a blueberry situation?"

"Good point," said Priya. "We need a neutralizing word." She thought a moment, to the sounds of my vigorous, second-round brushing. "*Rhinoceros*," she said. "If you're actually talking about blueberries, say *rhinoceros*."

"So if I say *blueberry* by mistake, you want me to casually drop the word *rhinoceros* into a sentence."

"Yes," said Priya, her grin broad and unapologetic. "Yes, I do."

ACH!!!

I jump back to the moment.

To the classroom.

To stupid Eddy, puckering by my ear. "You know you miss these lips," he says.

I palm his face and shove.

"All right, all right." Eddy swats me away. "I'm joining Skye and Ying's group. You're no fun."

"Class act, that man," I say wistfully when he switches seats. "With time you could be fast friends." Logan laughs, his green eyes crinkling in the corners. It feels like you've done something right when eyes like that begin to crinkle.

"So what about you?" asks Logan. "Who are your fast friends at Prewitt High?"

My stomach drops a step. Maybe I shouldn't care, but I don't want him knowing I'm a hermit. "Just people. I'm kind of a grazer."

"O . . . kay," he says, like I'm oh-so-mysterious. "Any big weekend plans? Parties I should crash?"

I don't have it in me to make something up, but I try to play it cool. "I'll probably chill. Keep it low-key. My mom's girlfriend and my little brother have been getting into home decorating, so maybe I'll help with some of that."

For a flickering moment, I can tell he's stuck on the word *girlfriend*. It wouldn't be the first time. But then he says, "That's cool," like a code for *Hey, so you know, I'm not a wacko bigot.* "One of my best friends back home has two moms."

"Oh," I say. I appreciate the sentiment, but that's not quite right. "Actually, Whit's not one of my *parents*. Not yet, anyway. I mean I have a dad. He and my mom got divorced when I was a kid. Since, you know, she wasn't really living her truth or whatever."

"Huh," says Logan. "That sounds . . . complicated."

I shrug. "My mom says life is messier than we want it to be. And that sexuality is a spectrum."

Logan knits his brow. "Yeah, I don't think I have a spectrum."

I lift my chin. "How very heteronormative of you."

For a moment we're just smiling. Then he nods to my back-pack. "You gonna get that?" I hadn't noticed, but now that I listen, the inside is buzzing and buzzing. I open the pouch and read through my texts. There's a whole flood of them from

Arturo, and from the number of capital letters he's using, you'd think the restaurant was undergoing some kind of culinary apocalypse.

Guess Sam didn't find that sub.

I text back quickly—**Ahhhh yes will be there ASAP**—and put the phone away before la Señora catches me.

"Everything okay?" asks Logan while he doodles on his page.

"Work," I tell him, thinking a minute. "I need to go as soon as school's over. I bet the bus will be messed up. It's always rerouted when the Cubs play."

"I could give you a ride," he says. "I'm right on the other side of the park."

"Oh," I say. "Um. Are you sure?"

He shrugs. "I've got nothing better to do. Meet me by the front entrance after school."

"Okay . . ." I say, frowning. "Thanks." I stare down at my packet. Did we just make a plan? I'm pretty sure the rule is *don't* get into cars with boys you know nothing about. But Logan doesn't strike me as an ax murderer.

"Hey, what's your deal, anyway?" I ask after a minute. "Why are small women dragging you around places?"

"Oh that?" He smirks. "That's nothing. That's just a thing we do for fun."

"I'm being serious."

"And so am I," he says, moving his pen in scratchy strokes.

41

"There's no deal. Trust me. I'm not nearly as interesting as you are."

I come closer, noting the gorgeous spiral of dark-inked vines he's etched into the margins. "I don't believe you," I say.

Then he catches me looking and turns the page.

"No."

"Yes."

"No."

And there we have it, folks. There is always, always a catch.

"You really think you're hilarious, don't you?"

"What?" says Logan. "It's a loaner from my aunt. The woman has flair."

The turquoise bike is secured to a street sign along the edge of the park, a whole garden of plastic daisies woven into its big metal basket, quivering in the wind. I check my transit app, frustrated to find that the buses have been rerouted as predicted. It's a long walk, and the nearest "L" stop is about a mile from here.

"You see, Logan, when someone offers to give you a ride, that typically implies four wheels and an engine."

"Don't be a wuss," he says, crouching down to jam a tiny key into the bike lock. "It'll be fun."

I let out an involuntary squeak of offendedness. "I am not a wuss. I'm the opposite of wuss. I simply cannot on principle let you put me in that basket. No one puts Zanny in a basket."

"You're being silly, Zan."

"Am I? Okay. Then how about *I* bike and *you* sit in the basket?"

"Maybe because I'm six two?" he says, standing.

"That can't be right." I look him up and down—well, admittedly mostly up. "And anyway, I'm the one who knows the way there," I say. "Plus, this is a woman's bike! *I* am the appropriate driver here!"

"Now who's being heteronormative?"

I glance down and see Arturo's latest text.

HELLLP!! The vegans are rioting!

"Do you want to help get me to work or not?"

"Fine." Logan sighs. "I'll take the basket. For feminism."

I sling my leg over the bar and skid to a park bench, feeling somehow both huffy and pleased. "You can hop on from up here."

I hold us steady and he lowers his narrow hips into the basket, grumbling, "I'm never giving you a ride again."

"I'd hold on if I were you," I say as we wobble down the gravel path. I have to stand to see over him. He's wearing his backpack on his front, like a baby carrier, and each time I lean forward I feel the heat of his skin through his T-shirt.

Without thinking, I cut down Priya's street and feel a sudden dip in my mood as we pass her house. I guess they haven't found tenants yet. The mailbox is stuffed, with newspapers piled at the door.

I speed up, unable to stand the sight, and turn abruptly onto Clark Street.

Logan clutches the handlebars and calls over his shoulder, "In case I wasn't clear, I would prefer to be alive at the end of this ride." I veer to the left to avoid a jaywalker and he grips the handles tighter. "Seriously! I'm really appreciating the fragility of life up here!"

"Don't worry!" A fire engine rips past us and I hike us up a curb, along the sidewalk, and back onto the street.

"We're definitely going to die," he says.

"Back there is Molly's Cupcakes," I call out, ignoring him. "If you're ever in need of a treat. They have swings hanging from the ceiling. It's fun." Priya and I used to go there all the time. I zoom through an intersection and Logan lightly squeals before clearing his throat. "And that's the Crêperie," I say, pointing. "In the summer they have checkered tablecloths on the patio outside. It's like a little piece of France." Another Priya place. I guess they all kind of are.

I turn a sharp corner, past a row of thrift shops and a street performer playing an amped keyboard with looped glow sticks around his neck. "Is he a staple of the neighborhood?" calls Logan.

"Glow-stick guy? Oh, big-time. Out here twice a week at least. Even in the snow!" I'm weirdly enjoying this—whisking this boy away on his bike, chatting him up with the wind in my face.

Even if he does think I'm about to get us killed.

We round another corner, past the little theater where Arturo does his shows. "Please tell me this is almost over."

"It's almost over," I say. And with that, we come to a halt.

"You're a madwoman," pants Logan. Through the window of the restaurant, I can see Arturo wiping down a booth. He looks up, shooting me a bulging stare before running out to meet us.

"I know, I know," I say, catching my breath. "I'm sorry. Are the vegans out for blood?"

"Huh? No, no," says Arturo hurriedly. "I managed to cover all the tables. I'm exhausted, but it's pretty much cleared out. You should have seen this place an hour ago."

I blink, wary. He's smiling like he froze that way. "What's with the face? Why so happy?"

"Zan!" Arturo bugs his eyes at me, like it's obvious, then leans in with a stage whisper: *"I'm not sure if you've noticed, but there's an actual human person with you right now."* He reaches out to shake Logan's hand. "I'm Arturo. I love you already. Please keep hanging out with her. She's been terribly lonely."

"Arturo!" I can feel my face burning.

"I don't mean that in a pathetic-loser sort of way," says my soon-to-be-dead boss, still shaking and shaking and shaking Logan's hand. "Not at all. Zan's the coolest. Way cool beyond her years. We all love her. Although I should warn you she is a bit stubborn, and bossy."

"So I've noticed," says Logan with a smirk. "Logan. Nice to meet you."

"You hungry?" asks Arturo, giving Logan a manly slap on the back.

"He was just leaving," I say.

Logan holds my stare, clearly enjoying this. "Actually, I'm starved."

Arturo opens the door and gestures happily to the inside. "It's all vegan," I tell Logan flatly. "You'll hate it."

"I'm sure I'll find something." He locks his bike to a pole and returns to us.

"Attaboy," says Arturo.

"I'm going to kill you," I whisper to my boss as I slip past.

"Worth it," he whispers back.

Inside it's empty, aside from a group of guys at a four-top still lingering, with cash already thrown down for the bill. "You two sit," says Arturo. "I'll have Manny whip something up." He swipes the other table's check and disappears into the kitchen with a skip.

Logan drums his fingers on the table, admiring the restaurant's glittery booths and poster-plastered walls. Above us, Ella Fitzgerald's voice comes slinking through the speakers—the soundtrack of my childhood, one of my dad's old favorites.

"Cool place," says Logan. I nod, feeling suddenly exposed

and fidgety. Even Ella can't calm me down. Logan studies my face from across the booth. "So . . ."

"So."

"You're on a no-human streak, huh? I must say I'm honored to be the exception."

I look at him, defeated. "Please don't laugh at me."

Logan's expression twists into something like worry. "I wouldn't . . . I wasn't . . ."

"It's okay." He's kind of sweet. "I guess I was having fun . . . talking to you. And I didn't feel like getting into the fact that I'm kind of a depressed and friendless loser at the moment."

"So you're not a grazer."

"Not a grazer. Just got dumped."

Logan frowns abruptly. "Well, then he's an idiot."

"Not a guy," I say, smiling a little. "My best friend. But . . . thanks."

He leans forward, elbows planted on the table. "So what happened?"

I meet his eyes, and it strikes me that I really want to tell him. There's something about Logan. He's so . . . clear. Like staring straight down to the bottom of a lake. And while I have no idea why, he seems to genuinely want to listen.

"Nothing happened," I say. "That's kind of the problem. She moved away. We hugged and cried and said we'd visit every break until summer. We were even planning to volunteer together in India after graduation. It was all we talked about.

And now . . . nothing. She won't pick up her phone, or write back to my texts or emails. It's been months but I still can't get over it. I hate how I feel. It's like nothing makes sense anymore. Like I've lost all control."

Logan nods. "And therein lies the danger in loving people."

"Speaking from experience?" I ask.

"Something like that."

"Being a hermit is definitely the safer option."

Logan thinks a moment. "Maybe she's depressed?"

"She hasn't had the easiest life," I say. "But I don't know. It doesn't seem like it from her posts." I grab my phone from my bag and pull up her account. "If anything, it's like she's being extra happy just to make me feel like crap."

Logan takes the phone to study it. "Priya, huh? She's cute."

I sigh. "As a button."

He gets out his own phone and does some typing. "I'm sending her a follow request."

"What, why? Don't!"

He shrugs. "Too late. Who were all those people she was talking to in the comments?"

"Friends from different places. Model UN, language classes, her dance team. No one I know too well. We didn't really share a group. It was usually just her and me."

He takes my phone back. "Were Priya and Eddy friends?"

"I mean, she tolerated his existence."

Logan studies the screen. "But the two of them . . . They weren't like, close."

"No," I say. "Not at all."

"It's Eddy Hays, right?"

"That's the one."

He turns the screen toward me. "Then why is Priya responding to his comments with little hearts?"

"What?" I lunge across the table. "Give me that."

Priya has posted a photo of a glistening pool, in a valley surrounded by desert. Fifty likes.

eddytheonly Priya, that pool is SICK

thepriyapatel514 @eddytheonly Thanks bud.🤍Miss you!!

"Miss you. *Miss you?!*" For a moment, I'm in shock. "What. The fuck."

Logan's eyes are lighting up. "You should write something, too. How can she keep freezing you out if she just responded to someone else you know?"

"I can't . . . This is so . . ." I'm babbling. "No, it's too weird. And anyway, she's already ignored like a zillion texts and calls from me."

"Then fuck it!" he says. "What's the harm? Say something really simple. Like there's nothing going on between you. Get into her head. This is different than texting. It's public! Make it

a question, so it's weird not to respond." He takes my cell again.
"Can I write it?"

"What? No!" I dive over the table to wrestle the phone from
his hands. "I'll do it. I'll say . . ." He's right. *Why not?* I tap the
space beneath her comment.

zanmartini I'm so jealous! Can I come?

"There." I let out a breath, immediately regretful. God, that
was pathetic. I should delete it. Is it too late to delete it?

"All right!" Arturo is standing over us with both hands full.
"Sweet potato fries, garlic white bean dip with house-made pita
chips, and some fresh-pressed juices. Not too scary, right, pal?"

"Not at all," says Logan. "This looks amazing."

The knot in my gut twists as I glance down at the phone. My
ears have begun to ring. "Anything else I can grab you two? . . .
Zan?" I hear them, but it's like they're far away. "Zan." It feels
like I've been blown backward, blasted straight onto the ground.
"You okay?" asks Arturo, the volume back to normal.

"Yeah," I say, looking up at them. "It's just . . . Priya wrote
back."

THREE

Saturday, September 8

It doesn't make any sense. She said, **Wish you were here!** I said, **Really?** She said, **Of course!** I said, **Can we catch up? Phone call tonight?** She said nothing.

Nothing.

Two whole days of nothing.

Bits of sun sneak in through cracks. I slept till noon, happy to find an empty house when I came downstairs. I foraged for snacks and brought them back up to my room, overcome by the oddly specific urge to stream *Beaches* in my bed. Now, an hour or so in, I brace myself for the Sad Half while the cookie level dips dangerously low on a bucket of Whole Foods oatmeal-raisins.

Priya and I thought Barbara Hershey was so elegant the first time we saw this movie. I remember flipping through cable channels on a lazy Sunday in her attic when we stumbled on the beginning. Something about the rain outside pulled us deep into the story, huddled up under blankets, the golf-ball chunks of hail clacking against the roof. Being twelve, we both quickly identified with Barbara (the Pretty One), but then she died and suddenly being funny old Bette Midler didn't seem so bad. I got choked up while Priya full-out blubbered to "Wind Beneath My Wings." When it ended, we wiped our eyes and laughed, never to speak of it again.

We were still getting to know each other then, but it felt like something miraculous was happening. It was easy, and natural, like we already knew how to be friends.

It was Mom and Ben who brought us together—forced us together, more like. Ben invited us over for dinner as a thank-you, the week he and Priya moved to Chicago, right before the start of seventh grade. Mom had helped Ben find the house here, a convenient walk from ours, and had gone above and beyond to help them get settled. I remember playing with Harrison on the kitchen floor while Mom whipped up a salad to bring with us to their house. She had this frantic energy about her.

"I wish you could have known her mom better," she said, whisking vinaigrette in a bowl and tasting it with her finger. "I have a really good feeling about you and Priya. And after everything those two have been through . . . I really want them to like it here. Priya was such a sweet girl when she was little. Do you remember her?"

"Not really," I said, though I did remember. Our first encounter just hadn't gone that well. We'd met them in Central Park when Mom and I were visiting New York. Priya opted to sit and chat with our moms as I dug for worms alone. She was like that—a tiny grown-up, blazing through chapter books while I was still Seeing Spot Run. She liked puzzles, and clothes, and often wore a purse to match her mother's. I was a simpler child. I preferred dirt.

As Mom and I walked down the block, pushing Harr in the stroller, I remember thinking I had no interest in having someone thrust upon me. But I could feel how important the night was to Mom. She needed to know these people. She needed to help her friend.

So I was polite as I handed Ben a bottle of wine and some sparkling cider when we walked in the door. Mom doled out armless hugs as she held the wooden salad bowl, with Harr on her hip. I trailed behind as Ben began the Tour, and Priya fell into step with me, appearing moderately embarrassed by Ben's enthusiasm for fixtures and new fancy cooking appliances.

As Ben led us onto the back deck, all strung up with lights, it struck me that Priya and I may as well have never met at all. She was someone new.

Over dinner at a glass patio table in the yard, Priya smiled each time Harr stood to reach his plate and smash a banana chunk into his face. Ben grilled enough swordfish, filet mignon, and veggie burgers for a party of ten, proudly donning a manly apron and refilling Mom's wine whenever it got low. He moved his hands a lot when he talked, I noticed—as if everything and anything was exciting.

Mom was doing that rapid-fire-question thing she always does when she's anxious for things to go well.

Priya was quiet through most of it. So was I.

Mom described her therapy practice—the parts she could divulge—and Ben bobbed his head with fascination. Ben told us about his new job, a step down from the Wall Street fast lane. After his old firm had gone belly-up, he felt lucky to have landed on his feet, and he could still help out at GRETA remotely. He and Priya liked the new house. They were getting their first family car—a Prius. They hadn't needed one in New York.

Midway through the meal, the conversation began to slow. You could feel it—a hole. Mom and Ben had one person in common. And that person was dead. After a long pause, Mom leaned across the table and squeezed Priya's arm. "God, you've grown up." She pulled back. "I'm sorry. You probably barely even remember me."

"No, I do," said Priya. "A little."

For a moment, Ben looked sad. Then Mom said, "Hey. I hear you're going to Zan's middle school. How awesome is that? Do you know which homeroom?"

Priya spoke into her plate. "Um. Ms. Haggerty's?"

Mom tapped my arm excitedly. "Did you hear that, Boop? Same one!"

Priya stole a glance at me from across the table, her expression confirming our shared mortification. I smiled. "That's great, Mom." And to Priya, I said, "I hear she's okay."

I startle at the sound of a knock and return to my room—to the movie on my computer.

Another knock.

"Boop?"

It's Mom. I hadn't heard anyone come home.

I hit the space bar and sit up in my bed. "Yeah."

She pokes her head inside, quizzical. "Did I hear Bette Midler?"

I close the laptop and cover it with a pillow. "Nope."

Mom blows a wavy strand of hair from her face, taking in the chaos of my room. "You okay?"

I shrug.

"You know," she says, weaving through piles of clothes on the floor to reach my window. She pulls the curtains apart and zips up the blind. "It's a really nice day out there. If you get out now, you could still catch a couple hours of sunlight."

"True," I say, unmoving.

Mom purses her lips. "Well, if you change your mind I'm here." Her eyes zero in on the bucket of cookies. "I think I'll confiscate these now."

"Fair," I say.

"Hey." Mom stands above me and takes hold of my chin.

"I'm fine, Mom."

"I'm sorry, but in my experience, fine is never fine. Trust me, I'm an expert."

"That'll be a hundred and fifty dollars," I say, but she doesn't laugh.

And then she gets that look of hers—that overwhelming optimism pouring out like a light so bright it makes you want to squint. "Let's go do something. Anything, you name it. Spa treatment? Fancy desserts?" She grabs my laundry basket and starts filling it with clothes from the floor. "Or maybe I'm not what you need right now. Want me to leave for a few hours so you can throw a kegger? I'm not even completely kidding." She hoists the basket on her hip. "I really think I'd prefer a healthy dose of rebellion to the look on your face right now."

I crawl out of bed and take the laundry from her. "I'm sorry to disappoint you, Mom, but I don't think I could draw much of a crowd." I set the basket on my dresser, my back to her.

After a moment, I feel Mom's chin on my shoulder. I glance down at the floor. She's popped up on her tiptoes to reach. Sometime during my colossal ninth-grade growth spurt, my mother became my mini-me. I'm over three inches taller than her, and her skin is not as fair or freckly, but we have the same blue-gray eyes and brownish-reddish hair. Nothing on us is a clear-cut color. People tell us we could be twins, but I think

Mom's face is rounder, sweeter. She's got this glow that makes people fall in love.

I soften, giving her my weight.

"I miss her too," she says into my hair. It's easy to forget I'm not the only one who's lost her. "I think . . . How do I say this? Maybe it all got to be . . . too much. It's a tough time of life to go through without a mom. Add the stress of college applications, moving to a new place, not to mention all those psycho teenager hormones."

I turn around. "Is that a clinical term?"

"I'm just saying, I hope you don't assume this is about you."

"I don't know, Mom. You really think that's all it is? She's . . . sad?"

"Well . . ." Mom doesn't quite meet my eyes. "She used to talk to me. Sometimes."

I frown. "What do you mean?"

"Nothing bad. But . . . Once in a while she would sort of . . . open up. Ask me questions. About the parts of life she wasn't there for, or couldn't remember anymore."

I climb back into bed. I guess that makes sense.

It's the one thing Mom and Priya have always shared without me—memories of this person I wish I knew but didn't really.

It makes me sort of sick to think that Sita was here the weekend before she died. I saw her for a bit that Friday, then spent the rest of the weekend at a sleepover at Lacey's.

I hate picturing Priya at that time. Or Mom, for that matter. She was pregnant with Harr then, and weirdly emotional. Sita came to hang and cheer her up. It's not like Mom made the car hit ice on the way back from Newark, but I sometimes get the sense she feels vaguely responsible.

"Look," says Mom. "I don't know what's going through Priya's head, but I have an idea. I think . . . I think she's figuring out who she is. And sometimes, when a person is struggling with something like that, they kind of go inward. They feel like they need to get some distance from the ones they love. To work it all out. And sometimes they come back, when they're ready. I see it in my work all the time."

"If something was bothering her I would have—"

"I know," says Mom, taking the spot beside me on the bed.

"I would have tried to help. Anything would have been better than this."

"I know," she says. "I hate that you have to feel this. People never tell you."

"What?"

Her eyes grow glossy, but she smiles. "How much it hurts to lose a friend."

I nod through the quiet. "I wish I could remember her."

Mom sighs with that nostalgic, happy look she always gets when she talks about Sita. "They were a lot alike. Only she was more . . . unpredictable."

"Like how?"

"Like . . ." Mom bites her lip, her face lighting up. "I remember once, back when we were roommates at Barnard—we'd been strolling around for hours doing nothing when we passed a free concert in the park. It was early and no one was watching these poor guys play. Next thing I knew Sita was pulling me toward the base of the stage, front and center, the whole area to ourselves. We danced like complete fools, until a crowd finally formed."

I laugh under my breath. "I can see how she and Ben got together, then. Both spontaneous like that."

"Yes and no," says Mom. She settles back against the bed, quiet a minute. "Sita could be impulsive, sure, but she always . . . She had a vision for her life, and she was methodical about it. Same as Priya in that way. Ben . . ." She frowns. "Ben was always the first one to jump when it came to the big stuff. Did you know he proposed only four months after they met?"

"Huh," I say. I didn't. "Yeah, I think I'd need to know someone for like, a decade, minimum, before committing to that. And maybe run a few background checks." Mom's eyes get that knowing glimmer for a second, as if to say, *You'll see, young one.*

"She was so . . . *happy,*" says Mom. "On the phone when she told me, I swear she sounded twenty years old again. They'd been on their way to pick up Priya from a friend's house when Ben passed the perfect ring in the window of Tiffany's. He brought Sita inside, got down on his knees, and begged until she said yes." Mom shrugs and smiles, as if this fact still baffles her a little.

It sounds right to me—the Ben part, anyway. He once brought Priya and me on a cruise to Mexico with only three days' notice. We had fun, though I'm not sure Priya ever recovered from watching him drink from a pineapple while dancing poolside to "Gangnam Style." (I can still see her face. "Dude," she muttered, with a slow shake of the head.) As for the whole "seeing Mexico" thing, I don't think petting a dolphin in a port for a couple of hours really counts, but it's one of the few stamps in my passport (I had to ask—they don't normally do it). Off the ship, other tourists kept coming up to Priya to practice their Spanish, assuming she was Mexican. Priya would sigh in my direction but respond, humoring them, in an accent so good they walked off none the wiser. Priya and I had our own room on that trip, our balcony jutting out over water, next to Ben's. Actually, there was a weird moment one night. I started to go outside when I thought I heard him crying. I never told Priya that. I figured it would just make her sad.

"Well," says Mom, as if coming up from a faraway thought. "Somehow Priya came out sensible."

I sink back against the headboard. "Maybe she got it from her dad's side."

"Maybe."

"You think it bothered Priya more than she let on?"

She pauses a moment. "What do you mean?"

"Her dad," I say. "Not knowing him. You think that could be part of this whole . . . whatever this is?"

Mom starts to say something but stops. "Oh, who knows, Boop?"

"Sita really never talked about him?"

"Wasn't much to talk about."

"I still don't get how she could know so little." This story always bothered me. I see no shame in sowing oats, but a last name seems bare minimum.

"It . . . happens," says Mom carefully. "I don't think the two of them had any plans to, er . . . stay in touch after . . . that night." Ha. Mom is getting awkward now.

"It's so weird to me that you met him," I say. "I don't know how Priya didn't just bombard you with questions all the time. That would drive me nuts."

"Well, it was really only briefly at the bar. I told you about it, right? All MIT kids? The menu on the wall painted to look like the periodic table?" I smile. She's told me on a number of occasions—Mom Brain, as she calls it—but I let her anyway. (P.S. Of course Priya's existence was predicated on a nerd bar.)

"It was supposed to be our big girls' trip to Boston, visiting our college friend Tasha at grad school." For a moment, Mom's expression is far away. "I still wonder whatever happened to Tasha. . . . Anyway, I was too tired to stay out very long. Everyone was giving me crap about it. Later they felt like jerks."

"Because you were actually pregnant with me," I say with a happy sigh. "I know. Thanks for not binge drinking, Mom."

She laughs, blinking in thought. "I do wish I could have talked to him more, though. I remember he wore glasses. And Sita said he got cuter with beer." Mom glares through a smirk. "If you ever do that, I will kill you."

The doorbell rings, and Mom and I look at each other, confused.

"I'll get it," she says. After a moment I muster the strength to get back out of bed. I grab a few handfuls of clothes and shove them in the basket, revealing a few more long-obscured patches of floor. From downstairs I faintly make out the sounds of chatting. And right away, Mom's shouting, "Zan, come down! There's someone here to see you!"

I walk out to the top of the stairs, startled to see Logan by the front door.

I rush the rest of the way down as Mom's eyes dart back and forth between us. There was a reason I didn't invite him inside when I gave myself a ride home on his bike the other day.

"Hi," I say.

He's a bit less raggedy tonight, his hair clean and neatly tied up, his T-shirt free of wrinkles. "Hi," he says back, shrugging with his hands in his pockets, like there's no need to explain his being here.

My mother's eyes sink into me like *OMG who is the cute guy and how come I don't know about him??* I shoot her a look and her face drops. "Right," she says. "Well, I've got some work . . . to do." She walks backward as she talks. "It was nice meeting you, um . . ."

"Logan," he says with a wave as she bumps into the bottom step. I've gone full death-stare now.

"Sorry," she says. "I'm not here."

"You really don't get out much, do you?" says Logan when her bedroom door finally closes upstairs.

I have no comeback, so I say nothing and he follows me to the couch. I feel weird. This is definitely weird. I tug at the hem of my tie-dyed shirt, suddenly wishing I hadn't chosen such tiny shorts to lounge in.

We haven't talked much since Thursday. We were placed in different groups in Spanish yesterday and had to do actual work. I've been pretty distracted these past couple of days, but I can't say I haven't thought about my afternoon with Logan. And seeing him here . . . It's like he has this way of filling up the room. It makes me oddly happy. It also makes me want to hide.

When he sits, I take the opposite end of the couch and grab a pillow for my lap.

"Do you need my Spanish notes or something?" I ask after a weird silence.

"No," he says. "Actually, it's about your friend. Remember how I sent her a follow request the other day? I noticed this morning that she accepted and followed me back."

"Oh," I say, still perplexed by the sight of him in my house.

It feels like worlds colliding.

"Maybe I should have minded my own business, but it was bugging me. The whole story you told me, and how that back-and-forth at the restaurant just sort of stopped. Anyway I got curious, so I wrote a comment on her photo. To see if she'd respond."

"Wait, what?" I snap to attention. "Why?"

"Thirst for knowledge?" he says, shrugging. "A general propensity for distracting myself with other people's lives?"

I frown at him. Logan does this thing, I've noticed, that makes the task of interpreting sarcasm versus sincerity nearly impossible. But right now, I'm too curious to care. "What'd you write?"

"Uh, I think I said, like, 'How's it going?'"

My face falls. "*That* was your comment."

"I admit, it wasn't the most creative line," he says with a grin. "But. Well, that's not why I came over." He moves next to me on the couch and gives me his phone. "Look."

thepriyapatel514 @loganhartist Things are going great! Hope the same is true for you, Logan!!

"It's weird, right? It almost seems like . . ."

Our eyes meet. "She's acting like she knows you."

We sit there quietly for a moment, staring down at the phone. My brain has hit a wall. It does not compute. None of this is right. Is she flirting with a stranger? And what's with all those cutesy exclamation points? Although, I don't know. I sigh. "Maybe she thinks you're . . . cute?"

"I mean." Logan stretches his long legs onto the coffee table, gesturing to himself.

"I take it back," I say, rolling my eyes.

"Can't," he says seriously. "Can't take it back."

"I bet she has you confused with someone else," I say, moving on. "But hey, you've got her talking. Maybe you should write back."

"Okay," he says. "How about this . . ."

loganhartist @thepriyapatel514 A lot of people miss you, you know.

"It's good," I say. "That could get us somewhere."

Logan scans the room. "I like your house, by the way. It's so . . . quiet."

"Quiet, huh? What, is your aunt keeping you up with ragers all night?"

He grins. "Hey. Bonnie can get down when she wants."

I relax into the cushions. "Well, it's usually more hectic here. My little brother's out."

"How old?" asks Logan.

"Seven."

"Huh. My sister's six." He pulls up a picture on his phone.

The girl's hair is even blonder than his, curled into ringlets around a beaming, tiny-toothed face. "Brittany." Our heads almost knock together as I take the phone in my hands, and I get a waft of clean boy smell. Priya loved that smell. #255, was it? *The best ones always smell like soap.* "We call her Bee."

"Cute," I say, feeling suddenly jumpy. I straighten up. "And uh . . . She's in Chicago with you? At your aunt's house?"

"She is." He collapses back into the couch. "She's not too happy about it. New house. New friends . . ."

I nod, all business again. "You should bring her over some-time. Let her meet my brother. Although I should warn you. He's something of a serial monogamist. The kid's had more dating experience than I have."

"Really," says Logan, an eyebrow raised. "Care to elaborate on that?"

"Nope," I say coolly, though I mentally smack my own fore-head—really walked into that one, didn't I? The numbers paint a sad picture. Guys kissed? Just one (unless you count Eddy, which—NEVER). Brian Poulos from my coed weeklong soc-cer camp two summers ago was cute and nice, and from our talks on the phone, Priya thought he sounded deserving of a romantic gesture. It was his last year, so in an effort to get the experience over with, I hit him with a cowardly I'll-never-see-you-again-anyway kiss on the day we were going home. It was a significant upgrade from Eddy's cold-dead-fish lips. The kiss was kind of funny, actually, both of us smiling and self-conscious as we pulled back. But it was also kind of . . . wet.

Afterward I felt no need to gush and cry and call everyone I knew. I didn't start relating to every love song on the radio. Not surprisingly, when it comes to actual boyfriends, the number is a big, fat zero.

Logan checks his phone. "Huh."

"What?" I say.

"Priya again. That was fast."

"Seriously?" My pulse quickens. "Read it."

He clears his throat, appearing suddenly dubious. "Sad face. Heart emoji. 'Miss you guys.'" He blinks. "Okay, she definitely thinks I'm someone else."

"Who?" I throw my hands up. "Who could she possibly be mistaking you for? We don't know another Logan at Prewitt. And who is *you guys*? She didn't have like . . . a big cohesive group or anything. Maybe she thinks you're one of her boy-friend's friends at Northwestern?"

"Older man, huh?"

"Yeah. He's British too, so that makes it extra sophisticated."

Logan thinks a moment as I pout into my throw pillow. "Have you tried talking to him? Maybe he could explain some of this."

"We never met. Wanted to, but it never happened. It's a hike up to Evanston and they'd only been dating a few months when she moved."

"How'd they meet?"

"In a class at Northwestern. Our school ran out of them."

Logan frowns. "Ran out of what?"

"Of classes. Priya is ridiculously smart. In most subjects, but languages especially. The girl speaks like a billion of them."

"A billion, huh?"

"Beyond English and Hindi, she's got Spanish pretty much down. She kept up great with the guys at the restaurant, even the jokes, which are the hardest. She taught herself some French online. And I think she and Nick met learning Arabic at Northwestern. Mandarin and German were on deck. Oh! And she can sign. I think she has it in her head that one day she'll be this, like, master communicator. She told me once that in a perfect world, she would travel all over and speak to every person she met in their own words—no barriers between them. I thought that was so cool." Logan's smile is soft and easy as he watches me talk. It makes me sort of squirmy. "Anyway. By the start of sophomore year she was too smart for the majority of the teaching staff at Prewitt. They didn't even try to deny it."

"So maybe that explains it," says Logan.

"What do you mean?"

"Aren't super-smart people sometimes a little . . ." He spins his pointer finger by his ear and whistles.

"No. Priya is, or at least was . . ." I shake my head. "She was great. Even when life just completely let her down. It never hardened her, you know? She was always loving people, and listening to them, and learning every single thing she could. And now she's this . . . I don't even know! I don't get it. I don't get *her*. And I hate that!" I cover my face with my throw pillow. After a moment, I peek out at him. "Am I crazy for not letting this go?"

"Does it matter?"

"I mean, a little. But hey, my mom's a therapist. Hopefully she can fix whatever damage I'm doing here."

Logan laughs lightly. "Do you want me to write back?"

I take the phone and push through the weepy feeling, scrolling until I find a picture of her face. It's an enthusiastic selfie with a homemade BLT from a few months back. I remember I was right outside the frame when she took this, probably telling her she was ridiculous. Her bright smile takes up the bulk of her face, her skin a warm brown. Her big eyes shine back at me—happy and direct. I want her to hear me. *What is up with you out there??*

I feel a hand on my shoulder and flinch.

"Sorry," says Logan, pulling back. "You looked . . . sad."

"Yeah." I can't quite meet his eyes. "I guess it was naive, but I really thought we would always be friends. Like pregnant-at-the-same-time kind of friends. Not that we were those girls. But we could have been. A version of them anyway."

"Hey," he says after a minute. "You wanna get out of here?"

I pause. "What'd you have in mind?"

He ponders a moment. "How about Evanston? We could explore the Northwestern campus. Maybe find ourselves an Englishman?"

A little rush courses through me. "You'd do that?"

"Why not? You know what he looks like, right?"

"Well . . . yeah." I scroll back further through photos until I find one of Priya posing beside her happy beau, her shoulder-length hair spread out over a blanket on the grassy quad. He's squinting, a hand blocking the sun, his shirt buttoned to the top.

Logan leans in. "Nicholas, huh?"

"That's the one."

I feel a sudden streak of panic. "What?" asks Logan, as if I've said the thought out loud.

"What if we actually find him and he tells Priya that I came searching for him? I've made myself seem pathetic enough as it is."

Logan taps his chin thoughtfully. "Perhaps. But I think there's a certain degree of freedom that comes with the total loss of dignity."

"Hmm," I say. "I suppose that's true."

"Is that a yes?" he asks, standing up to offer me a hand.

I think for a moment. *"Mom! I'm going out!"* I even let him help me up.

Upstairs, a door creaks open. "Really?!" Her giddy voice makes me cringe. "I mean . . . Cool, sure. Be safe. Text me later."

Logan and I share a smile before I notice my grass-stained shorts. "I should change."

"Why? You look fine."

"Ah," I say, already taking the steps up two by two. "But fine is never fine!"

Upstairs I find nothing in my drawers, so I flip the laundry basket over again, returning the semidirty clothes to their rightful place on the floor. I kneel into the pile until I come upon a pair of nice-fitting jeans and a loose white top. I brush the tangles from my hair and catch a glimpse of myself sniffing my pits in the mirror before lopping on deodorant.

Logan's right. No dignity left to lose.

"Okay!" I hurry down the stairs and scoop up my phone and keys. Logan waits by the door as I step into sandals, whip my hair into a high pony, and swipe a set of Mom's dangly earrings from the table by the door. "There," I say. "I feel less gross."

"Way less gross," he says with a smirk as he holds the door open. "Now tell me about our target."

"Right," I say as I lock up and lead us toward the train. "So he's from a suburb outside London, and Priya liked to call him by his full name, Nicholas Wallace Reid, because it made him sound like he was some sort of royalty. Priya thought he was cute in a nerdy way. And I guess he's super-smart. A math major, I think." It's warm out, and the sky is streaked with purple and gold. I can't believe how excited I feel.

I snap my fingers. "You know what—I'm positive he is. I remember because Priya told me he's in an a cappella group with only other math majors. They're called the AlgoRhythms."

Logan chuckles.

"Maybe they have a Facebook page or something," I say, almost giddy. "I'll search for it on the train. If we're lucky, maybe they'll be performing tonight." We stop at a crosswalk and I wait for the little light-up man, shifting my weight from side to side. I'm already antsy. The "L" stop is in view.

"What else?" asks Logan. "If not singing, what would Nicholas Wallace Reid be doing on a Saturday night?"

Finally, the light changes. "I get the sense he's a pretty social guy. Priya said he had joie de vivre. Anything festive and he's there, especially if costumes are involved. Priya's like that too, actually. As of last spring they were already planning Halloween. They were going to go as Napoleon Dynamite and Deb."

As I ramble on, I notice Logan has a funny look on his face, and I stop in the middle of the street. "What?"

"This is fun," he says. He raises an eyebrow. "I feel like a spy."

"Me too," I say, smiling wide. "We're being way creepy, and I love it."

"Excuse me! Hey! *Excuse Me!* Coming through . . ."

My body collapses into itself, impossibly, like a roach through a wall, as I squeeze through the maze of pressed-together people. Turns out the AlgoRhythms have a Twitter account, which provided details for a show earlier tonight. They were to perform along with several groups, but by the time we reached the chapel, we'd missed their set. I didn't spot Nick in the audience, but luckily a young lady from Tonal Destruction told us where most of the groups would be partying tonight.

"Sorry, coming through . . . Excuse me . . ."

We found the building easily enough, but it took us a while to locate the right suite. First we stumbled into a room full of Ultimate Frisbee types, eating bulk trail mix and dried fruits while giggling in a cloud of weed. We tried another party a few doors down, but it turned out all the noise had come from a small gathering of girls taking down-the-hatch shots followed by squeals. The correct room was another floor up. We heard music booming from the stairwell, and once inside I spot several members of the Sexy Pitches as confirmation.

This party appears to be more of a destination, disgusting as it may be. I guess a cappella fans come to rage. The furniture has been stashed away, the floors sticky with beer. The elbows in my back are sharp, the skin grazing mine sweaty. As someone who hates most forms of touching, this is pretty much my hell.

"I said, *excuse me!!!*"

I'm spit out from the crowd onto a patch of open dance floor. A bro-looking dude teeters before me in a worn-out pastel pink cap. "Hey!" I yell over the pulsing music. *"Hey you!"* I hold my phone up to his face, a picture of Nick zoomed in. "Do you know this kid?"

The bro shakes his head through half-closed eyes. "Wan' dance?" he asks, his body swaying slightly.

73

"Not even a little," I call back.

He purses his lips and talks to the floor. "Whatever."

I search for Logan's face before returning to the mob. My foot catches on someone's outstretched leg, and when I fly forward, a row of guys hold their Solo Cups above me like a canopy of swords. I steady myself as the song changes—prompting an excited "*Ohhhhh!*" from the room because new songs are apparently exciting.

I've been to parties, mostly with the older girls from soccer, but even on those rare occasions, you wouldn't find me shooting Jell-O shots or doing keg stands. It's not that I have some big stance on drinking. I just prefer to be in control. And for other people to not be idiots.

I realize my white shirt is glowing under a black light. Everyone's teeth look a little weird. "This is ridiculous," I mutter.

I see the light from another screen glowing across the room. A few girls in tube tops and miniskirts crowd Logan's phone and shake their heads. I watch them eye him hungrily as he heads for the next group. One whispers something that prompts a round of giggles, and I catch myself feeling strangely territorial.

I shake my head—moving on—and elbow my way to another patch of miraculously open space. A small brunette sits on the floor, her legs splayed out as she hurls into a miniature trash can. That may explain the breathing room. The friend holding the girl's hair calls out, "I guess we know she's a lightweight now!"

I crinkle my nose. "I don't envy you tonight!"

"It's my fault! I shouldn't have let her play beer pong. Some people just aren't coordinated." Puke Girl lifts up then, and for a moment the friend appears hopeful. Then the retching starts again.

I feel a hand on my shoulder. "Hey," says Logan. "Any luck?"

"No. This sucks."

He nods to Puke Girl. "We're having a better night than she is."

I hold out my screen to the friend. "You know this kid by any chance?"

She takes the phone with her free hand. "Yeah! That's British Nick!"

I feel my spirits lift. "Do you sing with him?"

"No, but he's in my psych class."

"Oh," I say. "Well, any idea where we might find him tonight?"

"Sorry," she says. "I don't know."

I think a moment. Nick likes festive. . . . What would be festive? "Do you know of any costume parties happening tonight?"

She considers this, and Puke Girl says something in her ear.

"What?" I ask.

"She saw a Tinker Bell earlier. Someone on campus must be doing Disney."

"Perfect," I say, giving Logan a nudge. "Sounds like we have our next party to track down."

"All right, then," he says, scanning the room once more. His face falls.

"What?"

"Nothing," says Logan as I follow his gaze. "Let's get out of here." The kid with the pink cap from the dance floor earlier is shoving his way through the crowd. "Come on," says Logan, ushering me toward the door.

"*Hey!*" calls a voice behind us. Several people look over, and Logan's whole body seems to stiffen with awareness. "I know you from somewhere." When I turn around, Drunk Bro is squinting at us.

I take a step closer. "Yeah. We met like five minutes ago. You asked me to dance?"

"Not you, sweetie." He's grinning. Like douchey-rich-guy-in-an-eighties-movie grinning. He reaches past me to ruffle Logan's hair.

Logan steps back. "Hey, don't touch me, man."

The boy laughs, too hard, and I'm immediately uncomfortable. "Of course. Now I remember. How could I forget those flowing locks? It's my favorite pizza delivery specialist." Logan's expression has gone flat, his nostrils flaring slightly. "Hey, ever'body!" cries Drunk Bro. "Say whatup to Little Caesar over here!"

Logan rubs the back of his neck, his eyes on the ground. "All right, you've had your fun. We're leaving now."

"Who let you in here anyway? I'm pretty sure I'd know if my favorite restaurateur went to my school."

Logan keeps his voice low. "We're just looking for a friend, man. I don't want any trouble."

The boy narrows his eyes, as if fascinated. "You're kind of a pussy, huh? I wouldn't have pegged you for one back in Indy. Although I must say I'm impressed. Your girl's got a sweet ass."

"*Hey!*" Logan and I both yell.

"Let me ask you a question." The boy comes forward, his face inches from Logan's. "If I were to give this lil' baby face a tap"—he hits Logan's cheek lightly, and Logan bristles—"would you hit back? Probably not wise, huh? With your whole . . . situation."

He does it again, but Logan doesn't move.

Again.

"Stop it!" I yell.

Logan doesn't touch the boy. He just turns and heads for the door. The boy calls after him, "What, you don't want a fight?"

He's staring at the back of Logan's head, a wild glint in his eye. Logan pauses a moment, his fists clenched, but keeps walking. And then I see what's about to happen, an instant before it does. The boy draws his arm back, winding up for a cheap shot, and suddenly I'm running into the space between them.

It's pure reflex. With a swift, low jab, I feel the boy's stomach sink—deep, soft. He stumbles back, and I brace myself for a return attack—hands up, elbows low, protecting my face and ribs.

When I learned to fight I'd come to hit stuff, but Reggie couldn't let me walk out without at least a basic self-defense sequence. Wrist to windpipe. Elbow to solar plexus. Knee to groin.

But the boy doesn't come at me. Instead he coughs, doubled over, stumbling back until he hits the wall behind him and slides down to sit.

I drop my stance, raw with shock. I've never pulled a move like this. Not in real life, anyway. I'm out of breath, and somewhere else, thinking of all those days with Reggie—testing jabs and blocks, the weight on my chest impossible to explain to anyone. There were so many nights spent alone in my room, pounding on that heavy bag, until slowly, slowly, the bad drained out. It was okay how Mom always hovered. Or how something in my dad had just extinguished. Maybe the ground was never solid. Maybe nothing and no one was certain. But I had myself.

That was before Priya, of course.

And now, here I am. Again.

The boy gasps for air, still clutching his belly. "You fucking . . . bitch!" It's like I've suddenly returned to this room. People are standing around us, watching and whispering.

I crouch down next to the boy. "You seem like an angry guy. Get help."

I get up and turn to Logan. "Should we go?" He stares as the onlookers begin to disperse, trickling back toward the dance floor.

I lead us down the stairwell and out into the night. Logan's lips stay sort of dumbly parted. "What . . ." He blinks for another moment. "What was that back there?"

"What? You've never met a girl who could fight before?" I may be laying on the bravado a little thick, but I'm kind of enjoying the stunned expression on his face.

There's a distinct reggaeton beat echoing from a distance. I walk in the direction of the sound, and Logan eyes me warily. "Remind me not to make you mad."

We wind our way through the leafy grounds, past sleepy buildings lit by tall streetlamps. This part of campus feels abandoned—enlivened only by the steady chirp of crickets, a reminder of all the life around us we can't see.

I keep glancing to my side. I can feel Logan thinking thoughts. Finally I shove him. "Okay, *what*?"

"Nothing. That was just . . . Thanks."

I watch the pavement, out of words again. The silence is a jarring reminder that we barely know each other. For a moment I have to steal a glance at his face just to remember how we got here.

I clear my throat. "So who was that guy?"

Logan slips his hands into his pockets. "Kid from basketball. We went to the same prep school."

"Prep school, huh? Fancy."

"I was there on an athletic scholarship. But I was in it for the art department. Place was amazing."

"I take it you two didn't get along?"

"We were kind of . . . rivals? I know it sounds ridiculous. It was mostly in his mind. Like he thought we were living out *The Karate Kid* or something. The truth is, I was a better basketball player than him, and I didn't even care. I just wanted to draw. I think that's the part he couldn't handle. When he found out about my job as a pizza delivery boy, he started ordering from us all the time. After a while he started requesting me. It was nonstop. I think he got a little obsessed."

"Couldn't you say no?"

Logan shakes his head, a stray piece of hair falling into his eyes. "I was already pushing my luck at work. There were a bunch of nights I had to cancel shifts to watch my sister. The manager was always pissed at me. He wasn't like your boss. I couldn't risk getting fired. We needed the money."

"So you kept bringing him pizza?"

"Till my last day on the job."

"And it never got old for him."

"Guess not," says Logan. "The guy could really hold a grudge. And he's from the part of town where kids can waste their parents' money on shit like that." We turn the corner and come upon a group of students in a circle on the grass. They're singing Bob Dylan's "Don't Think Twice, It's All Right" with eyes closed while one girl plays guitar. "They seem happy," says Logan.

"Yeah," I say, gazing out. For a second, I wonder what it

would feel like to be one of these "Kumbaya" types, surrendering myself to the night, to the music. I don't think they'd accept me into their little circle. I'd be cracking jokes before we even reached the chorus.

Logan's hand grazes mine and I pull away instinctively. Somehow touching makes me almost as squirmy as people singing their hearts out. Aside from Mom and Harr, Priya was the only other real exception. Maybe she just wore me down, after days upon days of her arms on my shoulders or her feet on my lap. After a while it felt normal. She couldn't invade my space because she belonged in it.

Logan clears his throat, eyeing the gap I've left between our fingers.

"So," I say. I start to walk again, leading us down the path. The distant music echoes off of buildings, drawing closer. "Are you going to play basketball for our school this season?"

"Maybe. I'm pretty rusty. I didn't play much last year."

"How come?"

He kicks a rock in his path and watches it sputter away. "It wasn't really up to me. I kinda got kicked off."

"For what?"

Logan stops walking, and for a moment there's no winning smile or eyebrow raise. "For getting expelled."

I study his face under the light of the moon. "Huh." I wonder if I've just seen a flicker of sadness or if that look was something else. "Are you a bad boy, Logan Hart?"

"Nah. You saw me back there."

I perk up suddenly.

"What?" he says.

"Mulan and Belle," I say. "Twelve o'clock." I pick up the pace as a third friend converges with them along a connecting path, waddling with her legs stuck close together. "Oh my God, it's Ariel! Follow that mermaid!"

We hurry past the glass entrance of a residence hall. I notice someone inside and start to glance back when Logan nudges me, pointing up ahead. A few buildings away from us, the girls are filing in. I spot a Snow White out front, already drunk, crying to a consoling Pinocchio on a smoke break. "Well, this should be good," says Logan.

I hesitate along the path. "No. Wait a minute," I say, turning back the way we came.

Logan follows until I stop in front of the entrance to squint. Amid a smattering of colorful chairs in a brightly lit common area, a boy stands in an undershirt and striped pajama pants, appearing deep in thought.

I get out my phone for reference, checking back and forth. After a moment, a student walks out, and I lunge to catch the door.

Inside, the common space is silent, and I realize the boy is studying a vending machine. He still hasn't moved. Like . . . at all. "Tough decision tonight?" I ask, coming forward.

The boy's shoulders lift for a silent, breathy laugh. "Sadly my evening snack has become one of life's happier moments. Best I choose wisely." He sighs to himself. "Do you have any opinions on Combos? I haven't managed to try them since my arrival to this innovative, snack-tacular country of yours." He vaguely glances back at us before returning his gaze to the rows of snacks. "It's sort of a strange name, *Combos*," he goes on, the emphasis on the word drawing out his crisp British accent. "It's as if they believe it's some unusual accomplishment, combining two foods into one. A peanut butter cup is a combo. So are yogurt raisins. You don't hear either of them raving about it." He thinks a moment. "Then again, I suppose by claiming the name *Combo* you are sort of suggesting that pretzels and synthetic cheese are the *ultimate* combination. So that's something."

Logan's eyes widen, amused, and I smile.

"All right, then." The boy inserts a dollar and presses the button. "I suppose it's time I take the leap." The machine releases the bag, and soon he's reaching down to cradle the snack in his hands like something altogether precious. "Combos, I've put my faith in you." When he turns around, my chest tightens but I take a deep breath.

"I hope they don't disappoint," says Logan. "It's Nick, right? Nicholas Reid?"

"Um . . ." The boy regards us there. "Yes. I'm sorry. Have we met?"

"No," I say, taking another step forward. "But I think we have a friend in common. I don't know if Priya ever mentioned me, but I'm—"

"Zan," he says, his face lighting up. "Of course!" He smacks his forehead with the snack bag still in hand. "I've seen your picture."

"Yes," I say, standing a little taller. *No dignity left to lose.* "I'm sure this is weird for you—me coming here like this. And I don't want to put you in a bad spot or get you in trouble with Priya. But I thought maybe if I came here and spoke to you . . ." I brace myself. "Has she said why she won't talk to me? I hate to ask. But I'm having a hard time dealing with all this. Even if it hurts, I think I really need to know the . . ." I trail off, distracted by Nick's expression. "Why are you looking at me like that?"

"I'm sorry. Really. I wish I could help you. But Priya broke up with me."

My mouth falls open. "What? When?"

"July."

"No way. That's not possible."

"If it makes you feel any better, she won't talk to me either," says Nick.

"I—" I'm stunned. "You have got to be fucking kidding me!"

"Wow," says Nick, pleasantly startled. "Thank you. I felt the same way."

"Wha—" I still can't believe it. "Did she say why?"

He scratches his head, his wispy hair gaining volume. "It was a very efficient breakup. Vague but firm. I know we hadn't been dating that long, but I certainly thought I deserved more than an email."

"She broke up with you over email?"

"I was in England with family, so I suppose doing it in person was off the table. A phone call would have been nice."

"That's so weird," I say. "Did she seem unhappy leading up to it?"

Nick thinks for a moment. "It's hard to say. We'd only been able to talk here and there on the phone in the days before. Tough with the time difference and all. I was actually planning to fly her out to London later that summer, once she got settled into her new place."

"And then just like that . . ." says Logan.

Nick rubs his tired eyes. "Pretty much. For a while she wasn't picking up her phone. I thought she was busy with the move at first, but then I started to get worried. Finally I sent her an email. She wrote back the next day and ended it."

I can't stop shaking my head. "This is not the Priya I know. Even if she couldn't stand you, she's too nice to end things that way. And, dude, she was crazy about you."

"Yeah . . . Well, I hate to think it. But there is another possibility."

"What?"

"I don't know how to put this delicately." He takes a moment to meet my eyes. "Did she ever mention anyone else?"

"No," I tell him honestly.

"Here's the thing." He runs a hand through his fluffy hair. "Before we split up, I sort of . . . peeked at her phone. She was in the other room and her phone dinged and I picked it up. It was wrong of me, I know that, but I was sort of . . . caught in a moment of weakness. Anyway, the contact was just an initial—J. Which I found strange. The message said, 'Can't wait, Priya.' With a happy-face emoji."

"Can't wait for what?"

"Don't know," says Nick. "I never snooped like that again. I put the phone back, and hoped it was a friend of hers. But to be honest, I'd been feeling for some time that there was something she wasn't telling me." Nick somehow manages to look even more miserable.

"Hey. Nick," I say. "Priya's not a cheater."

But as I say it, a flurry of thoughts surfaces. In the months before she left, she'd grown funny about her phone—never wanting anyone to touch it. I'm surprised she left it out that day with him. And there was that time outside the restaurant. I'd heard her laughing out back by the Dumpster, and when I walked out with the garbage, she was clutching her cell phone to her chest.

"Who was that?" I asked.

Her expression shifted suddenly, and she said, "Uh . . . Friend from Model UN."

Nick sighs down at his Combos. "Even with my suspicions, the breakup was still a shock. I really loved her." He opens the bag. "But if you ask me, the part about you is a bigger surprise. She always struck me as a 'sisters before misters'–type girl."

"Ladies before mateys," I say reflexively.

"What?"

I wave him off. "Nothing. You were saying?"

"I guess. Well. From the way she always talked about you . . ." He frowns. "I'd already assumed she was going through something. But to cut *you* out . . . It must be something big."

"Yeah," I say. "Maybe."

Nick furrows his brow as he chews, perking up. "These are actually quite good. Want one?"

I decline, gently, and clear my throat. "Sorry if this is weird, but do you think you could you show me the email she sent you? I'm trying to understand."

"Sure." Nick waves his free hand. "Have at it." He retrieves a phone from deep inside his pajama pocket, does some typing, and hands it over. "Pretty astonishing, really." He collapses into a puffy green armchair by the window. "Five little lines to rip my sodding heart out."

I take the couch across from him, my stomach clamping down with the words.

From: Priya Patel <pripatel514@gmail.com>

To: Nicholas Reid <nick.wallace.reid@gmail.com>

Date: Mon, Jul 2, 9:42 pm

Subject: Re: You okay?

Dear Nick,

I'm sorry it's come to this, but I think we should see other people. Please don't try to change my mind. It's hard to explain
but I can feel myself moving on and so should you. California is
great and I'm happy here. Take care of yourself. --Priya

Logan sits to read over my shoulder. "Brutal. Sorry, man."

I stare down at the screen. "What a"—I can't believe I'm
saying it—"bitch."

"I wonder why she ended things with Nick but left you in
the dark," says Logan.

I shrug. "Maybe she knew I wouldn't take no for an answer."

"I don't know," he says. "She could have put you out of your
misery if she wanted. Or tried, at least."

"Well . . ." Something is nagging at me. "I never actually tried
this email address. We still have our silly old ones from middle
school. We only used them for each other. Martini-weeny-
bikini? Priya-wouldn't-wanna-be-ya? We still loved them, but
we couldn't exactly use them for summer job applications."

Logan appears incredulous. "So, what, you think if you
emailed her on her grown-up account she would have responded

and everything would be normal between you two? You left her voice mails, and texts. Not to mention that whole back-and-forth the other day that she cut off out of nowhere. If you ask me, the girl is playing games."

"No." I scrunch my eyes shut and press my fingers to them. "Priya doesn't do games. She hates games—well, actually she loves games. But games like Taboo and Scattergories . . ." Nick nods appreciatively. "She doesn't play people games." I'm getting flustered. "I don't know why, but it feels like this address might matter." My heart is speeding up. There's a bad, sick feeling creeping up. "And she doesn't sign her name that way."

Nick frowns. "What do you mean?"

I sit up straighter. I don't care how it sounds. "With the double dash. She doesn't do that."

Nick shares a quick glance with Logan, as if agreeing they should proceed with caution. "Zan." Nick says it gently, like I'm either breakable or deranged. "People change. It seems that moving to California has brought out a new side of Priya. One that may have already been in the making, and that neither of us could have anticipated. People get swept up in their lives. They try out different selves. Maybe she's the sort of person who uses double dashes now." He thinks for a moment. "Do you know that people here call me 'British Nick'? Here in this country, at this university, I am British Nick. It's fantastic. Everyone thinks I'm so funny and charming. Someone actually called me 'nerdy-chic' the other day. Me! I referred to a professor as a 'wanker' and had people laughing and fawning all over me. I wasn't especially funny or charming in England. Over there, everyone has this accent. Everyone says wanker, and I am just plain old Nick."

"So you think she's getting swept up in something? Trying out a new identity?"

"Maybe," he says. "It's hard to imagine, but . . . well, who knows? The fact is we can't know. Because she doesn't want to tell us!" He tips the bag up above his open mouth. "I'm coping the best I know how, Zan. I suggest you do the same. The sooner you let it go, the sooner you'll feel better."

I raise an eyebrow. "You just said your nightly snack is the highlight of your life."

"Well," he says with a smirk. "Coping is a process."

"Well, I don't want to cope," I say. "And I'm sorry, but I don't particularly want to let it go either." I take out my phone and start typing as fast as my fingers will let me. "I want her to tell me the truth. I don't care if I look stupid, and I don't care if it hurts. I'm trying the other email address." I begin to check over my message but press send before there's time to change my mind.

From: Alexandra Martini <alexandra.j.martini@gmail.com>

To: Priya Patel <pripatel514@gmail.com>

Date: Sat, Sep 8, 11:54 pm

Subject: Really?

You broke up with Nick? NICHOLAS WALLACE REID?? What is going on with you? Write me back. I'm serious.

"You're wasting your energy," says Nick. He sinks deeper into the armchair. "I've tried that address many, many times, and she's never responded. Not since the one. As much as it kills me to accept this, I think she must really want a clean slate. For some people, when they decide something's done, it's really . . . done."

"You really think so?"

He stares into the empty Combos bag. "I do."

"Well, in that case, you're not as smart as your nerdy-chic accent makes you sound. She responded."

Logan leans into me. "Whoa, seriously?"

For a moment I'm too scared to look. Then I read it and something drops out from beneath me.

From: Priya Patel <pripatel514@gmail.com>

To: Alexandra Martini <alexandra.j.martini@gmail.com>

Date: Sat, Sep 8, 11:56 pm

Subject: Re: Really?

How did you know? It wasn't working out. Nothing's going on. All good. I've just been busy, and to be honest I need a little space right now. It's hard to explain, but I do miss you. Really.

I can feel the blood pump straight up to my face. "She needs *space*?" I hold the phone to my face and shout at it. *"Fuck! You!"* I can feel Nick and Logan watching worriedly as I let my fingers fly:

From: Alexandra Martini <alexandra.j.martini@gmail.com>

To: Priya Patel <pripatel514@gmail.com>

Date: Sat, Sep 8, 11:57 pm

Subject: Re: Really?

Fuck space, Priya. That's fucking bullshit and you know it. I want to talk to you. On the phone. Now. After all these years I think I deserve an explanation. One call and I'll never bother you again. I'm dialing. So pick the fuck up.

I dial her number. Voice mail. "Hey, it's Priya. You know what to do."

"Dammit!" I spike the phone into the couch cushion. It bounces and flops onto the floor.

"Whoa," says Logan. He touches my shoulder lightly. "Deep breaths."

The lump in my throat grows thicker. "Why won't she give me a fucking explanation? Is that really too much to ask?" Logan stares helplessly into my filling eyes.

The phone chirps on the ground and Logan strains to pick it up. Nick's gaze is kind, but I can't bear it. I'm embarrassed by the tears streaking my face.

"She wrote back," says Logan.

I wipe my eyes. "What?" But he just hands me the phone.

From: Priya Patel <pripatel514@gmail.com>

To: Alexandra Martini <alexandra.j.martini@gmail.com>

Date: Sat, Sep 8, 11:58 pm

Subject: Re: Really?

Sorry Zan. I can't. Maybe it's time to move on.

FOUR

Wednesday, September 12

When the last class lets out, Lacey and I converge in the crowd beneath the Exit sign.

"Where are you off to?" she asks brightly.

"To my dad's," I say as people talk around and over us. Everywhere I go, people seem to be jostling one another and making spectacles of their happy teenage lives. I kind of hate them for it.

"Nice," says Lacey. "What are you guys up to tonight?"

The stairwell is nearly gridlocked, but I push ahead. "I might talk him into a game of soccer. It's been forever since we played, but I think I need to kick the crap out of something right now."

"Wow," she says, squeezing through to follow me. "When did you get so intense?"

Since Sunday, Mom has been referring to me as Hurricane Zan, which is fair, I guess. I snapped at dinner when Harrison wouldn't stop telling knock-knock jokes. Kids are never funny when they try to be, and sometimes it's excruciating. I may have asked him to please shut up (GASP! the other other S-word!), and then Mom glanced meaningfully across the table and suddenly Whit was whisking Harr outside for a walk.

Mom and I had a standoff then, and I could feel her resisting the urge to go all "Let's talk while we do this puzzle" clinical therapist on me. I kept quiet, and she was careful to explain that she was more disappointed than angry. I think she was hoping the sudden presence of Logan in my life would turn me all gushy and fluttery until I magically forgot all my problems. I would like to point out that this Disneyesque narrative should theoretically horrify my mother, but I guess now we know what she's really made of.

I blast through the main entrance and out into the day. "Zan!" After a few paces, Lacey catches my arm. "Hey! What's the matter?"

I stop along the dusty path. "Sorry. I'm in a shitty mood."

Lacey stands there a moment. "Do you . . . want to talk about it?"

"I really don't."

She leans in like we're about to share a scintillating secret. "Okay, but does it have something to do with the new kid, Logan? I've seen you two together. He's super-cute. But be careful. I think he's trouble."

I look at her, reluctantly taking the bait. "What do you mean?"

"Okay," she says, her voice dropping low with excitement. "So I did a little online stalking with Skye and Ying when he first got here—as one does. He has like five pictures on his whole Instagram from forever ago but whatever. The point is, Skye recognized a bunch of his followers. Apparently he used to go to the same school as her cousin. Turns out? They had to kick him out of school."

"Yeah, I know," I say coolly.

"Well, do you know he was *arrested*?"

I frown. "Honestly, I didn't ask him for the details, but he seems harmless to me. Not that it matters. We're friends."

Lacey's expression calls bullshit. "I've seen how he looks at you."

"More like acquaintances, actually."

"Liar."

The truth is I've been avoiding him since he saw me cry on Saturday. We took the "L" back together but didn't talk much. I told him not to walk me home. He escorted me anyway, from a few paces behind. I guess because it was late, or because he'd left his bike at my house. Whatever the reason, he didn't try to pull me from my mood.

I skipped school for two glorious days at the start of the week—told Mom I was sick, though she barely believed me by yesterday. Today I went to the nurse's office instead of Spanish—said I had a stomachache and blamed it on a bad breakfast burrito. The nurse didn't seem entirely convinced either, but she gave me some Tums and let me lie down for a while. Logan texted midway through class (**you okay?**), but I never responded.

Lacey raises an eyebrow. "You're telling me there's nothing happening there."

"Not a thing."

I think of Logan's gentle wave from my doorstep. I was mortified that he'd seen me like that, all puffy and splotchy and sniffly. I think he tried to pat my back at one point on the train. That did not go well for him.

I didn't even say good night.

Lacey examines her nails. "Well, if you are lying, which you obviously are, be careful. People say he's dangerous. And sells drugs."

"No way," I say. "Who are your sources?"

"All right," she says, rolling her eyes. "So some of this may be conjecture." I smile. For a gossip, at least Lacey has a sense of humor about herself. Her face lights up. "Speaking of . . ."

I glance back and catch a glimmer of Logan's yellow hair in the distance. Without a thought I yank Lacey by the arm to hide behind a tree. "Ow!" she cries as I shush her. She rubs at the spot where I grabbed her, then pokes out below me to peek.

"Shit!"

He was facing this way, but I don't think he saw us. I sigh.

Lacey's delight is evident. "Acquaintances, huh?"

"Yep." I peer out again. He's walking toward the opposite end of the park, languid, his headphones in, a notebook tucked beneath one arm. I'm relieved as his wiry body gets smaller and smaller and disappears around a corner. "Phewf." I plop down on the ground to rest against the tree trunk, sending a cloud of dusty dirt into the air.

Lacey sighs down at me. "Alexandra Martini, what did you do? Were you mean to him?"

I crinkle my nose. "Maybe a little?"

At this, Lacey slides down the trunk beside me, letting her pristine white jeans squish right into the grass. "Tell me. Is it true you've never dated anyone?"

"There have been guys," I say. "I don't know. Little sparks. But it never goes anywhere. What?" I must sound defensive.

"Just curious," she says, her hands up. "If you wanna talk about it, it would stay between us. Believe it or not, I actually *can* keep my mouth shut from time to time."

"It's fine," I tell her. "Priya used to bug me about it, too. She and my mom diagnosed me with chronic boylessness."

"How is Priya anyway?" asks Lacey. "I've been following. The pictures are so pretty. Does she love California?"

"Yep," I say quickly. It's easier to lie by omission than get into it.

Lacey thinks a moment, then turns to me decisively. "So where *do* you think the chronic boylessness comes from?"

I shoot her a look. "Are you trying to therapist me right now? Because you may remember, I have enough of that at home."

"Oh right," says Lacey. "I forgot about that. I'm just saying. If it's a shyness thing, I would happily coach you. It's all about confidence."

"Well, that's very charitable of you," I tell her.

"Zan." She looks almost stricken. "I didn't mean it like that."

"No, I know," I say, smiling at her. "I'm just giving you shit. Anyway, I wouldn't say it's a shyness thing. It's more like . . . I don't know. Like maybe I'm just not a mushy person. And the thought of *losing* myself to someone? Sounds like a bad idea to me. People suck so much of the time."

"I get that," says Lacey. "I definitely get that. And I guess it doesn't help if the guy in question has a *past*."

She says that last word so dramatically it makes me flustered. "No, that's not . . . I don't know what people are saying, but I doubt you have your facts right."

"Okay," says Lacey. "Hey, if you trust him, I'm on board. I say go for it. Because, honestly, I think people forget—in cases like these, you have to consider the extenuating circumstances."

I meet her eyes, dubious. "Like what kind of circumstances?"

Lacey gets up, brushing herself off. "Like the kind where the guy is just really, really hot."

The track lights in Dad's new condo are dimmed, apart from a single low-hanging lantern that glows above the bright white kitchen table. It feels like Dad wants us to like this place, and I'll admit the Wicker Park location is pretty cool—in a self-aware hipster sort of way. Harr and I each have our own rooms now, which is nice. But it's probably a waste if I'm being honest. We're not here enough for it to matter.

Tonight, though, I'm happy to sleep somewhere that isn't mine—to leave the shit-storm-of-perpetual-misery that is my actual life behind for a night.

"Got any homework?" Dad asks, setting down a stack of plates and a handful of forks and spoons. We've both cleaned up since our one-on-one game. I can't remember the last time we played soccer together, but I was struck by how easily we picked it up again. I think Dad was surprised I suggested it.

Anyway, it turned out to be exactly what I needed—and I totally kicked his ass.

"Not really," I say as I take my seat. "Do you?"

He rips through the staples of a paper takeout bag. "I've got a presentation to go over before bed. Nothing major." Dad's an account executive for an advertising firm, like a modern-day Mad Man without the morning Scotches and submissive secretaries. In fact, I'm pretty sure their receptionist is a dude.

"Anything good?" I ask.

"Toilet paper," he says as he sets out the to-go containers one by one. "We're going with a luxurious angle."

I can't help but grin. "How about 'A little swipe of heaven'?"

He shudders. "You're a natural. . . . Don't be like me." Dad used to write the slogans for his agency—back when he was a "creative." I think he liked that better, but the promotion came with perks, and money, and it's not like cranking out one-liners for plug-in air fresheners ever filled his soul like John Coltrane or Dave Brubeck or Billie Holiday did. His standing bass still rests in the corner by the bookcase, unplayed and out of tune. Mom always says she wishes he'd pick it up again.

"All right," says Dad, crumpling the paper bag and tossing it in the recycling. "Get it while it's hot." He sets out chana bhaji and saag paneer. I take a scoop of both and rip off some naan before making a dash for the lamb vindaloo.

Dad stops my hand. "That's lamb."

"I know," I say.

He frowns. "I thought you were vegan."

"None of this is vegan, Dad. The chickpeas have ghee. And that's cheese in the spinach, not tofu."

"Oh. . . . Sorry."

"Don't be. I'm not vegan."

He still looks a bit puzzled.

"I just work at a vegan place?" I say, jogging his memory with a sigh. There are times my dad seems so in tune with the world around him. And then come the moments when I wonder if he's ever listened to a word I've said.

He mutters to himself—"Right"—and walks back behind the counter to grab a roll of paper towels. "And you're not a vegetarian."

"Nope."

"So . . . why haven't I been ordering more meat all this time? I very much like meat."

"Because of Priya," I say. She usually joined our weekly dinners. I never had to explain myself when I asked her to tag along, but I think she knew. She was a good buffer. She moved the conversation. Kept everything easy and fun.

Dad rips off a paper towel for each of us and I maintain a neutral face despite a sudden bout of misery. "This was her order," I say. "She's the vegetarian. Well, except for bacon."

At this, Dad smiles. "So her love of animals stops at pigs."

"Oh, she loves pigs, too. She just also thinks they're really, really delicious."

"Well, I can't argue with her there." He takes the seat across from me. "So is that whole thing still . . ."

I nod.

He has a look of predetermined regret, like he already knows he won't be able to conjure up the right thing to say. I don't mind. I kind of prefer it, actually. It's a nice break from Mom's X-ray eyes, slapping scans of my broken heart against the illuminated glass for daily checkups. Dad's eyes don't x-ray. In fact, there's a good amount he doesn't see when it's right in front of him.

Harrison emerges from his bedroom in footy pajamas, looking rosy and clean after a bath. Dad gets up to pour a Styrofoam container of mulligatawny soup into a bowl over the sink. He sets it in front of Harrison with some naan on a plate.

"Mmm," says Harr, his arms outstretched at the table as Dad punctures his mango lassi with a straw. "Come to me, my pretty."

"Hey, Harr," I say. "Tell Dad your joke. The one you told me while he was out getting the food."

Harr wipes his soup-covered lips with the back of his hand. "Knock-knock."

Dad grins. "Who's there?"

"To."

"To who?"

Harrison throws his head back with exasperation. "To! *Whom!!!*"

Dad cracks up, holding my gaze for a moment. "That wasn't awful, Harrison. Nicely done."

It's weird watching Dad with Harr sometimes. It's almost like he's picking up where he left off with me after a long, long gap. I never liked the sound of the term *daddy's girl,* but I guess that's what I was once. Until the weather hit below freezing—as it is apt to do in Chicago—Dad and I would play soccer before dinner every night, rain or shine. I remember having inside jokes, hundreds of them. They bounced between us without a thought. I remember Sunday mornings, after pancakes, when the plucky, low sounds of a bass filled our house for hours.

When he and Mom split up, all that went away, so fast it left me winded. He became a visitor. A fun uncle. The place he moved into felt sparse and sad. Harr was only a baby, so Dad never had us for long. He worked a lot. Took trips by himself.

At the very least, we always had our weekly dinner, but something had died. And every week, I got a little angrier. Until it all became numb and normal.

My brother perks up suddenly. "Can I watch a show while I eat? I promise I won't spill."

"Sure," says Dad. "But I'm putting down a towel." I don't know what possessed Dad to buy a white couch, but at least it's cheerful looking. Almost everything in here is new—the rug, the chairs, the dishes. There's an old-fashioned globe at the end of a high shelf full of books. Below is a row of framed pictures, and one is of me, as a roly-poly baby. In the kitchen, there are drawings from Harrison all over the refrigerator.

"So." Dad returns to his seat once Harr is set up. "How, uh . . . How are you?"

I look at him. Frown. "I'm . . . good?"

He blinks, staring at me as if I might detonate at any moment. "I don't want to pry here." He clears his throat. "But uh . . . Your mom called me before you guys came over. And she asked if I might try to . . ." He winces. "Well, she says you've been acting"—oh no, cue the eye roll—"depressed?"

"It's not depression when something bad happens," I spit back. "Then it's just regular old sadness. Mom of all people should know that."

His hands are up. "Of course she does. But I think she's . . .

worried. And she's not the only one." He scratches his head, thinking, and I can feel him winding up for a Talk. We don't do this. I don't know why he thinks we do this. "Believe it or not, I've been where you are before. I've lost a best friend. And so has Mom."

"Mom lost her best friend to a car accident. To life being shitty and unfair. She didn't lose Sita to, I don't know, a choice! To a completely unexplained thing that makes no sense."

He nods, calm, thoughtful. "That's true."

"Priya is *choosing* not to be my friend, Dad. I'm not saying it's worse. I'm saying it's different."

"And I'm sure that's hard. But it doesn't make it any healthier to pick the scab."

I swallow. "Who says I'm picking a scab?"

He hesitates. "Mom . . . She says you still check up on Priya sometimes. Online."

I drop my fork onto my plate. "So now she's spying on me?!"

Harrison looks up from his show and I smile like everything's fine. "*What the hell, Dad?*" I whisper.

"Hey. No one's spying on anyone."

"Then how would she know that?"

I glance over at the couch, where my brother has returned to his TV-induced trance. Dad's eyes fall to the table. "She said you've left Priya's Instagram account up on your laptop a couple times. It was just there—she wasn't checking. But she says this has been going on for months, and, I mean I hate to say this, but

I think maybe it's about time you say to yourself, I don't know, *Message received!*"

"Well, I can't." I can feel the heat rising to my face. "And honestly, I'm getting less and less sad, and more and more pissed off." Dad hasn't touched his food. He's just listening, waiting. "Her posts are so . . ." I'm fighting tears again. "It's like she decided to be this new, bouncy, California chick who wants nothing to do with me. And I just want to know what it is!"

Dad's eyes flit up to search mine. "What *what* is?"

I shrug. "What's wrong with me. Why I wasn't worth keeping in her life. Why I'm so . . ." I look at my lap. "Easy to leave." I clear my throat. "You should see the posts, Dad. It's like she hates the people we used to be." I take out my phone and scroll through her captions, narrating in my best Valley girl voice. "'I kinda miss the changing leaves, but who could argue with forever summer?'" I throw my hands up. "Do you see what I'm talking about? Priya knows perfectly well that *forever* is a noun, not an adjective!"

"Well, technically . . ." He frowns. "Wait, is it an adverb?"

"I don't care, Dad. Listen to the caption on this photo." I hold up an arty shot of color-boosted blueberries in a bowl. "'Berries, not chips! Getting healthy, woo hoo!'" I let out an exasperated groan. "She's so, like, chipper! And she's always writing cheesy crap now. Like, how you have to 'look through rain to see the rainbow,' or whatever." I stare at him, still baffled. "Who has she become? I want her to call me. Or better yet, to come back home and look me in the face. And then I want to scream at her." I meet his worried eyes. "So I'm not depressed. Okay, Dad? I'm furious." I shove some naan into my mouth. "Are we done?"

"Sure," he says.

I chew in silence for a moment, feeling a little like I briefly left my own skin. This isn't me. I don't bare my soul and fight off tears. Especially not here, with Dad.

He gets up to grab the water pitcher from the fridge, and I watch from across the kitchen as he pours two glasses, plus a plastic cup for Harr.

"Who did you lose?" I ask suddenly.

"Hm?" he says, settling back into his chair.

"You said you lost a best friend, too." Dad glances over at me before lifting his fork, and for a second I'm reminded of all the things I don't quite know about him. "Who was it?"

He smiles, almost. "Your mom."

And there it is. "Oh."

"Look." He studies me for a beat, clearly questioning his decision to keep talking. "I know this is hard. And it sucks. But eventually, you will get past this. And . . ." He braces himself. "I know this is a fairly sacrilegious thing to say to a teenage girl, but I think the first step is probably to put down the phone." I laugh as I scroll past another nauseating photo Priya posted this weekend (**Saturday Selfie! Love you, Cali**). She's tilting her head to one side with a mock model face, the blue water stretching out behind her. "Think we could try that?" he asks, reaching across the table to gently pry the phone from my hands.

I sigh with resignation, before my fingers clamp back down around the phone. I study the picture again. Priya's hair is swept back in a ponytail, revealing a pair of chandelier earrings. *Jhumke* in Hindi, she told me once. These are gold with little teal beads—the ones I gave her for her birthday.

My breath catches.

Holy shit.

"Boop?" I don't register Dad's voice at first. He hasn't called me that in years. "Hey. You okay?"

"Can I borrow your car?" I ask.

I interpret his flummoxed expression as a yes. "I'll be right back!" I say, swiping his keys from the kitchen counter and doubling back for another piece of naan.

"Wait . . ." Dad stands as I run around the apartment searching for shoes. "Your food will get cold."

I smash my feet into my sneakers until they're halfway on and make a beeline for the door. "I just need twenty minutes, half an hour tops."

I'm already halfway down the corridor when Dad's voice rings out behind me. "Okay, well . . . Permission granted! But be careful!"

I find the Subaru in the garage beneath the building, wedged into Dad's corner spot near a beam on the passenger side. I press hard on the accelerator and lurch out of the space with a solid inch to spare. Soon I'm barreling down North Avenue, cursing every light and crosswalk.

At the next red light, I have a standoff with my phone on the passenger seat. I bite my lip. I was horrible. I know. But I really want to talk to Logan.

"Come on . . ."

His phone goes straight to voice mail, and I'm surprised by how disappointed I feel. I hit another stoplight and send him a text.

> **Hey so . . . . If you keep hanging around me you will probably pick up on how much I suck at feelings. I'm sorry about before. Would you call me? Seriously—911!**

My phone chirps as I pull onto my street, but it's only Dad, probably worrying about his daughter's questionable mental state. I take the porch steps two by two, and soon I'm hoofing it up to my room.

Mom calls out from the first floor. "Hello?"

"It's me!" I shout. "Forgot a couple things!"

I shut my door and run over to my dresser. There are four small jewelry boxes stacked against the wall, hidden behind books and laundry.

I grab the first one. Mom brought it back from a trip to Denmark years ago. It's shaped like a treasure chest, carved like it's covered with vines. I swipe the dresser clear, sending clothes in all directions. I open the lid and spot the jangly bracelets Priya and I both got as presents from Anushka after one of her trips, back when she still traveled a lot to and from Mumbai, before GRETA hired someone local and the gifts stopped.

I turn the little chest upside down and spread knotted necklaces and mismatched earrings onto the wood surface.

"Dammit."

The next two boxes are less sentimental, the kind that come with cheap jewelry already inside. They yield nothing but some long-retired anklets and a few pairs of hoop earrings that look completely ridiculous on me.

I hold the last box in my hands. It was a handmade gift from Priya, upholstered in silk and bedazzled to the max. Priya always had a thing for bedazzling—posters, picture frames, her cell phone case. My thoughts keep veering off, buying time, and for a lingering moment I'm completely still. Like maybe I don't want to know.

But I do know. I've known from the moment I recognized the picture.

I set the box in front of me on the dresser and lift the lid. A little jolt courses through me and I step back. Because there, atop a heap of tangled chains, are Priya's teal beaded *jhumke* from that goddamned *Saturday Selfie*.

I don't fully remember driving back to Dad's. Some other part of my brain took over and got me there. It even helped me wedge the car back into the parking spot. Harr was still watching his show when I walked in, while Dad scrubbed at the bright white table with a Lysol wipe. He might have asked if I wanted my food reheated, but I think I mumbled "Maybe later" before slipping into my room.

I sink onto the edge of the bed, resting the earrings beside me on the comforter, and check the photo on my screen to compare for the millionth time. There's no mistaking it—they have the same intricate gold base, the same teal beads on chains that form a perfect V.

The more I stare, the more certain I become. That isn't the ocean in the background. It's Lake Michigan. It was that day on the beach on Mom's ratty yoga blanket. The week of Priya's birthday. When our to-go cups watched the sun go down.

I gave her the earrings early, because they were *so her* I couldn't wait. Then she left them at my house, sleeping over one night, and forgot to take them back.

Logan's name flashes silently across the screen. I lift the phone to my ear, unsteady.

"Hey," he says. "I'm downstairs."

My shoulders slump. "Shit. I'm sorry. I'm actually at my dad's."

"I know."

"Huh?"

"Your mom told me."

"What?"

"You said 911, so I biked over. And then she told me where to find you. So I'm here. Are you going to let me in?"

I slip Priya's earrings into my pocket and walk out to the living room, feeling like I've just woken up. I peer down from the floor-to-ceiling windows and see Logan's street-lit figure pacing in the glow.

"You still there?" says the voice in my ear.

I shake my head. "My mother is giving my coordinates to strange men in the night. She must really think I'm lonely." I watch Logan laugh under the streetlight, and when his eyes lift they lock with mine. "I'll buzz you in," I say. "Come to the fourth floor. First one on the left." I hang up. "Uh, Dad? My friend is coming up."

"Oh," says Dad. "Good." He looks me over. "You okay? You seem pale." I want to reassure him, but all I can manage is a nod. After a moment there's a knock at the door and Dad answers, surprise registering faintly across his face. For a moment I see Logan as a dad might—towering over everyone with his messy hair and snug jeans. The long, flat sneakers and purple hoodie zipped to the top. He borders on intimidating when he's serious.

He's the best thing I've seen all day.

"Hello," says Dad.

"He's Logan," I manage to spit out.

"Sir," says Logan, extending an ink-stained hand.

"Please," says Dad. "Just Chris."

"Uh . . ." I'm struggling to click into the moment. After a pause, I gesture toward the couch. "This is my brother."

Harrison glances up briefly from his show. "Pleasure," he says, making Logan's face break into an easy grin.

"Can we, um . . ." I point to the guest room. "I need to talk to you."

I tell myself to keep calm as I lead Logan to the bedroom. "Nice place," he says as I close the door. I shove past him toward the desk and turn on music. I don't need Dad or Harr listening to whatever's about to fly out of my mouth. But as I scroll through my playlist, each track makes me queasy. All songs Priya liked. I click at random. "Paper Planes" by M.I.A.

"Zan. What's the emergency?"

I try to concentrate, struggling to string together all the words getting tangled in my head. *I fly like paper, get high like planes* . . .

The sight of Logan does calm me down a little. It's weird, but I think I missed him.

"Zan?"

"Sorry," I say. "Um. Okay. So the way I see it, there are two ways to interpret this. One—Priya is lying online to make her life seem more interesting than it actually is, or to cover up whatever it is that she's actually doing." I pace the room. "Maybe it's embarrassing or boring or, I don't know . . . super secretive? I'm honestly not an imaginative enough person to work out what that could be. . . . Or, two—" I swallow hard, flinching as the gunshots go off in the chorus. *And take your money.*

"Oh Jesus, this is insane." I plop down on the edge of the bed and hold my head in my hands.

Logan takes a seat beside me and ducks down to meet my eyes. "Can we rewind for a second? I'm pretty lost." He leans over to the computer and lowers the volume a few notches.

I peek up at him. "Promise you won't think I'm crazy?"

He shoots me a reassuring smile. "Promise."

"What if someone else is writing her posts?"

His face grows serious. "Zan . . ."

My hand trembles as I take my cell phone from my pocket. "This picture that she posted . . . It wasn't taken on Saturday. I'm actually pretty positive I was there when she took it. Why would she lie about something like that?"

Logan nods slowly. "Okay . . . Well, is there any chance it's just a similar picture? I mean, don't selfies all kind of look the same?"

"They do. Only . . ." I pull her earrings from my other pocket. "She left these at my house before she moved. I gave them to her. For her birthday. I didn't notice them at first."

For a moment it's as if I can see the thoughts moving across his brain. "Is it possible she replaced them?"

"Maybe," I say. "But . . ." We sit there quietly together, thinking, our legs nearly touching. "All the other pictures she's posted . . . They haven't actually been of her." I scroll through weeks of beaches and sunsets. "All this time I've been saying it didn't sound like her." An eerie feeling is creeping up my throat. "What if that's because it wasn't?"

"So you think . . ." Logan holds up both hands. "Okay, let's back up. Why would someone post from her account? And why wouldn't she stop it?"

"I don't know." I start to stand and then sit back down.

"All right," says Logan. "Maybe this is too obvious, but have you tried calling her parents?"

I open my mouth, then close it. Somehow I hadn't thought of that. "I suppose I could try to talk to her stepdad."

"You have his number?"

"I mean . . . yeah. But what would I even say? Do you call your friends' parents?"

"What if I call?" he says. "I could make up some excuse. See if I can get anything useful out of him before we go jumping to conclusions."

"Okay," I say, nodding through my blurry thoughts. "Yeah, do that."

A knock makes me jump. Dad's voice comes through the door. "You guys hungry? There's plenty of takeout left."

"We'll get some in a little bit!" I holler. Dad's footsteps fall away. "If we're gonna call, we better do it now."

Logan takes down the number on his phone, pausing. "Your dad doesn't think we're like . . . doing stuff in here, does he? I'd like him to understand that I'm classier than that."

"Ew, no."

He laughs and sits up tall, stretching his lips into wide, exaggerated shapes. "Getting into character," he says. "What's his name?"

"Ben Grissom."

"Okay, it's ringing."

"Wait! What are you gonna—"

"I got this," he says, perking up. He raises a finger. "Hello? Is this Ben? . . . Hi. I'm David Johnson. I teach laboratory sciences over at Prewitt High School." His wide smile helps settle my nerves. He's actually pretty convincing. "Oh yes, I am aware. But I'm heading up the yearbook committee for our seniors this year, and even though Priya transferred, we'd like to include her in a few sections. She was such a star student after all. Mm-hm . . . Mm-hm . . . We have few questions for her. Any chance you can put her on the phone?"

My eyes go wide. I am not prepared for this.

Abort! Abort!

"Oh. Well, perhaps you can have her call us back?" I sigh with relief and he scratches his head. "I see." I bug my eyes out—*WHAT?*—and he covers the receiver to whisper, "Her phone broke."

I hover close, trying to listen in, but he waves me away. "Will she be in later tonight?" He raises his eyebrows at me. "Oh. Wow. That must be quite a change from the Chicago public schools. How did that—" He nods. "I see. . . . Mm-hmm."

I wish I could hear the other side. As if reading my thoughts, Logan leans in and whispers, "Boarding school."

"Huh," I say, taking this in. Priya had been researching private schools in California before she left. She figured if she had to make all new friends, she might as well get a leg up for college. "Will you hate me if I get one of those blazers?" she asked one day, Googling places on my bed. "With the little school crest on the pocket?" I told her it would be acceptable, so long as she maintained her sense of irony. Guess that part didn't pan out. Last I heard, there were hardly any transfer spots and most deadlines were long gone. But Ben is one of those connected types. I bet he pulled some strings.

"Well, hey. That's wonderful," Logan is saying. "Yes, have her give us a call when she gets her new phone. . . . Yes, this number. It's my personal cell. . . . Hm? Oh, nice. Indiana, yep." He puts on a snooty expression. "I may be a Harvard man, but it's always nice to have that little reminder of home." I give him the signal to wrap it up. No need for the backstory, Logan. But he winks.

"Hm?" His face falls. He closes one eye and starts counting back with his fingers. "Oh, uh . . . 2001?" His face goes pale and I mouth, *What??* But he relaxes. "Wow. Must have just missed each other."

Oh Jesus. I forgot Ben went to Harvard.

"Haha, yes . . . Er, Go, Crimson." I collapse back onto the bed and cover my face with my hands.

Logan clears his throat. "Sorry—what was the name of Priya's new school again? I didn't catch it before." I peek up at him and a smile beams back. "Got it. Saint Anne's. Wonderful. Tell her we look forward to hearing from her." I sit up, my body prickling with something like excitement.

Logan's face falls. "What's that?" He lunges toward the desk, scribbles on an open notebook, and holds it up.

What's my name???

"Er . . . Sorry. I can't hear you, Mr. Grissom." I jump out of bed and grab his pencil. "I think the call is cutting out a bit. Hello? . . . Hellooo . . . Can you hear me?"

I scratch the words *David Johnson you dummy,* my eyes bulging so violently they nearly launch from their sockets.

"Ah. There you are, Mr. Grissom." I let out a huge exhale and throw myself back onto the bed. I don't think the CIA will be recruiting Logan anytime soon. "What were you saying? . . . My name! Of course. I'm David Johnson, from Prewitt High. Absolutely. I . . . never had the pleasure of teaching Priya myself, but my students have told me so much about her. . . . Mm-hmm . . . Mm-hmm . . . Yes, you too. Have a good evening." And with that, he collapses on his back beside me.

He starts to laugh and I do, too, clutching my belly as I catch another whiff of that boy soap smell.

"You're a terrible liar," I say to the ceiling.

"Yes, I think we've established that tonight." I can still feel him grinning. "Saint Anne's, though. That's something. . . ."

"Yeah," I say, breathing a little easier. "That's something."

FIVE

Thursday, September 13

At a window booth at the cleared-out restaurant, Logan and I are both three Italian sodas deep when we start to go loopy. The glittery table has become something of a work space, covered with papers and used dishes from the afternoon.

One thing has become clear—I am now the *master* of the bullshit call.

For example, "Yes, hello, I'm calling on behalf of my niece, Priya Patel. My brother and I are planning a family vacation to the Wizarding World of Harry Potter in Orlando next month and we're hoping to pull Priya out of school for a few days. This really will be a dream come true for her. I'm sure you've seen her cape. So! How do we go about requesting an excused absence?"

Or, "Good afternoon. This is Dr. Anna Thermopolis, family physician for one of your students—Priya Patel? We recently got back some pre-tty interesting test results, and I'm not sure her stepdad's gonna love them. Trust me—whatever you're thinking, it's worse. I'm talking seriously disgusting stuff. Anyhoo. How might I get these results to her?"

Or better yet, "I'm calling from Guinness World Records. I'm doing a bit of follow-up on one of your students, Priya Patel? Did she mention she holds the world record for most consecutive consumption of human hair? Head hair only, of course. My legal team tells me we're contractually obligated to check in on the state of her gastrointestinal tract. Could you pass along a message for me?"

I keep wavering as to whether all this digging is justified or just batshit stalkerish, but we're in it this far. Between occasional tides of panic, I keep feeling what can only be described as slaphappy. I think I like making Logan laugh.

I sigh into the phone. "Well . . . thank you for your help." The woman clucked and said "Poor dear" when I told her of Priya's newly deceased cat, but a quick search produced no such student for a sympathy card. "You must have the wrong school," she said.

We've been hearing that all day.

"Not your best," says Logan from across the booth when I hang up.

I take off my apron—it's dead in here anyway—and walk to

the bar to refill our sodas. "Even geniuses run out of material eventually. I'm washed up. Old news." I add syrup. "The secretary sends her condolences, by the way."

Logan nods, solemn. "Poor Carl."

"Carl?"

"The cat," he says.

"Ah." I walk back to our table and hand Logan his drink. "Well. To Carl." We let our glasses touch and I slide in across from him.

Logan chews on ice as he studies the printed Google Maps search, scattered with Saint Annes all along the western coast. The margins are covered in phone numbers, scratched out in my lazy loops and Logan's jagged handwriting. "Another one bites the dust," I say, taking the map from him to draw another X.

I slump against the window. Rain streaks the glass, blurring headlights and neon signs against the gloomy sky.

"How many does that leave us?"

"Two," I say, defeated. "And I don't think they're boarding schools. Are there live-in Montessoris?"

Logan wobbles the pencil between his fingers. "Maybe I heard him wrong. Saint Anna's? Saint Andrew's?"

"He never said the school was in California." I tug on my bottom lip. "Maybe it's somewhere really random, like Delaware. Maybe that's why Priya's lying. Who would want to tell the world they go to school in Delaware?"

"Where is Delaware?" ponders Logan. "And what do people do there?"

I shake my head gravely. "No one knows."

I hear scuffling in the kitchen and after a moment the doors to the dining room swing open. Arturo walks over and sets down a bulging takeout bag onto the table behind ours. "Someone should be picking up soon. I think it's for a birthday party. Five orders of chickenless nuggets."

"Those are going to be some disappointed children," says Logan.

Arturo laughs. "Keep an eye out for me, Zan?"

"Sure," I say, scanning the empty dining room. It's early, and the Cubs got rained out. I should probably be mad (I've made exactly twelve dollars in tips so far), but there are worse ways to spend an afternoon. Arturo slips into a jacket and grabs an umbrella from behind the bar. "Where are you off to?"

"Rehearsal with my coach. Remember? My showcase is on Saturday. All solo acts. There's talk of agents coming, producers, scouts. It could be huge for me. There may even be *SNL* people."

"Holy shit," says Logan. "Hey, good luck, man."

I kick him under the table. "You're supposed to say break a leg."

Logan frowns. "People really say that?"

"Yes," says Arturo, a bit bashfully. "At least superstitious people like me. If you could, perhaps you could suggest that I sustain some kind of horrible injury?"

"Okay," says Logan with a smile. "Break your legs. And arms. If possible, please break all of your limbs."

"Thanks," says Arturo. He turns to me. "You'll be there, right? Laughing super hard at everything I say, even if I suck real bad?"

"I'll be there," I tell him.

"And you, Logan?"

Logan smirks in my direction. "Of course. I wouldn't want Zan to go alone. It'll be like a date."

"Not like a date," I say, straight-faced.

"Date adjacent."

"Not date adjacent."

"Date analogous."

"Date antithetical."

"Ooo, good word," says Logan.

I nod. "SAT prep."

Arturo watches happily. "I love this so hard."

The doors swing open and Samantha walks out, her hands buried in her apron pockets. "You off to rehearsal?"

"Yeah," says Arturo.

They kiss quickly. After a pause she says, "You'll be great," like giving compliments is just a tiny bit painful.

Logan glances at the clock above. "Crap. I better go, too. I have to pick up my sister from after-school." He stands and slips a pen into his bag. "But uh . . . Thanks for the sodas."

Samantha hesitates a moment, then walks to the takeout bag on the next table over. "These the chickenless nuggets?"

"In all their glory," I say.

She and Arturo share a look. "You know what? It's dead in here. There's no sense in both of us staying, and I've got studying to keep me busy. You should go with your"—Logan slips a sweatshirt overhead and Sam smirks my way—"friend."

"Oh yeah, you should," says Logan, popping through the neckhole. "That'd be great. You could meet my sister. Stay for dinner. She'll love it."

A part of me wants to disappoint my smug, smiling colleague with her all-knowing face, but something makes me say, "Sure," and before I can change my mind, I head for the kitchen to clock out.

I. Am. The champion!

But I'm too out of breath to gloat.

I'm soaked and dripping inside the school entrance, heaving as I grip the banister. We sprinted the whole way from where the bus dropped us, an edge of giddy competition coursing palpably between us. "Goddamn," says Logan. The doors click shut behind us, silencing the rain. He pushes back the wet hair clinging to his forehead. "You're fast."

"Yeah," I pant, swallowing hard. "I'm a sore loser too. So it's a good thing I whupped you."

"Hey now," he says, still winded. "I think we both know . . .

that 'whupped' . . . is an overstatement. Also, it wasn't . . . a race."

"Losers always say it wasn't a race."

"Fine," he concedes with a grin. "But for the record, you're also a sore winner."

Pleased with myself, I follow Logan down the steps to the school's basement, past dull cement walls offset by colorful kid-painted murals. We turn a corner, our energy settling, and Logan greets the counselor standing guard at a set of propped-open doors.

"Brittany Hart," says Logan.

The man checks his list and gestures ruefully to the other side of the cafeteria. The back wall is lined with backpacks on hooks and rain boots on trays. The counselor hesitates. "She's been a little—"

Logan raises one hand, quieting him gently. "It's okay. Thanks, man." I trail behind as Logan weaves through a sea of directionless children. After a moment I spot her—the girl from Logan's phone. She's sitting in the corner, staring at the pink windbreaker folded in her lap.

Logan jogs the last few paces. "You okay, killer Bee?" I hang back as he crouches down and tucks the girl's hair behind one ear. Her bottom lip begins to quiver. "Hey . . ." he says. His worry makes me worry. And it's strange to see him in this light. Logan is someone's big brother.

The girl notices me suddenly, her big, curious eyes staring, unblinking.

"Hi there." I do this weird little wave. "I'm Zan." I wonder if I sound too casual. "Rough day at the office?" I ask, deciding to just run with it.

She stands to lean against her brother's rain-soaked hip, and he hoists her up until her little legs clasp around his waist. "You're okay," he says into her hair. He gives me a reassuring look as he swipes a yellow backpack covered in cartoon pugs from a hook and heaps it over his own.

Back at the entrance, the counselor checks Bee's name off a list and gives her a cautious pat on the shoulder. "Weren't quite yourself again today, were you, kiddo?" But she stays buried in her brother's neck.

The bus is pulling away from the stop as we arrive. "Noooo," cries Logan, abandoning his sprint. The rain is pouring down in sheets and there's not one umbrella between us. It feels like I have fallen in a dunk-tank, save for a few dry patches—which I do appreciate. At the very thought, a little stream makes its way into the space between my bra and skin, and I shriek.

I hear Bee giggling softly as her brother groans. I look past him, to the bar-studded strip glittering ahead. A little ways up the block, by the will of some merciful traffic god, our bus has hit a red light.

"Hold on!"

I sprint into the intersection, plunging through puddles until I've caught up. I bang on the glass doors, but the driver keeps her eyes ahead. "Hey!" I pound again, with both fists, but I may as well be invisible. The water is well above my ankles now, seeping deep into my defenseless canvas sneakers. "Come on!" I whine to the stone-faced woman. "*Please?* We've got a kid out here!" After a moment, the driver shifts her gaze, and I point an emphatic thumb behind me. Logan has caught up with Bee in his arms. The driver squints, something shifting in her expression, and I know that I have broken her.

Within two blocks, Bee is passed out in her brother's lap, soothed by the stop-and-start brakes and the bus's rumbling engine.

"She's not usually like this," says Logan. "Quiet, I mean."

"She okay?"

"She's been through a lot. And now, on top of everything she's come up against some, I don't know, mean girls? They must get younger every year."

I narrow my eyes. "Do I need to rough up some six-year-olds?"

"She's been asking Bonnie to take her shopping. I think her old wardrobe isn't cutting it here. Kids in Lincoln Park are very trendy."

I nod, understanding now. "Silver light-up shoes."

"What?"

"All the hot bitches in Harr's class have silver light-up shoes. I'm telling you. It's, like, a key component in the little-girl pecking order."

"You probably shouldn't call children bitches."

"Eh." I wave him off. "Kids are just small people. They can't all be nice."

Logan laughs. "I guess we've got some shopping to do. Honestly, it's nice to have a solvable problem." Bee shifts in his lap, her eyes fluttering slightly. He adjusts in his seat and a little river trickles down onto the floor from his rain-soaked jeans. "Well, this was fun." He holds my gaze, green eyes glinting.

"Yeah," I say, and we watch the oversize windshield wipers fend against the night.

Logan's building is close to the lake. I've been to places like it—midrise, prewar, a friendly doorman in the lobby. We take the elevator to the top floor, with Bee still half-asleep, though standing on her own. She and I wait in the hall, peeling off wet socks while Logan tiptoes inside. With the door propped open I can hear him rummaging around. He starts Bee's bath and comes back to guide her toward the sounds of running water. When I step inside, he hands me a towel, reaching over my shoulder to bolt the door behind us.

"Back in a sec," he says, leaving me to drip over a welcome mat. He disappears into a bedroom off of the hallway. I hear drawers open and close, and soon he comes back with a pair of satiny pink pajamas. "There's another bathroom down the hall."

I run my thumb along the silky fabric. "Wouldn't have pegged these as your style."

"My aunt's," he clarifies.

When I emerge minutes later, it is painfully clear that I am much, much taller than Logan's aunt. Holding my wet clothes balled up at a distance from my body, I round the corner from the long hallway. Logan is changed and dry, chopping onions in a big, open kitchen that spills into a living room. He brightens when he sees me, his eyes already streaming with oniony tears. "You look ready for a flood."

"Oh *ha ha,*" I say.

He wipes his hands on a dish towel and takes my wet clothes from me. "Hungry?" he asks, careful, I notice, not to pay too much attention to my sopping wet bra as he stuffs it in the dryer.

"Starved," I say, taking in the place. The open layout is bright and airy, accented with a smattering of antiques and a small jungle of hanging window plants. Logan returns to his post at the stove and I sink onto a bar stool at the kitchen island. I watch him slide the onions into a sizzling skillet doused in olive oil. The smell is immediately intoxicating. He digs out carrots from the fridge next and chops them up small. Then he adds them to the onions, grinding sea salt and pepper before lifting the pan by the handle to give it a hearty shake.

Rain chatters on skylights above us. "So . . ." He unfolds brown butcher paper from a ball of what looks like ground turkey, which he drops into a glass bowl with a thud.

"So," I say back to him. He laughs, accepting the silence, and I watch contentedly as he adds eggs, bread crumbs, parsley, a squeeze of lemon, and finally the cooked-down carrots and onions from the pan. He mixes the meaty goo with bare hands, balling up pieces to throw back into the skillet.

"Meatball?" He reaches across the island with a raw one in his palm.

I swat him away. "No thanks." And then, feeling I should contribute something to the conversation, I say, "I've never seen someone put carrots in meatballs before."

He shrugs. "It's the only way to get Bee to eat her vegetables. I put broccoli in pesto. And mushrooms in hamburgers. If you cut them up small enough she can't tell the difference." He glances up from the pan. "What?"

I drop the smile that's crept up my face. "Nothing. That's just . . . nice."

"Yuuum-my," says a little voice from down the hall. With the skillet still hissing, Logan washes his hands and brings the dirty dishes to the sink. Bee walks up to inspect the stove, her blond hair soaking the back of her nightie.

Logan sighs down at his sister. "Go get your brush. And a towel. You're dripping all over the place." She nods obediently and runs off.

Logan turns the meatballs in the pan. "You seem like you know your way around a kitchen," I say. I noticed his methodical chopping earlier. Everything so neat and even.

"Yeah," he says. "I like it."

A thought strikes me. "Arturo mentioned hiring another

guy to help with prep before the night shifts. And we could use a sub once in a while now that Priya's gone. Would you ever want to—"

"Yes," he says immediately. He shrugs, sheepish. "I'm saving for a car."

"Okay, cool," I say. "I'll mention it to him."

Bee comes scampering back down the hall with a brush in hand and a towel over one shoulder. She runs the bristles through her hair at odd angles, making slow, modest improvements to the pile atop her head.

"Your hair is a bit messy too, Zan," she says when she's finished, her first full sentence of the evening. "Would you like me to fix it for you?"

Logan catches my eye and I turn to her. "That would be delightful." The bar stool is too tall for her, so we move to the living room floor.

"Tell me if I'm hurting you," she says expertly. I can feel her childlike concentration as she runs the thick brush along my scalp. Despite the occasional yank, it actually feels quite nice. "I like your hair," she says, turning to face me as she brushes the front pieces from my eyes. For a moment we're just inches apart. "It's pretty." Her smile reveals a missing bottom tooth.

In the kitchen, Logan removes the lid from a pot of boiling water. "Hey, kiddo. Elbows or bow ties?"

"Bow ties," she says decisively, and Logan rummages through the upper cabinets as the landline begins to ring. "I'll get it!"

says Bee, dropping the brush. She sprints to the old-fashioned rotary phone mounted to the wall and stands on tippy toes to reach. She takes in a big gulp of air. "Good evening Hart residence Brittany speaking."

I turn to Logan, charmed, and he explains with a whisper, "Our aunt taught her that." He takes the skillet off the burner and moves it to the oven.

Bee listens a moment, her face lighting up. "Oh hi, Mommy."

The oven door slams shut. "Brittany, give me the phone." She ignores him, still listening along. "Give it," he says. But she doesn't move.

Logan charges over to pull the receiver from her hands, and in a flash, she's running down the hall with tears in her eyes. He pauses before lifting the phone to his ear. "You know you can't call like this"—his voice has completely changed—"Mom." I wonder if I should see myself out. Then I remember the satiny pajamas I'm wearing and my own clothes bouncing in the dryer.

I point in the direction Bee ran and mouth the words *Should I . . . ?* He nods, appreciative. His voice seems to soften as I creep down the hall. "Mom, come on. Don't cry." I feel bad for being curious, so I make myself walk faster, until I'm out of earshot. I can tell he doesn't want me hearing any more.

I find Bee sitting on the carpet in her room, staring blankly at a tattered, purple-clad doll with bright pink hair. The doll's clothes suggest a hard life of turning tricks, her oversize head a vague advertisement for bulimia. "Who's she?" I ask from the doorway.

"Gwendolyn," says Bee. "My mommy gave it to me."

The bedroom window is cracked, letting in the swirling sounds of wind and rain. "Gwendolyn, huh?" I say, stepping into the room. The bed is crisply made, with fluffy pink pillows, a canopy overhead, and a big stuffed bear in one corner. Shelves of kids' books take up an entire wall. Bee's eyes are red and puffy. She wipes them as I sink down onto the carpet beside her. "That's a good name. Is she a princess?"

"No," she says, somewhat scandalized. "She's a senator."

I have to stifle a smile to match her serious expression. "Wow." I peer down at the doll with newfound respect, my mind drifting to Priya. She would frickin' love this kid. "Good for you, Gwendolyn."

Bee pulls a tiny silver outfit from a box at the foot of her bed and begins stripping Gwen down to her emaciated figure. "Logan doesn't like princess games," she offers up after a moment.

I keep my eyes on Gwendolyn. "Oh? And why is that?"

Bee slips the crotch-length dress up the little lady's torso and fastens it closed at the back. "He says princesses don't get to do anything cool. They just like . . . put on lipstick and wait for boys to marry them and stuff." She wipes her eyes with a strong little sniff. "He says he'll be very, very sad if that's all I want when I grow up."

I feel a pang of warmth for Logan and have to fight the urge to extract more information from this innocent little person.

For a split second, I feel like I'm not quite myself, because I have the strongest urge to call up Priya and tell her about a boy. The thought makes me feel queasy and sad, giddy and deflated. It's too many feelings all at once. "So Gwendolyn is a senator," I say, shaking it off.

"Yes," says Bee, pulling the pink hair into a ponytail. "A very pretty senator."

Down the hall, the front door opens, followed by huffing and puffing. "It's like a monsoon out there!" calls a woman's voice. The heavy door slams and moments later a head pops into the doorway. "Hey, Honey Bee . . . Oh." Logan's aunt, who I now remember I once observed from behind a trash can, regards me curiously. "Hello."

"This is Logan's friend Zan," says Bee as I stand. "She's wearing your pajamas."

The woman laughs, her deep-set eyes lifted by rosy cheeks as she reaches out to take my hand. "Pleased to meet you, Zan. I'm Bonnie." She removes a trench coat and shakes out her short, brown hair. "You're welcome to my pj's anytime."

"Thanks," I say, crossing my arms around the loose-fitting top. The open door has brought in a draft. "Nice to meet you."

Bonnie kicks off kitten heels, losing another inch. "Where's your brother?" she asks Bee.

Bee's shoulders drop. "Phone."

A flash of understanding registers on Bonnie's face, and I wonder if this is nothing new. "I . . . better check on him."

When Logan calls us for dinner, Bee is showing me her extensive library—a gift from her aunt upon moving to Chicago. She doesn't falter as she reads from *Angelina Ballerina,* not quite looking at the page. I suspect she's memorized it.

"Brittany," says Logan for the second time, tossing a dish towel over one shoulder as he steps into the room. "I said come eat."

Bee slaps the book shut. "Sorry, Zan. We'll have to finish the story later." Logan grins and we follow him toward the scent of meatballs.

"So, Zan," says Bonnie as we sit around the table. She scoops a second helping of salad onto her plate from a big ceramic bowl. "What do you think of my nephew's cooking?"

"It's amazing," I say, dabbing my mouth with a cloth napkin.

"I'll tell you," says Bonnie. "This kitchen has gotten more use in the last month than it has in the previous three years combined." She reaches across the table to take Logan's bashful face in hand. "How about you try for local colleges next year, hm? Stick around and cook for me?"

"He wants to go to the Art Institute of Chicago," says Bee through a mouthful of pasta. "He could still cook for us if he went there."

"Is that so?" says Bonnie with a glance at her nephew. "Well, I think that would be terrific."

Bee seems cheered by her aunt's mood. "It's only three miles from here. I looked it up on the computer. He should definitely go there."

"How do you know about the Art Institute?" asks Logan.

Bee's eyes dart to her lap. "I saw some papers in your room."

"I told you not to go through my stuff." She sulks and Logan seems to soften a little. "Anyway I wouldn't get your hopes up. My grades sucked last year."

"Well, that's what this year's for," says Bonnie, making another dive for the meatballs. "And you're more than what's on paper, my darling. But what about you, Zan? What are your plans for next year?"

"I'm not sure," I say honestly. Every adult seems to ask this question, and I never know what to say. My ambivalence toward the future used to baffle Priya. Unlike me, she had the picture in her head. Ivy League school. Nice, big family. A career in something like global health or public policy.

"You must have some idea," says Bonnie—parroting Priya to a tee.

Whenever we had this talk and I *didn't* have some idea, Priya would spin out into a list-making frenzy. *Teacher? Doctor?? Zoo-keeper???*

"I guess it's weird to me," I remember telling her once on the futon in her attic. "We're supposed to make these huge decisions when we haven't done enough or seen enough to know who we are or what we even want." Priya sat cross-legged above me,

137

listening in her thoughtful way. "But wherever I end up, I hope I do some good," I told her.

I can still remember Priya's face—how she'd looked so unbelievably certain. "'Course you will, ZanaBanana."

I startle as a cell phone rattles against the coffee table in Logan's living room, bringing me back. It's mine, actually.

"Sorry," I say, getting up. "I'll turn it off. It's just my"—the screen flashes MOM, but my stomach catches at the thought of Bee—"friend."

"Please," says Bonnie. "We're not exactly formal around here. Take your call."

I walk down the hall and hit the button. "Hey, what's up? I'm kind of in the middle of something."

"Real quick," says Mom. "Are you working tomorrow?"

"No, I think I'm off." I lean against the wall by a cracked-open bedroom door.

"Great," she says with relief. "Can you pick up Harr from after-school and bring him to Dad's?"

I frown. "But we were just there."

"Well, Whit and I are going to her work thing and he offered. Harr had a sleepover but it fell through. Anyway, Dad can't get there until seven." She pauses. "You know you can eat dinner with your dad more than once a week."

"I know," I say. "I didn't mean it like it was a bad thing." I peek in through the crack in the door and nudge it open a little more. Big sheets of paper covered in ink and charcoal are tacked all over the walls. It must be Logan's room. The drawings are mostly faces, peering out from shadows. Grief seems to pour from each pair of eyes, even the smiling ones.

"Some medical group is putting on a big banquet for the doctors," Mom is saying. "Whit's actually getting an award! I'll just be the arm candy."

I laugh. "Nice. You should definitely go. You two will have fun." I catch a glimpse of a sketch pad leaning against the base of Logan's desk and do a double take. Is that me?

"So you'll pick up your brother?"

"Um . . . yeah. No problem," I tell her. When I hang up I'm still staring. The sketch is loose and messy, but it's definitely me. I've locked eyes with myself, emerging from a charcoal-smudged page. I'm smirking, an eyebrow raised, like a challenge. Unlike the other faces, mine is somewhat hopeful. Strong and soft all at once. My cheeks are round, my freckles brought out.

For a moment I'm slightly sickened by the warm and fuzzy feeling rising up in me.

"Okay, I'm back," I announce, crossing my arms over the pj top as I return to the dinner table. I was careful to leave Logan's door the way I found it before creeping back down the hall. "Where were we?"

"You were telling us what you're going to do with your life," says Bee, making Bonnie chuckle.

"Ah, that," I say. "I'll tell you the truth, Bee. I have no idea."

"Really," says Bonnie.

I shrug. "I guess I've never felt like I was one of those kids with some big, great destiny. You know? Maybe the world isn't begging for my achievements."

Bonnie frowns. "Sounds to me like you might be under-selling yourself a bit, if you don't mind my saying." My phone beeps again and her eyebrows raise. "Popular lady."

"Sorry," I say. "Let me silence this." It's an email from an address I don't recognize.

From: <thegrissoms@yahoo.com>

To: Zan Martini <martiniweenybikini12@gmail.com>

Date: Thu, Sep 13, 8:32 pm

Subject: <no subject>

ZZWelcome way in/d.344itspdfiiiihauhlep

"What is it?" asks Logan.

"Nothing." I turn the phone facedown. "Just spam. Anyway, enough about me. Any big plans in your future, Bee?"

"I've been thinking a lot about Halloween," she says seriously. "I'm pretty sure I want to be a doughnut."

I laugh out loud and Logan looks happy for a moment. "That is amazing," I tell her. "Please do that. I'll help make the sprinkles."

After dinner, Logan places a bundle of dry clothes in my

arms. Bonnie and Bee load the dishwasher while "Lady Marmalade" booms from built-in speakers.

Logan and I hover in the kitchen to watch. Bonnie hands Bee everything that isn't sharp or glass, and Bee takes intermittent breaks to sing into spatulas and wooden spoons. The little diva pauses as Aguilera and the crew sing the chorus: *Voulez-vous coucher avec moi?* "What does all that French stuff mean?" she asks.

"Oh," says Bonnie, smacking her lips. "I uh . . . I don't know."

Logan smiles and clears his throat. "My aunt's going to call you a car, when you're ready."

I return a few minutes later in warm, dry clothes. Bee and Bonnie have since moved on to Prince's "1999." They briefly break from dancing to say good night.

"I'll come down with you," Logan says as we walk the narrow hall. He jolts up as we approach his room, subtly rushing ahead to close the door. I try to look oblivious.

Waiting for the elevator, I fight the urge to ask about that call from his mom. I can tell we're both thinking about it. The longer the silence lasts, the harder it is to break.

The elevator arrives and he lets me on first.

He reaches past me to press the button, and for a second I'm startled by how close we are. The elevator stops with a bounce and we step into the old-fashioned lobby.

"Logan, my man!" says a new doorman through a thick,

eastern European accent.

"Hey, Frank," says Logan as the man pauses something streaming on his laptop. "Don't let us interrupt," says Logan.

"*Scandal*," Frank says to me. "Wonderful program. I'm late to this party. Please. No spoilers."

"I would never," I say seriously.

A car rolls up and Logan makes a rush for the door before Frank can get out from behind the desk. "You going to put me out of job!" he calls over the sounds of wind and rain.

"It'll be our secret," says Logan, opening an umbrella through the doorway.

I tuck myself next to Logan as we scurry out from the protection of the awning. With the umbrella still above us, Logan opens the door to the slick black car, and before I slip inside, I stop and catch his eye. We are safe and dry, our faces inches apart as the rain pours down around us. He looks at me but doesn't move. I don't move either.

My gaze slides to his lips. I imagine what it would be like to lean just the littlest bit forward. Instead, I take a step back. "That was fun," I say over the rain. I'm not sure if I'm disappointed or relieved.

"Yeah," he breathes.

"Well . . . g'night," I say, and I disappear behind tinted glass.

I lurch up in my bed, awakened by a dream.

Mouth dry. Stomach plummeting.

Heart beating.

I was the bus driver in the storm, staring straight ahead, with Logan's grieving charcoal faces all behind me. Priya stood outside, screaming soundlessly as she pounded against the rain-streaked doors.

"ZZ," I say aloud.

She used to call me ZZ.

Hellooooooo. *taps mike* Is this thing on?

Priya here.

Oof, this feels weird. But I guess I'm doing it.

I never keep journals up after I start them. Maybe because deep down I know it's just a glorified way of talking to yourself. And who wants to admit they talk to themselves? But I don't know. I guess lately I could use the company.

This isn't even mine. I stole it off Amanda—packed in the same box as her computer. It's the nice kind, from the good stationery store, and the cover says Follow Your Heart. She'll never miss it. I'm convinced she's recovering from a bit of a shopping problem. (This wasn't even the only journal in the box. The other one said Love Your Life.)

Amanda hasn't let up on her exhaustive positivity any since we became roomies. So. Much. Singing. Think you could tone it down there, Mandy? And while we're at it, the LIVE LAUGH LOVE blocks you've got mounted above the minifridge are a bit much.

Today Amanda was stuck on that Judy Garland song "Get Happy." Which, okay, can I just be grouchy for a minute? Because what is the takeaway supposed to be from this little ditty? You want to be happy? Oh okay. Get that way! Thanks a lot, Judy Garland. I guess the rest of us were just overcomplicating things.

Listen to me. I sound like Zan with all this grumpitude.

Ugh. Why did I bring her up? I can't think about her right now. Can't think about anyone.

OKAY BEING POSITIVE FOR A MINUTE!

I got a shiny new textbook this week. I'm learning Mandarin, and can now write the characters for "I am a student," "You are a student," and "You (respected) are a student." As for pronunciation, thaaat will have to wait a while.

I keep on scarfing down blueberries. They are a superb study food, I always say. And great for any diet. ☺

Before I forget,
TO DO:
Daily, relentless positive affirmations
~~Project dial up~~
~~Loose documents—remind!~~
Photo suggestions? Think back.
Jumping jacks and sit-ups (for health)
Cut back on TV (to prevent brain decay)
Speaking of my brain—request one more textbook
More blueberries

(PS. Yes—you got me. I put already-done things on to-do lists. It makes me feel accomplished, all right? Even if the aforementioned completed tasks were only debatably successful.)

Anyway, I'm signing off now. Probably forever because I have historic journal commitment issues. We'll see how bored I get.

¡Adiós! Ciao! Auf Wiedersehen!

(Principle #301: Judy Garland would be a sucky therapist.)

SIX

Friday, September 14

I know there are rules. Basic human etiquette or whatever. I know, for example, that I should wait until a socially acceptable hour to call Logan. I watch the sun come up over the trees from my bedroom window, already dressed for the day. Then I decide that six thirty in the morning is absolutely a socially acceptable time to call someone. It goes to voice mail, so I text.

Are you awake? Call me!

I keep seeing it during breakfast. Smashed together among the other colorful letter magnets on the fridge. On my phone, over toast, smack-dab in the center of the word *BuzzFeed*. In

Harrison's morning funnies, repeated over and over above a sleeping cartoon cat.

ZZ

zz

zzzzzzzzzzzz

If Mom weren't so tyrannical about sugary cereals, I'd probably see it floating in my Alpha-Bits. That nagging, tugging, bad feeling is back, and for some reason I know that I can only talk to Logan about it.

As of eight, he still hasn't responded. The unanswered texts go as follows:

> **Helloooooooo?**
>
> **Roger, text me back, Roger. 10-4**
>
> **What does 10-4 mean?**
>
> **And who is Roger?**
>
> **Okay this is not a drill, I have abandonment issues, where are you?**
>
> **I don't really have abandonment issues. I don't think. But please call me at your earliest convenience.**
>
> **You are THE WORST!**
>
> **. . . Okay you're not the worst.**
>
> **(You might be the worst.)**

I don't pass him in the halls on the way to either of my first two classes. I keep checking to make sure my phone is getting service. I need to look at his assuring face. To know if he can see what I do.

From the back row, I tune out a lecture about Puritans, or Pilgrims? I try to remember Logan's second-period class today. Biology, maybe. I think I've seen him walking toward the labs when I've had history. For a moment I actually listen to the lecture—"Corn was also a significant source of sustenance"— annnnnnnnd I imagine myself face-planting into my desk.

The clock on the wall is taunting me, the second hand moving effortfully, through thick, invisible sludge. No one seems to notice as I get up, which is good because I am suddenly convinced I will drown from this rising tide of simultaneous angst and boredom without the refuge of the bathroom pass.

I close the door behind me and gulp the glorious hallway air. The corridor is mostly silent, aside from the clacking of my ankle boots. I actually put in some effort getting ready this morning, because I had time on my hands and nervous energy to expel. And yeah, okay—maybe a little bit because some part of me enjoyed the thought of looking nice for someone else. I settled on a paisley top and snug jeans. I even put on bronzer. Before I left for school, I caught sight of my reflection in the mirror and stood still. It felt like the first time I'd really seen myself in ages.

I round a corner, relieved to find an empty hallway, and peek into the bio lab. Through the tiny window in the classroom door, I can see Logan in profile, slumped in his seat for a lecture. It appears he's watching the clock too, perhaps mes-merized by that same torturous, slow-motion phenomenon that nearly killed me earlier.

I can't seem to catch his attention. *Look at me! Or your phone, you dummy!* I've read somewhere that our bodies know when we're being watched, so I stare extra hard at him, figuring it's worth a shot, and it works. He's staring back.

So are a couple people, actually. Skye from soccer meets my eyes with a tilted head, chewing a wad of gum with concentra-tion. I duck out of the way before the teacher sees me. After a moment the classroom door opens and Logan slips out with a hall pass.

"You okay?" he asks. "Why are you dressed like that?"

"Like what?"

"I don't know," he says, scratching at his jaw. "A girl?"

"Shut up. Why haven't you texted me back?"

"Sorry, I had to turn off my phone. Long story. What's up?"

I pull up last night's email. I've practically memorized it.

From: <thegrissoms@yahoo.com>

To: Zan Martini <martiniweenybikini12@gmail.com>

Date: Thu, Sep 13, 8:32 pm

Subject: <no subject>

ZZWelcome way in/d.344itspdfiiiihauhlep

Logan reads it, blank faced. "Am I missing something? This is gibberish."

"Mostly, yes."

"So . . ."

"Priya called me ZZ sometimes. In emails. She called me a lot of things, though, which is why I didn't catch it at first. ZanaBanana, Mrs. Zantantic, Zanita, Ma Petite Zan . . . Priya had endless resources when it came to pet names for me. But in a rush, in emails, she would call me ZZ."

"And the first two letters here are ZZ."

"Yes."

"So now you think she sent this. A gibberish email."

"Yes," I say again. "And it's not all gibberish. There are three full words in the beginning."

"'Welcome way in.'" He blinks. "Does that mean anything to you?"

"Well . . . no. But look at the last part. The last few letters."

He squints to read. "How-lep?"

"The last four," I say, taking the phone back to shove it in his face. "H-L-E-P. What if she was trying to write 'help'? Maybe she was trying to get the words out. Maybe she couldn't." Saying it out loud makes it more real, more possible. The knot in my stomach is screaming at me. "It was sent to my middle school email address. She's the only one who ever used it."

Logan contemplates this. "Weird. Who's the sender?"

"Right! That's the other thing. The Grissoms. Grissom! As in Ben's last name."

Logan leans in. "Wait. You don't think . . ."

"I don't know what I think! He said her phone was broken, right? Maybe she wrote it from his."

"Have you seen this email address before?"

"Well . . . no. And the fact that it's 'The Grissoms' plural is strange, for sure. I mean, it's just him. No other Grissoms."

"Is a 'butt email' a thing?" he asks.

I laugh under my breath as I gnaw on one fingernail. All of this seems crazy. And the *this* is still all fuzzy. Whatever it is, it goes from possible, to crazy, to possible all over again.

"I want to go to her house," I tell him. "They were going to rent it out, but I don't think anyone's moved in yet. The other day I noticed a bunch of mail piled up. Come with me?" Logan appears doubtful. "It's a feeling, okay? I need to be there. In her space. It'll help me think."

"Okay," he says gently. "Well, how about after school?"

"Actually, you have work," I say. "I meant to tell you. My boss texted me back this morning and asked if you could come in for some job training."

"Oh," says Logan, perking up. "Yes. Thanks. Okay, how about after that?"

He pulls my hand from my mouth, saving what little there is left of my nail, and I feel my breath start to slow a little at his touch. I don't know what to make of that. "I was thinking now. Like after this class? We could stay through lunch and skip Spanish if we need to."

He inhales through his teeth. "I shouldn't. I've missed a bunch of classes already and the school year's barely started."

"You know what? It's fine. I'll tell you if I find anything." I start to back away but grow dizzy. I have to balance against a locker, my vision filled with spots.

"Whoa there." He holds my shoulders to steady me.

"I can't stay here," I say softly.

"All right. Meet me at the exit by the caf. We'll take off after the bell."

"You don't have to—"

"I want to," he says. "Hey." He comes closer, willing me to look at him. "If there's something that needs finding, we'll find it. Okay?"

I whisper, "Okay."

The ride takes us all of five minutes on Logan's bike. And because my nerves are shot, I even let him drive.

The bike slows as I point to the house. "This is it."

It's somehow bigger than I remembered—one of the few ornate wooden homes you find sprinkled in with all the brick and brownstone. Being here feels both foreign and familiar, and as I take in the sight—the porch lanterns, the yard, the blossoming vines climbing up wood—I'm barraged with memories wrapped up in a place I realize no longer exists.

"So they're rich," says Logan, steadying the bike. "What's the stepdad do for work?"

"I don't really know," I say. "Numbers? Money?" I press myself up from the basket and hop down. "He used to work on Wall Street before they moved here. My mom says his expense account back then was bigger than her salary."

Logan drops the bike in a patch of grass and follows me to the gate. "Sounds nice."

"Yes and no. Priya said they practically had a staff when it was just the two of them because he had to work so much. Housekeeper, nanny, tutor. She never liked having all those people fuss over her."

"Huh," says Logan.

"Anyway, all that ended when they moved here. Priya was older, and she had my mom to do the fussing instead." I stop. "Did I tell you our moms were best friends?"

"You didn't."

My heart speeds up as I pull the latch to the black iron gate. The last time I walked this path was to say goodbye. I would have stayed until the second they drove off, but I was supposed to be leaving for soccer camp that day. My mom kept texting me. I was going to miss my bus.

Somehow I was the collected one in those final moments together. Priya cried and threw her arms around my neck, and as she pulled away she said, "Don't you dare forget about me." The night before, we'd gorged ourselves on cookies and numbed the pain with old episodes of *Will & Grace* in the attic. I remember thinking I was Will, because I'm grumpy. And she was Grace because she sparkled.

After a few more hugs, I unlatched this gate, and we said we'd visit at Christmas. We said we'd write. We said we'd count the days until summer, until India. And in that moment, it wasn't so much a thought as it was a fact. We would always be friends. Because some love can't dissolve, or fall apart, or get complicated.

Some love just is.

In the side yard, Logan makes binoculars with his hands to peek into a pane of the downstairs bay window. "They left a couch."

I snap out of it. "I thought they were taking everything."

"An armchair too. Bunch of stuff." I march up the porch steps to see the mailbox completely stuffed. I scan the street for onlookers before digging through. "Anything good?" calls Logan.

My arms filled with envelopes, I lower myself to sit cross-legged against the front door. The pile is massive. "Menswear catalog . . . Trader Joe's newsletter . . . Something from the cable company . . . Credit card promotion . . ." I glance up as Logan joins me on the porch. "This looks like a bill." I dig for more. "Another bill. Another bill. *Another* bill. Jesus, did Ben not forward anything? He can be such a disaster. Once he forgot to pay the electric bill and they were stuck in the dark for like three days. Priya made him automate all the utility payments after that."

"You gonna open one?" asks Logan.

"Uh, no," I say, scandalized. "Tampering with mail is a *felony*." I stand and stuff the envelopes back into the box. A thought strikes me.

"What?" says Logan.

"I wonder if the garage is open. We could get into the house through there."

"Because opening someone's mail would be reckless but breaking and entering is totally reasonable."

I lift my chin. "I'm nothing if not unpredictable."

I leave him there and make my way to the narrow strip of grass that leads to the back. After a moment he calls out behind me, "Are you sure you want to—"

"Yep!" I trudge ahead and he follows until we're spit out into the alleyway, where garages meet in neat rows and trash bins soak up sun.

I rest my fingertips against the garage door.

"This is illegal, too," says Logan. When I glance back, he's standing in the center of the alley, a good distance away. "You know, if that was something you were worried about."

"Details," I say. And then, to myself, "Here goes." I push up on the door. And like a tiny miracle, it slides. The garage is filled with boxes. We weave through and find the back door open.

Jackpot.

The whole first floor is scattered with stray furniture. Upstairs, Priya's room is almost bare except for the bed, stripped down to the mattress, and the wooden desk she hardly ever used. In Ben's room, the closet is empty, the men's products cleared from his bathroom. There are no running shoes strewn on the floor or earbuds resting on the dresser.

I tug at the tightly wedged door that leads to the attic. I steady myself on the railing, suddenly hit with a transporting, indescribable smell. Is it pine? Laundry detergent? Whatever it is, it reminds me of Priya—the girl, not the mystery. There was a time when this place meant study sessions and laughing fits and epic discussions over cold leftovers from the restaurant. I used to race these steps without a second thought, careful only to avoid bumping my head at the top. The attic was a bubble, far away from my mother's well-intentioned check-ins and just out of Ben's willing-to-travel radius.

Now it's just a futon on a frame.

I sit down, winded by the emptiness, and run my nails along the scratchy canvas cover. A tiny whimper escapes me. *Where are you, Priya?*

I go downstairs and head for the kitchen. The tapestries Sita brought back from India have been removed from the walls, taking with them their colorful warmth. I always thought of them as a touch of her. Priya would pat the one with the elephant in passing—a sort of absentminded affection. And I'd often find myself staring into the next one over, sucked in by the hypnotic circular patterns, so full of motion, like a slow-turning kaleidoscope.

A couch and armchair still face the spot where a TV used to be. I walk the length of the naked hallway, clutching the straps of my backpack just for something to hold on to. The more I think, the harder it is to fill my lungs.

I find Logan rifling through kitchen drawers. At the table, I thumb through a few printed pages. It's a copy of the California lease. Logan jumps when he sees me. "Sorry," he says, panting slightly. "I feel like a bank robber in here." There used to be pots and pans hanging from these walls, drawers filled with every kitchen gadget imaginable. Once in a while, Ben would get in a mood and whip up something fancy.

I walk to the office, only to stop short. "What?" calls Logan from the other room. I turn back but can't speak.

Because there, in the doorway, is Priya's bedazzled cell phone, shattered on the ground.

"Ben did say her phone broke," says Logan after a long, heavy silence.

"I know," I say. "I know. But . . . This doesn't feel right." I scrunch my eyes shut. "Do you think we should call the police?"

Logan flinches slightly, stepping the rest of the way into the office. "To say what? That we broke into your friend's house and it feels weird?"

"It *is* weird. They left all this stuff!"

"It's their house. They don't have to take their stuff if they don't want to."

"Yes," I say, growing frustrated. "But why leave so much? I could have sworn Ben said they were getting tenants. How do you rent out a house *from* California when it's full of stuff? And what about the phone?"

"I don't know," he says. "Maybe they were in a rush and Priya dropped it and they left it to deal with later. Anyway, it doesn't change the fact that we weren't supposed to be inside to see it in the first place."

I hate that he's resisting this. I sit and swivel back and forth in the desk chair to calm my nerves. Logan crouches down, his shoulder brushing against my leg, and pulls back with a few loose papers. I'm not even sure if he's cute anymore. In fact, his face is kind of stupid. "What are these?" he asks, tidying the stack.

I take the papers—email chains and memos and documents covered in numbers. As I sift through, I spot the familiar logo of a little girl, reading in a cozy corner. "Must be something for GRETA—the charity Priya's mom started. Ben's still on their board."

It's a little strange, actually. Not once have I seen even a trace of paperwork left out in this office, let alone on the ground. Ben can be a mess sometimes, but usually not when it comes to his work. I shuffle through the stack, reading the emails.

There's one from back in May, sent by Yasmine to one Head-master Modi, with the subject "Fire at Friends Elementary."

Vijay,

We are so glad all the students were all right. Is there really nothing we can do? It seems a shame to let the school shut down. If you are open to the possibility of rebuilding, this is certainly something we could explore together.

Another is from April, addressed to Anushka.

Dear Ms. Jha,

I am happy to tell you that we at Priti have received a large international grant.

After speaking with our accountant, it would appear we no longer qualify for your aid, but I would like to express my deepest gratitude to all of you at GRETA.

Wishing you the very best.

Amrit Ganglani
Head of Students

The last one makes me pause. It's from Ben, to an email address without a full name attached: j.karim565@gmail.com.

Please take my call.

"Mean anything to you?" asks Logan.

"Not really," I say. I take off my backpack and slip the papers inside. "But I'll hold on to them just in case." I catch a glimpse of a picture frame that's fallen beneath the desk. "Oh whoa," I say. "This is her, Sita. Priya's mom."

I pick up the photo. She looked so much like Priya. Kind, warm eyes that make you feel at ease. I'm surprised Ben would leave this behind.

Logan takes the frame. "You said she had her own charity?"

"Yep. Inherited a shit-ton of money and then gave it all away."

"Huh," he says. "Why?"

"She was amazing, basically. Priya's grandfather had, like, an empire. Textiles, hotels, all over Mumbai. Priya told me one time, as a teen, her mom snuck into one of their factories when she wasn't supposed to. Totally freaked her out. Girls younger than her, working fourteen-hour days. She and her family never fought, but after she went to New York for college, she didn't come back. Got some nonprofit job and started over. Then one day a check arrived."

I hoist myself up, taking in the room once more. I open the closet. It's mostly empty, with a few stacks of paperwork in files on the floor.

Every time my eyes land on the shattered phone, I get a little shiver. "I really think we should report this," I say again.

Logan doesn't answer. Doesn't even look at me. "What's the charity?"

I check the file cabinet—still full—and snap it shut, annoyed. "The GRETA Fund. Girls Reaching Equality Through Academics. They fund girls' schools around Mumbai and in some rural areas."

"And you and Priya were involved?"

"Yeah. GRETA is getting ready to send student volunteers for the first time this summer. It was Priya's idea, actually. We were going to work for them after graduation."

"The India trip," he says, his face getting slightly less stupid. "I remember now." He glances at the clock. "Crap. We're missing Spanish. We should get going."

I drag my hand along the wooden desk and open one last drawer. There's a slip of paper inside. It's creased like a letter, and when I open it, I see a single sentence, typed.

Found you

Logan reads over my shoulder. "What is that supposed to mean?"

"No idea," I say, feeling winded again. I fold the note and drop it into my bag. "I'll file it into evidence." I heave a sigh. "This is definitely weird. You have to admit, it's weird, right?"

"It's weird," Logan concedes, slinging on his backpack. He

swivels back when I don't follow.

"You go ahead, actually," I say. "I . . . I don't know, I need a minute."

I can tell he's concerned. "Are you sure? I can stay if you—"

"No, no," I say. "I already made you miss one class. Go. I'll be right behind you."

When he's gone, I wander through the house. I sit on the couch where we sometimes studied and slide my hand along the cold granite kitchen counter.

I stop in a doorway and peer in. Even the bathroom is sentimental.

The inspirational plaque was displayed prominently—albeit begrudgingly—over the sink for the rare occasions when Ben's mother came to visit. This was hardly necessary by the time they moved. She hadn't come in years. Maybe the whimsical fonts just grew on them.

EVERY FAMILY HAS A STORY. WELCOME TO OURS.

I guess this particular slab of pseudo-Buddhist wisdom didn't make it into first-round packing. I take the stairs and check the second-floor bathroom.

A true love story never ends.

I stare at the mirror, noting my tired eyes. What makes it a love story, anyway? Something about this particular plaque always made me sad. As I'd wash my hands up here, I'd find myself wondering about Sita and Ben. Or Sita and Priya. Or my mom and my dad. Everyone who's ever loved and lost. But as the attic bathroom will tell you,

Better to have loved and lost than to have never loved at all

Cheesy, yes, but probably true. Who knows? Maybe Bed Bath & Beyond really is the great purveyor of wisdom when it comes to the human heart.

I take it all in one last time as I return to the first floor. I really shouldn't miss another class. I lock up from the inside and step out into the sun. As the door shuts, I realize that I locked the back door too. That was dumb. Now I won't be able to get in again if I think of something.

I notice a man outside the gate then. He has tan skin and dark hair, and he's staring intensely in my direction through thick black-rimmed glasses. I check behind me, in the weak hope that he's looking anywhere else.

"Who are you?" he asks as I walk down the porch steps.

Shit. Shit shit shit.

"Oh, uh…" I plaster on my best totally normal expression. "I'm a friend. Of the people who own this house. I was dropping in to . . . water the plants. Because, you know. No one likes a dead plant." I hear myself—*What?*—but the man seems too preoccupied to notice.

"So you know these guys? Ben and Priya?"

"Oh, uh. Yeah," I say. "Priya. She's . . . Well, she's kinda my best friend."

"Oh," he says. "Okay. So . . ." He frowns. "So they still live here?"

"Um." I bite my lip—I guess that's what I just said, isn't it? "Yes?" I peek at the gate between us, which the man is continuing to block. "Sorry, who are you?"

"Family friend. Just came by for a visit." Odd. I've never seen him before.

"Well, they're not here right now," I tell him. I look at the gate again and clear my throat, an obvious hint that I want to leave. But he doesn't move. "I should . . . go."

"Right," he says, stepping out of the way. "After you." I graze past him and start heading down the street. To my back, I think I hear, "Bye, Zan."

I'm halfway to school when I realize I never told him my name.

My next class has already started when I slip back into school, the garbled thoughts competing for space in my head. I missed lunch and my stomach is growling. I'm glad I left some popcorn in my locker.

"Alejandra."

I close the locker with a jump. Señora O'Connell is standing in the center of the hallway, with a purse on her arm and keys in her hand. My stomach tightens, but I try to come off cool and collected. "Oh, hey. Sorry about missing class. Logan and I both had a test. It ran long, and—"

"Just stop," she says through a sigh. "I saw you leaving school." I open my mouth but come up short. "For future reference, the teachers' lounge has windows. Big ones. And they look over the park."

"Oh," I say, my shoulders slumping. "Look, I'm sorry. This really isn't like me. Or Logan."

"I believe you," she says. "And one unexcused absence isn't going to kill you, Zan. But you might want to work on being a better influence. Logan's off to a bad start with his attendance. If he keeps this up, he could be suspended." My heart sinks a little. Logan said he couldn't afford to miss another class, and I went and made him do it anyway. "Now, if you don't mind me," says la Señora, "this is the one day a week I get out early, so I am off to have a long, romantic evening with two very handsome golden retrievers."

She turns to leave and I hear myself say, *Wait!*

I look down, surprised to see my own hand gripping her tightly by the upper arm. "Sorry," I say, my wide eyes mirroring hers. "I shouldn't have done that." This time she really leaves. "No, please! Hold on!" I trail her down the hall. "Is there any way you could excuse Logan's absence today? It wasn't his fault. He didn't even want to go with me."

"Then he shouldn't have," she says as I struggle to keep up with the fast clip of her heels.

"But if you knew the whole story . . . He was only being a good friend."

She shakes her head, a long fiery ponytail swinging side to side. "I'll admit, Logan seems like a super-sweet kid, and I'm totally rooting for him, but faculty members overhear things through the grapevine, too, you know. Not every young guy gets the kind of second chance he's been given here. After what he pulled, if he wants to go and get himself into more trouble, I'm sorry but that's on him."

I study her face, confused, and she stops beneath the Exit sign. "Señora O'Connell. What are you talking about?"

A look of understanding clicks in and she winces. "He hasn't told you. . . . Has he?"

"Told me what?"

Jamming her fingers into her eye sockets, she says, "*Goddammit, Megan,*" apparently berating herself.

"Hey." I take a step closer, my heartbeat speeding up. "Told me what?"

Her face falls. "Okay. Zan? I'm really sorry. I shouldn't have . . . I don't even know the whole . . ." She looks to the ceiling. "That wasn't cool of me. Ugh. I am literally failing at so many aspects of my life right now." She collects herself, meeting my eyes again. "If you were wondering? All the adults around you pretending they have their shit together? They don't."

I'm still waiting for my answer. For a moment, I imagine shaking her like a piñata just to get it out.

"Look." She steels herself. "I didn't mean to reveal, or suggest, anything . . . confidential about a student. Logan has the right to a clean slate. Whatever the story is there, you should be hearing from him, not me." She bites her lip. "Is there any way we could forget I said anything?" After a beat, despite the rising angst inside, I manage a nod. Her shoulders relax. "Thank you, Zan." She walks backward toward the stairs. "And don't worry about class today. Let's just . . . call it even."

Midway through English, I'm pulled out for a guidance counselor meeting. We talk about college, and I answer most questions with, "I don't know." *Would you like a small school? Greek life? Any majors calling to you? How about nature? Do you like big cities? Come on, Zan. Work with me a little. Where do you see yourself next year?*

Even if I weren't so distracted, I'm not sure I'd have an answer to that question. The bell rings and I say goodbye. The meeting is unsuccessful.

After school, I walk with Logan to the restaurant. He pushes his bike. I don't ask him about what la Señora said, but I find myself watching him more closely. I'm still trying to make sense of it—this whole swirling mess of a day. Every time I picture Priya's house—the phone, the note—my stomach plummets. I wasn't scheduled to work, but I figured I could help Sam teach Logan the ropes. The restaurant is where I want to be.

My mood somehow perfectly matches Manny's never-ending banda playlist. There's something sort of melancholy about the elephant-like honk of the baseline tuba. Once in a while, Arturo pops in and takes me for a spin around the kitchen against my will. It sort of helps. No matter how stressed or down I feel, Arturo always finds a way to make me laugh.

"It's not rocket science," Samantha is saying. "These are purple onions." She hoists a big box from off the ground and drops it on the counter. "You slice them into rings and store them in bins." She lifts a dripping wet container from the dishwasher. "The bins slide right into the salad bar."

"Got it," says Logan, following her in his apron as she buzzes around the kitchen.

"Make extra," says Sam. "So we don't run out." She pulls hard against the heavy door to the walk-in fridge. "Then stack the bins you're not using in here to stay cold."

Logan steps into the steaming air and rubs his hands together. "I'm ready, Coach. Put me in."

Samantha rolls her eyes, smirking. "Cherry tomatoes you cut in half. Cucumbers, maybe a quarter of an inch thick. Olives are ready to roll, just refill the bin when they're running low."

"I see cabbage," says Logan. "Impart your wisdom, Samantha. What do I do to the cabbage?"

"You cut it," she says, straight-faced. "And then stick it in a bin."

The volume to the music lowers. "Hungry, *flaca*?"

When I turn back, Manny is pulling yucca from hot grease. "Sure," I say. "Thanks." He slides the dish across the window and I gobble up a few chalky, salty bites.

Manny steps out from his cook's lair, wiping grease onto striped pants as he takes the place beside me. "He's okay," he says, nodding toward Logan after a thoughtful silence. I smile. For Manny, that's a pretty major compliment.

My mind jumps to Lacey and her rumors. And the look on la Señora's face today in the hall. I should have pressed her. What had she meant by "more trouble"?

I'm not sure how much time has passed when Manny whistles and starts slipping aluminum containers through the window. Arturo comes over and stacks them up in a big paper bag, then staples it shut. He calls out, "Sam, you want to bring this out to Reggie?"

I perk up. "Reggie's here?"

"Who's Reggie?" asks Logan.

I take the bag myself. "I'll bring it to him."

"You know you're not on the clock," says Arturo.

"Uh-huh," I say, hurrying out through the swinging doors.

Reggie's waiting by the Please Wait to Be Seated sign in gym clothes, a duffel bag on one shoulder. "Can I ask you something?" I say without a hello. It feels like a sign that he's here. I have to tell him about Priya. I can't keep it in anymore.

He takes the paper bag. "Um, sure. What's up?"

I look around. "Out there," I say, pointing to the street.

I hurry for the door, pulling him by the arm.

It's getting dark. "Zan," says Reggie, staring me down. "What is it?"

A young couple is walking toward us on the sidewalk. As they pass, I take a big breath. "How do you know if you should report a missing person?"

His chin juts back. "What?"

"You know her. It's my friend Priya. She used to be a server here."

"Oh right," he says. "I've worked with her stepdad, actually."

I frown. "What do you mean you've worked with Ben?"

"At the community center. Last spring. He started coming in for the Thursday self-defense class. Somehow this place came up and we figured out the connection."

"Huh," I say. "I didn't know that."

"I thought they moved," says Reggie.

"They did."

Reggie looks worried now. "Okay, back up. Did Ben not file a report? I'm happy to be a resource, but he should really go through the precinct out there."

"Well, okay." I brace myself. "So, no one else actually thinks she's missing. Right now she's at some boarding school. I mean, *allegedly*. But I haven't been hearing from her and her posts online have felt weird. She's my best friend, you know? And I really . . ." I hold his gaze, eyes pleading. "Reggie, I really don't believe she'd cut me off like that."

"So. Let me get this straight." I see the sequence move across his face: understanding, relief, sympathy. It's obvious he's working to look like he's still taking me seriously. "Your friend moved away and stopped staying in touch?"

I break from his dubious stare as a streetlamp comes on. "Yes."

"And now you're wondering if you should file a missing person's case."

My mouth falls open stupidly. "Well. When you put it like that."

He holds my gaze, gentle. "Come on, Zan. You must realize how this sounds."

"Okay, yeah," I say. "I know. But there's more. I kind of . . ." How to put this? "Okay, so I sort of broke into her old house and—"

"You what?" Reggie takes a step back. "Zan, why would you tell me that? I'm a cop!"

"I know," I say, bracing the air between us. "But it wasn't that bad. The back door was open and I didn't take any—"

"La la la la," he sings, plugging his fingers into his ears, the takeout bag hitting his shoulder. He starts walking down the street and I follow, waving my hands to get his attention.

"Okay," I say. "Okay! I won't get into details."

He unplugs his ears and stops. "No more illegal stuff, okay? And definitely no telling me about it after."

"All *right*. But, well, the thing is, I found a weird note inside their house and—"

"Just stop," he says, his voice booming with authority. "Has anyone talked to Ben lately?"

My shoulders slump. "Yes."

"Is he worried about Priya at this boarding school?"

"Well, no, but—"

"What about other friends? Is there anyone else who's concerned?"

I close my eyes a moment. "Reggie, I'm telling you . . ."

When he sighs down at me, I can see it's no use. "Get some rest," he says, gentler now. "You look like hell, kiddo."

I'm sitting on the bench outside the restaurant when the bell above the door rings. I've been staring at the streetlamp, willing myself not to fall apart.

Logan has my backpack with him, his face falling a little when he sees me. "It didn't look like you were coming back inside. Thought you might want this."

"Thanks," I say, taking it.

He pulls off his apron and lowers himself beside me. "Did I miss something?"

"I was just talking to a friend," I say. "Reggie. He's a police officer. I tried to tell him what's been going on—the weird posts, the note at Priya's house . . ."

Logan stares. "Wait. You told a *cop* we broke into Priya's house?"

"It's fine," I say.

He scoffs. "Oh, is that right? Christ, Zan. Did you use my name?"

His eyes are worried, hands wringing. I'm exhausted, and fed up, and it dawns on me. He's really hiding something. "Why didn't you want to report it?" I ask. "What we saw back at the house?"

"There was nothing to report."

"Are you in some kind of trouble, Logan?"

For a moment he just blinks. "What makes you say that?"

"You were so . . . skittish at Priya's house. Like you were so sure we'd get caught. Worried about missing class, about starting over. And you should have seen your face just now when I mentioned Reggie. I'm not dumb, okay? I've only heard bits and pieces, and it's hard to know what to believe. But, well, people have been . . ." I brace myself. "Talking."

Something in his expression shifts, his jaw tightening. "And I guess now you're someone who cares what 'people' have to say?"

"You're not exactly an open book, Logan. If you've done

nothing wrong, why dodge everything I ask?"

He furrows his brow, like he's just uncovered something fascinating. "You don't trust me."

I sigh. "I never said—"

"You didn't have to. But hey, why should I be any different? You don't trust anybody, Zan."

"That is not true," I say, straightening up in defense. "I trust people. I mean I obviously trusted—"

"Let me guess," he says coolly. "Priya?" Something in the air changes, and I suddenly can't look at him. "As in one friend? Out of everybody? It's a lot to put on one person, don't you think?" His laughter actually stings. "You know, maybe all this digging really *is* crazy of us. Maybe it's simple. Maybe the poor girl just needed a break from you."

It would have been better if he'd punched me in the gut.

It's quiet for a minute, and when I glance over, I can tell he knows he's gone too far. "I shouldn't have . . ." He stands. "Look, I should get back inside, but how about I come by later? We should . . . probably talk."

As he reaches for the door I feel the hurt, the rage and frustration, all rising up inside my throat. "Don't bother," I say to his back. "You know, Logan, I may be sad and pathetic, but at least I'm not a liar. Or some kind of *fucking criminal*."

"Really?" he says, turning around. "It's like that?"

But I'm already running down the sidewalk as fast as I can.

✳ ✳ ✳

Dad's at my house when I walk in. I close the door, confused. "She's here," he says into his phone. He's got a serious look on his face, all hunched over the receiver like he's handling something delicate.

Harrison walks straight to me, his hands balled up in tight fists. "I can't believe you forgot me!"

"Oh no." My backpack drops to the ground, as does my stomach, and Harr crosses his angry little arms. "*Shit*—I mean shoot! Oh, buddy, I really am so sorry. I completely—"

"I was stuck there for *twenty-eight minutes*!" His cheeks are turning red, his plump bottom lip jutting out. My heart always breaks when his lip does that.

I crouch down to Harr's level, but he refuses to meet my eyes. "Hey. Buddy. Really, I am so, so sorry."

He takes in a choppy inhale, trying not to cry. "The after-school teacher got all annoyed and made me wait in the cafeteria while the janitor mopped, and all the other kids went home. A bunch of girls made fun of me. Even Matilda laughed."

I pout and try to hug him, but Harrison rips himself away.

"No, no," Dad grumbles into the phone. "Really, we're okay here. Go enjoy your dinner." He hangs up and looks at my brother. "Harrison, could you go watch some TV?" My brother pauses dubiously for a moment, then scampers off, ever the opportunist.

"What's going on with you?" asks Dad once Harr is settled on the couch and out of earshot.

I lean into the counter. "I'm sorry. It's been a shit day. I got caught up, and I forgot." I realize my stomach is growling. "Are we staying here or going to your place? I'm starving."

"We'll go back to my place in a little while," he says, clearly thrown by the deviation. "I wasn't sure when you'd get here, so I ordered delivery. Leftovers are in the fridge. But . . . Zan, what happened today can't ever happen again."

"I know," I say as I walk over to scour the refrigerator. After the day I've just had, I want something heavy, possibly artery clogging, but it appears Dad has ordered nothing with meat. There are little tubs of hummus, fava beans, and lentils, plus a salad and one lonely piece of falafel.

"Look," says Dad to my back. "I won't pretend to know what's happening in your head right now. But it seems like it's getting to be a problem."

I lean into the open fridge, the cold air on my face. Salad. I guess I'll go with stupid salad. Or maybe lentils would be better.

"Mom says you've been moping around. Feigning sick to get out of school. This is not a good time to start melting down. You're going to start college next year and Mom says you haven't researched where you want to go. Then today, we both receive calls from your guidance counselor saying that you barely seem interested in applying."

"I'm really not that focused on next year right now," I say.

"Well, you should be."

"Well, I'm not." I slam the refrigerator door. "And for the love of God, Dad, I am *still not a vegetarian!*" My voice rings out and Harr glances over, a worried look on his face. "Sorry, buddy," I say. "Just watch your show." I go back for the solo falafel and bring it to the table. Dad gets up to pour me some water, finding the cabinet for glasses on his first try. It's sort of odd to see him here in our house, still knowing where everything is.

He sets a glass down and takes the chair across from me, waiting for me to speak.

"I honestly don't know what to tell you," I say, wolfing down the little ball in two bites.

"Then . . ." He seems flustered. "Help me understand."

"Dad. Stop, okay?" I finish chewing and take a sip. "You don't need to do this. We both know you're not the dad who *tries to understand.* And I'm okay with it. Because that's Mom's job. And she may be a relentless, meddling psychopath, but she's earned the right to be. But with you and me . . . If it gets too real, it's weird." My eyes stay glued to the table. "Kind of like it is right now."

When I finally peek up, Dad has gone all stiff. "See?" I say. I swallow, shrug. "We aren't that dad and daughter anymore. Haven't been in years." There's some kind of Disney tween sit-com rattling from the living room, but I don't think this house has ever felt so quiet. "I'm sorry, okay? Maybe it won't be this way for you and Harr. But . . ." I feel the words rising up, desperate to pour out of me. "He can't remember how everything changed. How you went from this person I trusted completely, one of two parents, who knew every tiny thing about me—to this . . . *dude*. Who I saw once a week for takeout and strained conversations. I know things are better now, and maybe you can start again with Harrison. But me?" I throw up my hands, laughing though it isn't funny. "I can still remember the time in my life when you barely even tried."

"Zan . . ."

"Let's stop, okay? Let's just eat this meatless food, go back to your apartment, and watch something on TV." I can't look up.

"I didn't—I didn't know you felt . . ." Dad trails off. "Oh, Boop. If I could go back."

"It's fine." I look around the room, feeling as if I've returned to my own body. "I'm sorry. I didn't mean to get so . . . I told you it was a shit day." I stand, smiling weakly. "I think I need some air. You guys go on without me."

"Hold on," says Dad. "Can we please talk?"

"Nothing to talk about," I say. I walk into the living room and smack a kiss on Harr's head with a whisper: "I'll make it up to you, buddy." Then I hurry out the door and don't look back.

I wander the neighborhood for an hour or so, with my phone powered off. My heart beats palpably, the thoughts churning in my head so fast they almost seem to hum. When I get back, I can still see Dad through the kitchen window—waiting up. So I sit on a stoop down the street and wait, watching, until he and Harr finally pile into the Subaru and drive away.

I've almost made it to the staircase when a lamp comes on in the living room. "I hear you had quite a day, Boop."

I turn back. Mom is sitting in the armchair, her hair pinned up, still wearing her sequined gown from the banquet. "Whit's still out," she says, as if answering a question. "I came home early. Talked to your dad."

"Oh."

She extends her palm. "Phone."

"What?"

"You're grounded, Zan." I sigh and walk over to hand it to her. For my mother, this is pretty extreme. She is, after all, a Progressive Parent Who Encourages a Dialogue. But right now I don't even care. She nods toward the couch across from her. "Sit," she says, so I do. She arranges her legs in the chair and stares.

I stare back.

"Let's recap, shall we? You forgot your brother. Yelled at your dad. And then stormed off, at night, without telling anyone where you were or when you'd be coming back. Did I get it all?"

I scrunch my eyes closed. "I know."

"Care to tell me what's going on with you?"

"I don't know, Mom."

She crosses her arms. "You don't know."

"I have . . . a lot on my mind."

"Zan. You're grounded either way. But if you want to tell

me what's going on, I may consider shortening the sentence."

I sink back into the couch. After a minute, I say, "It's Priya."

"Oh, Boop," says Mom. "Still?"

I shrug, a reluctant yes. "I've been feeling really . . . To be honest, I feel scared."

She looks at me strangely. "What do you mean?"

I swallow. "Mom, it's hard to explain, but I think something isn't right. The way she's been writing in her posts. And cutting people off like this? Not just me. Did I tell you she broke up with Nick?"

"Nicholas Wallace Reid?" She sounds surprised.

"Yes," I say. "And remember how much she talked about him?"

"I do. He sounded like a keeper."

"He is *such* a keeper, Mom. I actually met him recently and you should have seen him. She totally broke his heart. Over *email*. And he was so, so sad about it. And, I don't know, a part of me doesn't believe it could have been her."

A wary expression flits across her face. "Zan. What are you talking about?"

Here goes.

"What if it's not her, Mom? What if the statuses, the emails, *the silence*—what if none of it is in her control? She posted a selfie of herself the other day that was like four months old! Who does that?"

"Okay, you're losing me now," says Mom. "What's wrong

with a picture that's four months old?"

"Never mind." *Ugh.* None of this is coming out right. "It doesn't add up, okay?"

"Of course it doesn't. She hurt you. And it makes no sense. But honey? As you get older, more and more you realize people make no sense! Maybe she'll come back to you, and maybe she won't. But I think for now, for your sanity, you have to learn to live in the world where she won't."

"I don't believe it."

She groans, breaking my name into frustrated bits. "Za-ha-hann! We lose people in life, for one reason or another. And sometimes there isn't a moral, or a takeaway, or a . . . satisfying explanation. Sometimes life just isn't fucking fair!" Her eyes widen a little, like she's surprised by her own outburst. "Listen. I truly, truly don't mean to belittle your pain here, but I'm telling you, you have to start getting over this. I think Priya is going through some heavy stuff. It's not about you. You have to let her go. At least for now."

I think of Priya's house today. The shattered phone. Mom would flip if she knew I broke in like that. After a moment, I let her eyes meet mine. "What if you're wrong?"

"Honey." She shakes her head, baffled. "If Priya were in some kind of trouble, I think we would know."

I try not to let my voice crack, but it does a little. "How?"

"Well, for one thing, Ben would have called us. Or Anushka? Yaz? Hon, I think we're officially crossing over into paranoia territory here. It's normal to try and negotiate with your new reality. You lost someone. You're hurting. You're searching for some explanation that doesn't feel like a rejection. But this—"

I take a throw pillow over my head and proceed to shout into it.

"Hey!" says Mom.

"Don't talk to me like that," I say into the cushion. "I'm not some mental patient."

I don't have to see it to know the face she's making. "Okay, first of all, going to therapy doesn't make you a mental patient. You know that perfectly well. And second of all, if we're being completely honest here, if anyone is acting like a mental patient right now, it's you!" I lift the pillow to let her see my shock. She doesn't back down. After a moment, she sighs. "I wish you would trust me on this."

"Trust you? Why don't *you* trust *me*?"

"Fine. You really want to get to the bottom of it?" Mom strains to reach the purse on the coffee table and pulls out her cell phone.

"What are you doing?"

She holds the phone up to her ear. "I'm calling Ben."

I lunge across the coffee table. "No! Wait." I try to take it from her.

"I'm not going to make a big deal out of it," she says, fending me off. "I'm just going to check in."

"No. Mom! Hang up the phone!"

"Would you rather talk to him?" She holds the phone between us. I can hear it ringing. "It's you or me."

For a moment, I freeze.

I take the phone. *Breathe, Zan. Breathe.* . . . "Alice! Hi."

I clear my throat and Mom sinks back into her chair, her eyes locked with mine. When I don't speak, she waves me along. "Uh, hey, Ben. It's Zan, actually."

"Oh," he says. "Hi. Give me a second. I'm gonna step outside." I hear shuffling in the background. After a minute he says, "Is everything okay?"

"Well." I swallow, still eyeing Mom. "So, I'm not sure if you know this, but Priya and I sort of . . . aren't talking anymore."

"Yeah," he says, his exhale scratching at my ear. "I've been wondering how you might be taking that."

"I mean, it sucks."

"I'm sure," he says gently. "And, well, not to get involved, but I don't totally get her reasoning with this one."

"Which is . . . ?"

He breathes out. "That's what I mean. I don't entirely know. I think she's, I don't know, maybe going through a period where she needs some space."

"Yeah," I say, my heart sinking. "Well, I don't expect you to tell me anything personal. But I guess I was starting to feel worried. You'd tell us if something was wrong, right? I mean. Like . . . she's okay?"

He hesitates. "She's fine. It's . . . complicated. But she's fine."

"Okay . . ." I say, my worry spiking. "Wait, no, Ben. What the heck does that mean?"

He laughs lightly. "I just mean she's . . . going through some stuff. She's not talking to me much, though, either."

"Oh." I'm still not sure what to do with that. I look at Mom. "Hey, one second, okay?" I walk to the kitchen, out of earshot. I know Mom will respect my privacy enough not to follow me, but I keep my voice low anyway. "Did something happen at your house before you guys left? I . . . sort of went by today."

"What do you mean?"

I think a moment and decide to go with partial honesty. "I was there, so I . . . peeked in the window. I noticed you didn't bring all your furniture. And it was a mess inside."

"Ah," he says. "Well, we had to get the truck back by a certain hour here in Santa Monica. The bulk of our stuff was supposed to end up in storage, but we were so behind, rushing around. We just skipped it." He laughs. "It was a truly chaotic day."

"I gotcha," I say, bobbing my head. "Well. I don't know. I guess something just felt off." I perk up, suddenly remembering. "And there was a guy there."

"At our house?"

"Yeah. Like, sort of lurking around. He said he knew you and Priya, but I'd never seen him."

"Huh," says Ben. "What'd he look like?"

"Tan skin. Dark hair and eyes. Glasses. I can't remember much else."

"Weird," he says, clearing his throat. A pause. "Hey, I know it's not my place, Zan, and I wish I could be more helpful, but I do hope she'll come around. She's been . . . changing. Nothing bad. I'm not sure when you two stopped talking, so maybe you already know this, but she's at a boarding school right now."

"Oh," I say. "I, uh. No, I didn't know that."

"A spot opened up last minute," he says. "The environment there is pretty different from Prewitt. It's possible she's bending to peer pressure or struggling to adjust. I'm not sure, but I think it could explain some of this."

"Huh," I say, nodding slowly. "But you still see her?"

"We Skype sometimes in the mornings before her classes. I'm actually visiting tomorrow. It's a bit of a drive, but I go when I can."

"So the school is driving distance?" As it flies from my mouth I realize how obsessive it must sound, but I'm saved by a click.

"Hey, Zan? Hold on one second. I have another call. It's . . . Well, it's Priya."

"Oh," I say, my heart constricting. "Please don't tell her I—"

"I won't," he says. "Just a sec."

I wait on the line, my thoughts swirling. I feel like I've woken up in the middle of this crazy conversation. This is crazy. I sound crazy.

He comes back. "Sorry about that. She needs me to send

over some paperwork for school. I should call her back, but uh..
Sorry, what were we saying?"

"Nothing. It's okay. Thanks for talking to me."

After a pause he says, "Take care of yourself, Zan, all right?"

"Yeah," I say. "Thanks." I drift into the living room, where
Mom is clearly straining to listen as she runs a hand along the
sequins of her dress. "Bye."

I take a few breaths as Mom's X-ray eyes scan through me.
I'm sure she can see the way my throat is closing—the way my
whole entire body wants to cry. She's trying not to seem smug.
Trying not to say, *I told you so.*

I return the phone before heading for the stairs. I seriously
can't stand to look at her. "Boop?" she calls after me. "You're
going to be okay."

"Don't!" I say, not turning back. My walk turns to a run and
soon the door is slamming shut behind me. I lock it, my pulse
racing as my chest rises and falls.

I see the standing bag in the corner of my room and run
to it. I throw a punch, hard. From the shoulder, with all my
weight. Again and again. I punch the shit out of that bag, until
I lose myself. Until my knuckles ache. Until I'm breathless and
heaving, with tears all down my face.

Nǐ hǎo.

Me again. (Who else would it be?)

DONGGGG-GEE-DONG-GEE-CCCCHHHHHH

See above for the soundtrack of my brain. It's like a looming question mark, and I seriously can't stop hearing it. I suppose it's a nice break from Amanda's tunes, though.

"When You're Smiling" is competing for space in this tortured mind, though I only sort of know the words. Something something, repeat repeat, "The whole world smiles with you . . ." If we're sticking with this chipper theme, could I at least put in a request, Mr. DJ? How 'bout a little "Happy" by Pharrell? Actually, no. I was incredibly immune to how overplayed that song got, but Amanda would find a way to destroy it. It's the mother—

flipping jam. (If anyone disagrees, we can fight. This is a hill I will die on.)

Non Sequitur I Feel Compelled to Share:

When I was a kid, any time I started a journal I was always vaguely concerned it would wind up published for posterity. What if there was something really embarrassing in there? Like how I thought "approximately" meant "exactly" for like . . . years? Until Ben finally cracked up and told me? Or how I spent all of third and fourth grade convinced I was bound to convert to Judaism whenever Adam Eidelman and I inevitably married? (He was super nice, and he always shared the matzo from his school lunch.) TO BE CLEAR: if anyone's wondering, this journal is SO NOT THAT KIND OF THING. I just need to get stuff out. No posterity, please. ☺

Anyway. I've had a day. Days.

AHAHAHA that is an understatement.

Ben and I aren't in what you'd call a *great place* at the moment. It's been a whole lot of either fights or long stretches of not talking. Even during our less prickly times when he's come down, I've kept the chitchat to a minimum. But we can't stop talking now. That'll just make things worse.

I was decent about it today. He came bearing muffins and a new textbook he'd picked up for me. He said he talked to Zan last night, and that she was worried. He tends to overshare these days, I've noticed. Weirdly enough, I think he misses me.

"What'd you tell her?" I asked.

"Mentioned boarding school. Alluded to some changes. Think you really hurt that friend of yours."

I refused to let his words affect me. "C'est possible," I said, with a little French shrug. I couldn't help but complain a smidge. Told him I wished the muffin had been blueberry. "Always blueberry."

"So you've mentioned," he said. I'll pump the brakes for a bit.

I'm now officially switching from Mandarin to German. I'm lacking my usual determination with the former. It's too damn hard. German grammar is admittedly bananas, but I think I'll have more luck. Plus, I already enjoy shouting, "SCHEISSE!" when I'm angry, and I'd love to be able to fold that into a full-on German rant.

I need more expletives in my life.

Besides anger, I've also been feeling this, like . . . aching guilt. Toward Mom, mostly. And let me tell you, feeling simultaneously angry and guilty toward a dead person is one of the more exhausting emotions out there.

I keep seeing that photo in the box of her things. That lively smiling group in front of the bar. Mom and Alice looked so young. They looked like liars. I guess we all keep secrets. I did from Zan. I did from Nick.

At the same time, I can't believe how much I let Mom down.

There was an opening. I could have done something. And I didn't.

I find myself wishing there was a way to say I'm sorry, and to hear her say it back. I don't know what the point is in thinking this way. I'm not expecting some Disney Mufasa moment or anything. But I guess I could use, like, a sign? Now I feel ridiculous. (No posterity, okay?!)

Well, Mom, if you're somehow listening, or sensing, or whatever . . . I'm sorry. I guess you could say I'm still "working things out." But you and me? As far as I'm concerned, we're okay, okay?

I keep thinking about how optimistic you were. When things went wrong, more often than not, you managed to laugh! You'd turn the whole ordeal into a story. A story that you loved! I've tried to be like that. Though sometimes I just want to say, "This sucks! Can't we admit this just sucks?" If you were here, maybe you'd be looking for the silver lining in all this—in you leaving me here all alone. But I don't know. That one might actually stump you.

I will not cry. I WILL NOT CRY.

(Okay, I'm taking a break.)

I'm better now.
Pharrell voice with background claps "Happy happy
happy happy . . ."

TO DO:
More positive affirmations.
(See anything owned by Amanda for inspiration.)

(Principle #302: When admitting things suck, swear in
German as needed.)

SEVEN

Saturday, September 15

I woke up early this morning and stayed in bed through the muted scuffle of people leaving the breakfast table, packing up, and scattering. Around eleven, I snuck downstairs to scour the kitchen for treats. I was disappointed to find that Mom had done the latest round of shopping (it's Whit who has the sweet tooth). I settled for an apple with peanut butter, which I promptly brought back to bed.

My vision has gone hazy, strained by computer light in the otherwise dark room. I've gone into an internet sinkhole. Onion articles and memes, and clips of people falling down. I cried at a video of a three-legged dog conquering a stair step, and again when a baby got her first pair of glasses and saw her mom.

Anyway. Now I'm numb again.

The apple's whittled-down core is diluted but still tart. I study it a moment before chucking it into the basket across the room with a satisfying *swish*. My eyes return to the screen and I fill my mouth with an enormous, sticky spoonful straight from the peanut butter jar.

"Well, that's attractive," says a little voice. Harr is standing in the doorway with a backpack on one shoulder.

It takes a minute to swallow. "When did you get here?"

"Dad just dropped me off," he says. "Mom told me to ask if you want lunch." My little brother appears to be mildly exasperated, like for once he wishes I'd act my own age. It's a little unsettling, actually. "Well? You want anything?"

I shake my head.

"Okay," he says, and he shuts the door behind him.

I make a mental note to be a better sister later. Then comes another knock, and the guilt seems to vanish. "Ugh, what now, Harrison?"

But it's Mom who walks in, looking clean and fresh—a person well into her day.

"I told Harr I'm not hungry," I mutter. She stops a few feet from my bed to look me over. "What?"

"OkayseriouslyI'vehadenough!" Her reply comes out as a single word. I brace myself for a Big Talk, for the forced excavation of buried thoughts and feelings.

Instead, I feel a cold rush as the comforter vanishes from my bed. "Mom!" I catch the laptop before it flies away. Our eyes lock for a suspended moment before she pulls me, rough, by the top of my arm, up to my feet.

"Get out," says Mom.

I falter. "What?"

"Out! Out of this house!"

I rub my arm on the spot where she grabbed me, shivering in my pantslessness. "I thought I was grounded."

"Yeah, well." Mom slaps my cell phone into my palm. "I changed my mind." She bends down to scoop a pair of cutoff denim shorts from the floor. "Put these on." I take the shorts, my mouth agape.

"I said put them on!"

"Okay!" I step into the tattered legs and slip the phone in the back pocket, afraid to disturb the beast.

"Great, you're dressed," she says, shoving me toward the door. "See ya!"

"Am I allowed to put a bra on?"

"Fine," she says, unhanding me. I find one in a pile by the door and slink it through the armholes of my shirt, wary of the woman watching.

Mom holds out a hoodie when I'm finished. "You should probably take this too. In case it gets cold." The moment I take the sweatshirt in my arms, she begins pushing—out the door and toward the hallway, down the stairs, and into the foyer.

"Wait, I need to brush my—"

"Have some gum," says Mom, placing a pack into my hands along with my wallet. She opens the door, the daylight pouring in. I blink, adjusting, and she tosses my flip-flops onto the front porch, one at a time.

"I was going to say hair." Mom turns back to the shelf by the door and produces a brush. I stare at her. Well played.

"I know you're still a little mad at me," she says as I work through the sizable snarl that has formed along the underside of my untamed waves. "And to be honest, I'm a little mad at you too. But we'll just have to deal with that later." After a few more painful strokes, Mom takes the brush and holds my cheek in her hand. "In the meantime, I think you've sufficiently wallowed. So hear me when I say, with all the love in my heart: Get the hell out of my house."

I shake her off me. "God, do you talk to your clients this way?"

With a happy sigh, she guides me across the threshold, out into the breeze. "Honestly? There are days when I'd like to. But my clients pay me lots of money. You, on the other hand, cost a fortune." I scrunch my toes into flip-flops, eyes squinting to fend off the daylight. "Anyhoo . . ."

"Mom, you can't be seriou—"

She closes my lips with her fingers. "Bye, sweetie. Don't come back before sundown."

"But—" The door slams shut and I hear the click of a lock. I look at the pile in my hands. She gave me everything but my keys.

I stomp down my front steps. No direction seems to speak to me, so I let my legs take over, guiding me through the tree-lined streets. Wind tussles with trees, sun beaming through cracks. With each step I feel my eyes grow clearer, my limbs less heavy, skin tingling and awake.

Out in the fresh air, it's a little like I've broken from a spell. I'm on the lakefront path by the docks. Shiny white boats bob in neat lines, cheerful against the rocky water. It's blustery out, a whisper of fall in the air, and despite the hot sun I'm happy to have my sweatshirt.

The joggers are out in full force today, some pushing strollers, others chatting breathlessly in pairs. A shirtless man on Rollerblades whizzes past, half pulling, half pulled by a big dog on a leash. Coming toward me, a gray-haired couple teaches a little girl to pedal her trike, calling out directions in what sounds like Chinese. I step out of the way as the girl makes a break for it, sending the poor old folks running. I smile as I watch her go. This is a place where people are their best selves, happy and free under the enormous midwestern sky.

"Huh," I say aloud. I didn't come here once this summer.

I pass a patch of beach set up with volleyball nets. A few scrawny college-age guys dive after balls in the sand, unabashed by their obvious athletic ineptitude. By the water's edge, two toddlers in frilly suits dip their toes in, overwhelmed and euphoric, with shovels in hand.

Everyone I see seems to be really living, and right here.

My legs take over again and I find myself climbing the bridge over Lake Shore Drive. A shortcut through the park spits me out near a gas station, and I head north for a while, until I see a familiar wall of brick draped in vines.

I catch the door as someone comes out and cut through the basketball court, a stray ball nearly taking me out within seconds. Something in the way I jolt makes me click in with where I am. All around, kids are practicing shots on top of shots. Through the window, I see senior citizens learning to belly dance in the movement studio.

It's been years since I've set foot in the community center.

It's strange to think, but I've finally found one—a wholly Priya-less place.

The weight room is home to its usual loners. The boxing stuff is still off to one corner. A stocky, older guy works the speed bag clumsily. It's not quite the right height for him, and he can't seem to find the rhythm. A part of me wants to step in and show him how, but I'm not sure he's looking for advice.

As I walk onto the open mat, I get a waft of sweat and rubber and feel myself transported. For a second, I'm a smaller version of myself, all full of wordless fury. After Dad moved out, there was a long stretch when I loathed talking. I hated feelings. And talking about feelings. There was something in me, ready to burst and gush like a fire hydrant. If it opened, I wasn't certain it would stop.

Reggie got it, anyway. He didn't ask stupid questions. He

just let me hit stuff. It was here—slowly—that I put myself back together. It's a comfort to think about, actually. I did it once. Maybe I can do it again.

I walk toward a heavy red bag that dangles from a hook. I give it a push and watch it sway.

Maybe . . .

With a deep breath, I make myself complete the thought.

Maybe I have to let her go.

I kill time in Lincoln Park, winding along the nature board-walk and up through the archway to the zoo. I'm pretty sure Mom was serious about keeping me out until sundown, and it's as good a place as any.

I pay my respects to the snowy owl, the red panda, and a naked mole rat (who is, incredibly, just as ugly as he sounds). Inside the Ape House, the smell is pungent, an unfortunate marriage of mulch and shit. A mother nurses a baby in faraway corner, her back turned to the people straining to see.

Priya always got sad at zoos. I guess I can see why.

But none of that.

I'm letting go.

One tiny little thought at a time.

I suddenly remember the phone that's been returned to me. I pull it out and see the screen lit up with texts. It does make me feel better. Less hermit-like. The messages are from Lacey, sent this morning.

The soccer girls are going to the movies this afternoon. Come if you want, and bring the stud muffin. Together we can stop chronic boylessness!

I laugh into the screen, though the mention of said stud muffin does sour my stomach a little. The next one comes with a photo.

Look what I found!!

We're maybe nine in the picture, in matching soccer uniforms. My hair is messy and matted with sweat, while hers remains intact in the perfectly symmetrical French braids she always used to wear. She's got her arm slung around me like I'm a prized possession. We're both missing several teeth.

I write back.

Omg, so cute!
And sorry, didn't see this. Ps. you're ridiculous.

Lacey and I may never be soul sisters, but it wouldn't kill me to make an effort. I follow up with another message.

Next time. ☺

The crowd around me gasps, and my attention returns to the scene in front of me. The mother gorilla has set down her baby, who is now toddling this way like some adorable, bizarre near human. The reflections of gleeful spectators overlap the captives—little kids pressing noses to glass and parents wielding cameras.

Suddenly I land on a familiar face.

It takes me a minute to place him. It's the man who spoke to me outside Priya's gate the other day. His dark eyes widen behind glasses when they meet mine.

I jump. "Jesus!" The baby gorilla cackles through spread teeth, having smashed a handful of feces against the glass. I catch my breath as the mother lumbers over to scoop up the little rascal, and the phone in my hand buzzes—again, and then again. The texts are from Arturo.

911!!! Panicking.

You are still coming to the show, right?

RIGHT?? Starts at 4. HURRY!

"Crap," I mutter, immediately running for the exit. I'm officially a jerk. I completely forgot about Arturo's showcase. I weave through people, past food carts and rock candy stands, my flip-flops slapping the bottoms of my feet with every stride.

If I hurry, I still might make it there in time. I head north, then west, toward another Cubs game overtaking the streets. Buses are rerouted, cars gridlocked. I run through hordes of fratty fans and kids on shoulders, a sea of matching jerseys and hats.

At five minutes to four I come stumbling into the theater and throw down money for a ticket. The place is packed with grown men dressed like college kids and hipster girls cracking jokes at the bar. There are no windows, so it feels like night. I note a general smattering of plaid throughout, just as Sam described, and there are several mustaches, possibly ironic. In the audience, a penis-adorned bachelorette party is already woo-ing, despite the empty stage.

"Pssst!" I look around. "Zan!"

I spot Arturo's floating head against a wall of dingy black curtains. I push through the crowd until I reach him and he yanks me by the arm in through the opening.

"Thank God you're here!" he whisper-yells. "I'm freaking out!" I've never been behind a stage like this before. Some performers are chatting and finishing up beers while others stand with their backs to the wall, humming and talking to themselves.

"Hey," I say with as much authority as I can muster. "The people in that audience are going to love you. I'm sure you're exactly what these fancy agents and producer types are looking for."

"It's not that," says Arturo. "Sam finally listened to me and brought her mom to a show. It happens to be the most important one of my entire career, but you know, I'm not resentful or anything."

I frown. He may be turning slightly green. "Why would Sam pick tonight?"

"She didn't mean to. She was trying to talk me up, saying tonight could be my big break . . ." He scratches his head, looking dazed. "I guess she did such a good job her mom decided to come." He locks eyes with me, pleading, though I can't help.

I bite my lip and pull open the curtain to look. "Front row, to the left," he says. They're easy to spot—stiff and silent among the commotion. Samantha's lips are sucked in, a crossed leg bobbing as she sits beside a pretty, older woman with short-cropped hair. I try to see the place how this put-together woman might—noting the mismatched audience chairs and mingling smells of beer-stained wood and bathroom cleaner.

Arturo shakes his head as I close the curtain. "This is a nightmare. What if she hates me?"

"Aw." I palm his cheek, only to snap my hand away. He's quite sweaty. "You can't worry about that. Just . . . be funny, okay?"

"You can leave now," he says with a sigh, pushing me back through the opening. For a moment, I'm alone on the empty stage, the bright lights blinding me. When my eyes adjust I'm surprised to see Logan sitting on Sam's other side.

I'm sneaking toward the back row when I hear, "Zan!"

Dammit. I've been caught.

"How's he doing?" Sam asks as I come over, my eyes decidedly *not* on Logan.

Samantha and I don't sugarcoat. "I'm gonna say, bad?"

"Shit," she whispers to herself. She removes a jacket from the empty seat beside her. "We'll move down so you can sit with Logan."

"Oh," I say, still unable to look at him. "No, no." But it's already done, and soon I'm lowering myself stiffly into the spot beside him.

Sam says something in Korean and turns to me. "Zan, this is my mother, Connie. Umma, this is Zan." Connie reaches across to shake my hand, with a weak smile that has me worried for Arturo. "They sell wine here," says Sam. "Maybe we should get some?"

"I think we'd better," her mother agrees.

Logan and I are quiet as they head for the bar, leaving jackets in their places. After a minute I glance over. Logan, infuriatingly, says nothing. I roll my eyes, finally breaking. "What are you doing here?"

"Arturo asked me, remember?"

I cross my arms. "Well, I wasn't expecting you."

The lights flicker and Sam returns with her mom, each of them holding a small plastic glass filled to the brim. "He's gonna be great," Sam says between gulps. "Right?"

"Right," I say as convincingly as I can manage.

After another flicker, some feel-good hip-hop starts blaring through the sound system. "Hey hey hey!" shouts a sprightly guy in skinny jeans, clasping his palms together as the spotlight comes on. The cheering ramps up and I realize just how many people are packed into this little place. After the host does his bit, he tells us to turn off our cell phones, and the energy settles. Sam squeezes my hand as the lights go out.

Silence.

After a scuffle, something moves past me in the dark. A chair screeches and someone sits. The lights come up on Arturo, sitting front and center. I didn't realize he was going first. It must be harder to go first. I meet his stare from a few feet away. A bead of sweat slides along his hairline. Does he know he's looking at me? And why isn't he speaking? *Speak, Arturo. Speak!*

Finally, like a computer screen unglitching, Arturo's eyes leave mine, shifting off to a point in the middle distance. Beside me, Sam is pulling on her first finger. I hear the knuckle pop.

Arturo clears his throat. "Life is weird, in'it?" he says in a thick New Zealand accent. There's a small murmur of laughter around us. The accent in itself is funny. Arturo's arms rest in his lap, his posture sunken. "You work hard, get yourself a nice chrysalis, and you think to yourself—You've done it, Glen. Now it's time to relax." Arturo doesn't look as nervous anymore, but I can tell he hasn't fully settled in. There's a staleness to the air as people shift in seats. "And then, well . . ." Arturo shakes his head, a look of genuine pain filling his eyes. "Then someone comes along and tells you it's all about to change. *This is the Before Part, Glen,*" he says, doing a voice. "*No need to get emotional, Glen.*" He clucks to himself. "I don't know about you, but I quite like the before part." He shrugs. "It's cozy."

He looks out meekly to the audience. "I'm a caterpillar, by the way." There's a little snort from a couple seats down. "Probably should have mentioned that." Sam nudges me, a stunned look on her face as she tilts her head toward the smiling woman beside her. The laugh came from her mom.

I grin back at Sam before my gaze shifts to the bar behind her. I spot a man standing there, a beer in hand.

I look away, then double-check.

It's definitely him. The guy from Priya's house. The same guy from the zoo.

The audience roars with laughter. I must have missed something. When I peek over again, the man's expression hasn't changed. He drains his glass and sets it down, looking almost nervous as he runs a hand over his stubble.

I jump when Sam clutches my arm, laughing breathlessly. Beside her, Connie rears her head back, wiping away a happy tear. Music has started playing—a booming house party beat. I'm pretty lost, but I think Arturo is expressing Glen the Caterpillar's metamorphosis through dance. He prances and gyrates, his face so heartbreakingly earnest. It's all so perfectly bizarre.

When I steal another glance at the bar, the man is staring straight at me.

I jolt, and Logan leans in to whisper, "Hey, you okay?"

"Fine," I say tersely, watching as Arturo flits about the stage, morphing into character after character, impression after impression. All people with different accents, all in their Before Parts. I'm only getting bits and pieces, though, because the man's eyes are burned into my vision, my breath growing shallow.

I'm not sure how much time passes before Arturo's voice brings me back—his real voice—as a calm settles over the crowd.

"Please let her like me." Something in the energy around us shifts, and Arturo is somehow impossible to look away from as he ties an invisible tie onstage. "You know what? No. I mean I'm praying here, right, God? Go big or go home!" Arturo looks to the ceiling, and his arms spread out wide. "I meant *love,* God! Let her love me! I get that it's only a date. But *goddamn*—" He grimaces. "Whoops, sorry. It's just . . . With some people, you just know, you know?"

I catch Sam and her mom in a brief, meaningful look. Sam's cheeks are flushed, her eyes a little glassy from laughing. I'm not sure I've ever seen her look like that. I wonder if I'm even capable of the expression.

Around me people are still and silent, absorbed by this open view into my boss's weird, adorable heart. My eyes float to the bar again, and the hairs on my arms begin to stick up as a piano rings out. The man is gone.

Arturo is back to being Glen the Butterfly now, fluttering and singing while the crowd claps. I listen in on the song for a moment as I scan the place— "Nothing like landing on your first bologna sandwich!" *What?*

I spot the man slinking behind the standing-room-only crowd in the back row, making his way to my side of the theater. He looks . . . intense? Determined? It's freaking me out. I twist in my seat, looking for a clear path. I'd have to cross the stage to get to the main doors. But there's a back exit.

Sam gives me an odd look as I get up. I mouth the word *sorry,* my eyes fixed on the man still weaving his way through the tight space in back. I lean over to whisper another apology to Connie before slipping out, and Arturo catches my hunched-over exit while belting out a long note. He doesn't look mad. I think he's too high on the night to care. I give an emphatic thumbs-up and rush for the exit, the sounds of a joyful crowd dampening as the door closes behind me.

Out in the alley, I check over my shoulder and hurry toward the main street. I step into a busy intersection, swarming with Cubs fans, and a crossing guard trills her whistle. "Sorry. Sorry!" I say, darting back onto the curb.

Someone comes up from behind me and I whip around.

"It's me," says Logan, his hands up. "Is something wrong?"

"No." I shake my head, heart racing. "Maybe . . . I don't

know." I look at the gum-pocked sidewalk. "I think someone might be following me."

For the first time today, Logan looks straight at me. "Seriously?"

I feel suddenly sheepish as I meet his eyes. "I think so. I met him yesterday. Saw him again earlier today. And now here, at the theater." I search the moving crowds, but there's no sign of the man. "So yeah. Seemed like I should probably leave."

"Jesus," says Logan. He checks over his shoulder. "What'd he look like? Do you see him anywhere?"

"No, I think I lost him." I look down the block, back toward the theater. "I feel bad for running out on Arturo like that."

"I think you saw what you needed to," says Logan. "Our man killed it in there."

"Yeah, seemed like it. But I was so distracted by that stupid guy that I spaced out for a lot of it. What do you think he was getting at?"

Logan shrugs. "Meaning of life?"

"Damn," I say, smiling despite myself. "That would have been good to know."

For a moment, I'm tempted to slide back into our easy banter, but I know it's not that simple. It won't change what Logan said about me. Or what I said. He must feel it too, because he clears his throat, back to business. "I should walk you home."

I squint up at the sky. It's still a ways to sundown. "How about I walk you home instead?"

He groans. "Is this another gender role thing? I don't think it's patronizing of me to offer when strange men are literally stalking you."

"I'm just not allowed to come home yet," I say, smiling though I don't mean to. "Mom's punishment for . . . wallowing, I guess." We pass a stream of bustling bars before turning down a quiet side street.

Logan seems lost in his thoughts for a while. "So . . . how'd you meet this guy?"

"We met outside Priya's house. After you left."

He scratches at his jaw. "Did he say who he was?"

"A family friend, supposedly. Something was off. Anyway, I'm fine. No use dwelling on it."

"Oh, I plan to dwell on it," says Logan. "You might be a pain in the ass, but I don't want you getting hurt."

"Gee," I say. "How nice of you."

"Hey. Zan," he says, reaching out to stop me on the sidewalk. "What I said? The stuff about Priya?"

"It's fine," I say, a mess of emotion rising up inside me. "We were both . . ." I'm not quite sure what it is I want to tell him. I'm mad, and I'm sorry. It's strange. These aren't good feelings, and yet, even now, it's so much better to be with him than without. "I think you were right, anyway," I say finally. "I'm . . . giving up on all that." We're at the path to Logan's building, where one door stays propped open with a big rock.

Someone is shouting nearby. I listen close. "Whoa." There's a loud crash and I hurry toward it, stopping at the entrance to the lobby.

A small stained glass lamp lies in pieces on the ground. Frank the doorman is standing with his chest out, a petite woman yelling up at him. "*It's my kid!* Do you get that? I'm trying to see my *kid*!" On that last word, the woman's spittle hits his face.

"Is not up to me, lady," says Frank, wiping his eye. "I call upstairs, maybe we sort this out." The woman makes a break for the elevator, but he blocks her with his body. "Please. Don't make me dial police." She tries to run again, but he grabs her by the wrist, a pained look on his face. "I'm just doorman. Not security guard."

I can feel Logan standing behind me in the entrance now.

"It's my kid," the woman says through a whimper. Frank releases her and she crumples to the ground, a mess of blond hair covering her face. "My babies." As the woman's back heaves up and down, I turn to Logan and suddenly understand.

"Hi, Mom."

Frank and I share a look.

"Logan." She scrambles to stand and a few glass shards sprinkle down from her long skirt. "Logan, honey." She wipes away a trail of mascara, a frantic, pretty smile taking up her whole face. "Thank God you're here. Let's get inside, baby."

"You can't be here," he says evenly.

211

"I want to see Bee."

For a flickering moment, I see those haunted charcoal faces in his eyes, and all I want is to take them away. "You know you can't do that," he says. "And even if you could, it wouldn't be like this."

"Honey . . ."

"How'd you get here, Mom?"

She shrugs. "Got a ride." She walks over to touch his cheek, her eyes filling all over again. "I love you so much, baby. More than you'll ever . . ."

Logan takes her hand from his face to hold it, and for a moment I forget to breathe. "I know," he says. "I love you, too. But it's time for you to go."

When I get home I find the door unlocked and charge straight into the kitchen to hug Mom. As I pull away, she looks a little stunned, but in a good way, I think. "You okay?" she asks after an odd silence.

"Yeah," I say, the haze around me slowly dissipating. "Sorry."

"Don't be," says Mom.

I pause a moment, trying to place the lingering smells. "What's on the menu tonight?"

"Quiche and kale salad," says Whit, slipping into the room.

"Actually, Zan has plans," says Mom.

"I do?"

She nods. "Dad called. Asked if I would persuade you to come by. Consider yourself persuaded. I told him you'd be there at eight."

I hang my head. "I shouldn't have blown up at him like that. It's gonna be weird."

"He's your dad, Zan."

I pout there a moment, feeling especially indulgent, and Whit shoots me a kind look that makes me feel even worse. "Sorry about yesterday," I say to her. "I know it was your big night."

Whit shrugs. "It was just a party. It's what I signed up for with all this, isn't it?" She gestures to the home around us. "The kids come first."

"Where's Harr?" I ask, relaxing a little.

"The sleepover was rescheduled," says Mom. "You know that girl Claire?"

My jaw drops. "Claire as in *a girl*? You think that's a good idea?"

"Honey, he's seven."

"Uh, seven and a freaking Casanova," I say, making Whit snort.

"We'll see," says Mom. "He claims he's stepping out of the dating game for a little while, at least until he's ten."

"Huh," I say. Something in this house still isn't right. I peer down the open hallway. "What's different in here? Why does everything feel so nice?" Mom grins, waiting for me to catch up. I look at Whit. "You unpacked!"

Mom squeals and claps her hands. "We had a stoop sale while you were out."

"I'm still mourning a few items," says Whit, slumping down to rest her chin on Mom, who promptly takes the opportunity to palm her face and cover it in kisses. Whit laughs. "I suppose it was worth it."

"Oh! And we made a hundred bucks!" says Mom. "Here, buy yourself something pretty." She hands me a twenty from the counter. "And I forgot," she says to Whit. "This came for you." She sighs, handing her an envelope. "I still love seeing mail with your name on it."

Whit rips through the top corner and pulls out a photo. "One of my old patients," she explains, handing me the picture. "This little baby came out early. Four pounds. Now look at her," she says, showing us. "So sweet and chubby you just wanna eat her like a turkey leg." Mom and Whit both linger on the photo.

"Wait," I say. "You guys aren't thinking about having another—"

"No," Whit interrupts, though Mom sort of teeters her head from side to side. Whit laughs. "Not yet, anyway. I think we've got our hands full here."

I smile, surprised by the welling emotions inside.

"Hey." Mom bumps me with her shoulder. "Did you know

214

your dad always said you were the world's most eatable baby?"

I did not know that. The thought actually makes me a bit queasy, but I shake it off and say, "I believe the official title would have been world's fattest blob of freckles."

"You were adorable," corrects Mom, pretending to be stern. "I swear you were even cute in the sonograms—from the day Dad started calling you Boop."

The welling feeling grows. "That was Dad's name for me?"

Mom's eyes do a quick Zan-scan. "What?"

"Just. Go easy on him, okay? I think you made him . . . afraid." I cringe at the impending awkwardness. "Better get moving."

"Yeah, yeah," I say.

Mom pulls me to her, and though it feels a little abrupt, I stop to hug Whit too. She squeezes me back, and a pang of sadness shoots through me. *Hug a lot. Even if it's weird.*

But actually, this time, it isn't.

I walk through the warm night, in a fog from the strange day. I think of Logan, and his mom, and all the good in my life I take for granted. Thoughts of Priya slip in and out, but I send them away. It isn't easy, but I'll get it.

I'm living here, now. I'm letting go.

It's only when I reach the apartment that I really emerge. I turn the knob and stop short. Under the big low-hanging lamp in Dad's apartment, a small army of plastic takeout containers has overtaken the dining room table.

"Whoa," I say. I scan the dishes row by row—the bright reds, greens, and oranges smashed against the see-through sides. It smells amazing.

Dad walks in and I look around, confused. "Is all of this for us?"

"It is," he says. "And it's meat. It's all meat." I laugh, feeling oddly winded, and Dad says, "I'm so sorry, Boop."

"Look, we don't have to—"

"Yes we do," he says. "Those things you said? You were right. When your mom and I . . ." He shakes his head. "I did check out, for a long time—on you, and your brother too, though he was too little to understand." He tries to smile. "But I didn't love you any less."

I can officially no longer stand the sincerity in his eyes, but he grins and says, "We might get a little real here, and you're gonna have to deal with it." Something in my chest tightens, but I breathe through it. "It's hard to explain. My world sort of crashed, you know? I should have put you first, but you were such an obvious reminder of what I'd lost. And you know how intense your mom is." He sighs. "I guess I figured she had it covered. In my mind, you didn't need me. But that's no excuse."

I nod to the floor. "It's okay."

He walks to the cupboard and sets out two plates, alongside forks and serving spoons. "I know it's not that simple. But for now, at the very least, I should know that my daughter eats meat. And . . ." He waits for me to look at him again. "I'd like to be *the dad*. If you'll let me. And maybe even meddle in your life sometimes. Once I've earned the right. By being there, and . . ." He shrugs. "And by ordering the meat." I laugh. "Would that be okay?"

He pulls out a chair for me and I smile through a sniff.

"Yeah," I tell him. "That'd be good."

From: Zan Martini <martiniweenybikini12@gmail.com>

To: Priya Patel <priyawouldntwannabeya514@gmail.com>

Date: Sat, Sep 15, 11:58 pm

Subject: if you're out there . . .

I just thought you should know that if you're okay, then I'm okay.

Or I will be.

I'll miss you though.

Always.

Amanda's beginning to break my heart. I bet you liked her, Mom.

Look for the silver lining
Whene'er a cloud appears in the blue.
Remember somewhere the sun is shining,
And so the right thing to do is make it shine for you.

I keep thinking about my three-day sleepover. With Yaz and Anushka. It's not that I didn't want you around, but we'd been hyping it up, and I'd been counting down the days. You were flying out to see Alice. She was going through a tough time, you said. It was reason enough for me. Ben was on a work trip. He flew so much we rarely asked where to.

The moment you said goodbye to me is fuzzy. I was reading on Yaz's chair. I looked up for just a sec, just long enough for you to smack a kiss on my face and remind me to take my vitamins.

Yaz's place in Harlem had a huge four-poster bed.

Anushka slept over too. She made biryani, and brought a lifetime supply of chick flicks and candy.

On Saturday we went skating at Rockefeller Center and we saw a man propose to his girlfriend in the middle of the ice. Anushka got teary-eyed, and Yaz said, "Pull it together, woman." I thought it was hysterical.

Sunday I was reading in Yaz's chair again when the two of them came and sat down on the rug in front of me. I remember losing my breath.

A heart full of joy and gladness
Will always banish sadness and strife.
So always look for the silver lining
And try to find the sunny side of life.

I'm trying, Mom. I swear.

(Principle #303: Somewhere, the sun is shining.)

EIGHT

Sunday, September 16

I'm not quite asleep when my phone goes off. It's a text from Logan.

You get home alright?

I sit up in bed and text him back.

Yeah, I'm here. You okay?

I look at the time—2:30 a.m. exactly—and wonder if that might be some indication of the night he just had. When I last saw him, his mom had yet to leave the lobby, the glass still everywhere.

I pull back the blankets and slip into a pair of fuzzy socks from the floor before swigging from the water by my bed. The house is dead quiet, and worry bubbles up with each passing second. As of 2:38 he has not texted back. I can't take it. And so I'm up. Energized. *Cleaning.*

I straighten the papers on my desk and stack books in neat piles. I scoop jewelry into boxes and tidy the contents of my wardrobe. Moving dirty clothes into baskets, my fingers graze something solid. My heart sinks and the productive mojo promptly dies. It's the little lime-green notebook, buried in the pile.

I bring the book to bed with me and text Logan again.

Should I take that as a no?

But he doesn't write back. I peer down at the cover and send the pages fluttering with my thumb.

#5
When Zan is sad, JUST ADD COOKIES!!

It's actually very true. I wonder if we have any downstairs. I skip ahead to an old favorite.

#19
Life is like brie. It kinda stinks, but it's also weirdly good.

It's strange to think of Priya admitting life could ever stink. She was the one always telling me to be positive.

I've lost track of the origins for some of these, which does add an element of intrigue.

#36
They should have puppies at peace talks.

#87
We must band together to end egg salad on airplanes!

#267
One day, our kids will laugh at all the mustaches.

I leaf through the rest until I find the spot where the pages go blank. I notice the last entry and catch my breath. I didn't write this one. In fact, I've never even seen it.

#300
We can never, EVER, give up on each other.
(K ZanaBanana? PS. I'm gonna miss you a buttload.)

I touch the grooves in the paper where her pen carved out the words, and for a moment Priya is exactly who she always was—the master of many tongues who still sometimes used words like buttload. Priya. The real Priya. My friend.

I jolt at the sound of my phone. Logan.

Sorry. I'm okay. It's a long story.

I write him back.

I've got time.

The phone chirps again, and I smile down at the message.

In that case, wanna come outside? I'm kind of on your porch.

I slip on a sweatshirt and pad down to the darkened first floor. When I step outside, I find Logan sitting on the top porch step, his messy hair reflecting moonlight. "Hi," I whisper, closing the door.

He straightens up when he sees me. "Sorry about earlier. After you left I realized I shouldn't have let you walk home alone."

"Don't be sorry." I take the step below his and lean back against the railing. "I can take care of myself." He nods, relaxing somewhat as I drink in the crisp, clean air. The fireflies are out tonight, their little green orbs appearing and vanishing without a sound. Priya and I loved fireflies when we were younger. I always wanted to catch them. She always made me let them go.

I reach out to nudge Logan with my foot. "I hope you didn't come all this way in the middle of the night to say that."

"Well, no." He looks at me and I remind myself to breathe. "I guess I felt like if I saw you, I'd feel better."

"Oh." I clear my throat. "Do you? Feel better?"

He smiles. "A little."

"So that was your mom." It sounds so useless and obvious as it tumbles from my mouth. I tug at the drawstring of my hoodie. "Is she always—" I recoil. "I mean, is that why you guys had to move here?" He winces and a tide of regret rises up in me. "We don't have to get into it if you don't want."

"It's fine," he says. A car drives by, its moving headlights drowning out the fireflies. But the little orbs return soon enough, the engine's rumble fading.

I clear my throat. "Is she . . ."

"An addict?"

I look at him, startled by his directness, and he nods.

"It's been like that for a while."

"How long is a while?"

He laughs ruefully. "Since I was little. But it was getting worse. Or at least harder to ignore."

"Like how?" I ask, as gently as I can manage. He looks a little dazed. "Sorry," I say. "Too many questions?"

"No. I'm just . . . not sure where to start. I guess . . . It kind of crept up on me. The rough patches got closer and closer together. There were nights my mom wouldn't make it home.

She'd go out for a walk and wouldn't come back. I'd have to make Bee stay behind, get out the flashlight, and go looking for her. I never liked leaving my sister with her for long stretches, but I had to go to work. My mom would usually get herself back together eventually. She'd go out and get another job after the one she'd lost. She'd get energized, and start making plans for the future. And then we'd be good for a while. We were always a little on edge, but"—he shrugs—"I felt like I could keep it under control."

"So." I swallow. "What happened?"

He lets out a breath. "One night she borrowed my car and crashed it into a neighbor's tree."

My stomach drops. "Jesus."

"Yeah, that wasn't great."

"Was she okay?"

"She split the skin of her forehead. Hurt her arm. She was freaking out, crying. Wouldn't let me dial an ambulance."

"Wait. You were with her?"

"No, but she called me all upset so I came and found her. But then a neighbor must have called 911, because we heard sirens and she started panicking. She ran home and I sat behind the wheel until they came. Figured it would save her from the DUI."

"So . . . No one ever found out she crashed the car?"

"Nope. But that wasn't really the important part."

"What do you mean?"

He studies his hands a moment, his expression lost in the shadows. "When the cops got there, they found a bag of oxy in the glove compartment. It was a big one." My eyes shoot up to his. "It was . . . pretty bad. But my aunt came down to fight the charges, hired the best lawyers she could find. I barely skirted serving time, which I know was extremely lucky. Not every kid has someone fighting in their corner like that. I got off with community service and probation. But then my school found out—my old teammate from that party at Northwestern made sure of it. I lost my scholarship, my art studio." He looks at me and shrugs. "Eventually I came here."

"So that's why . . ." My shoulders sink. "The rumors."

He nods. "I don't know how it's getting out."

"What is it," I say, "six degrees of separation? A girl I know from soccer may have mentioned a source."

"Ah," he says, nodding his head. "Well. It probably comes up if you Google hard enough anyway. But yeah. Kids keep coming up to me and asking if I can get them drugs." His laugh makes me relax a little. "I've been disappointing people left and right."

I let out a big breath, and we're quiet for a while. I move up a step to sit beside him. "I guess I still don't understand. Why didn't you tell the cops the pills weren't yours? Why didn't your mom tell them?"

Logan considers this a moment. "I think my mom and I both knew it would be the end. DCFS had already been making home visits after a report from Bee's teacher. And my aunt wanted us out of there. All she needed was the proof, but I wouldn't give it to her for some reason."

I watch him closely, the way he's looking so intently at a point off in the street. "What do you think was stopping you?"

"I guess . . ." He looks at me, cutting through the space between us. "I told myself I was doing it for Bee. I couldn't make her leave her home, her friends. But really, I think I couldn't leave my mom. I was scared of what might happen to her."

"What made you change your mind?"

His eyes drift back to the street. "Nothing. It wasn't up to me." His stare seems more deliberate now, the muscle of his jaw twitching. "A few weeks later my mom's friend OD'd at our house."

"Like . . ." I blink. "As in . . ."

"Died?" The little shake to his voice makes me think I might be sick. "Right there on our living room floor. I was out and my mom was too messed up to handle it. Bee had to call 911."

I can't quite bring myself speak. When I do, it comes out like a whisper: "*Fuck*." Logan watches the fireflies and I look down at the space between us, surprised to find that I'm squeezing his hand.

"How's a kid supposed to get over something like that?" When I meet his eyes, I realize that he's really asking.

"I don't know," I say. "But having you must help."

He lets my hand slip away. "I think I knew something was coming. There was this voice telling me . . . But I was too scared to listen." I nod, calm despite the swelling in my chest. I think I know exactly what he means.

"Hey," I say, pulling myself together. "I'm really sorry about before. I shouldn't have doubted you like that."

"Stop," he says. "I was a jerk."

"No you weren't." I smile. "Okay, maybe a little. But so was I."

A long silence swallows us up, more comfortable than not. When I shiver, he gestures to the space beside him, and I wedge myself in close. For a few long moments, I can feel two sets of lungs breathing. Still, but fiercely alive. "Hey," he says, his jaw grazing the top of my head. "Did you mean what you said about Priya earlier? Are you really giving up?"

I look at him and realize I don't have an answer. When I close my eyes, I can almost see her knowing stare pouring into me. *We can never, EVER, give up on each other. K ZanaBanana?*

"All I have is this . . . feeling," I say after a minute. "Like you said. Like a voice, telling me it can't be her. This doesn't feel like her. Maybe I've got no solid proof to go on, but I'm still scared of what will happen if I don't listen."

Logan nods, taking this in, as another lonely car comes whirring past—loud to soft to silent, lights bright to faded to nothing at all. With a sigh, I lean into Logan's side once more— giving my weight, eyes on the street, searching for fireflies in the dark.

Guten Morgen! . . . Afternoon, actually. I just can't remember how to say that.

Today's Amanda Jam is "Here Comes the Sun," which— okay, I'm kind of into. (Yes, posterity that is not supposed to read this, I am super original and "discovered" the Beatles when I was twelve.)

Not much new here. Although! My German textbook has a delightful little section on vocabulary words without direct English translations. For example,

Fisselig: Being flustered to the point of incompetence. (Omg. Someone in Germany has met my stepdad.) Or,

Backpfeifengesicht: A face in need of a punch. (Okay,

staaawp. Was Ben like, THERE, when they made German? And why don't we have words like this in English??)

I'm a lifelong fan of these types of words, actually—even the ones with less relevance to my life. Like age-otori, the Japanese term for when you look worse after a haircut. Or my fave, gattara, the Italian word for old women who devote themselves to stray cats. (I mean come on, how sweet is that?) Jugaad is sort of like that, too. It's an Indian word with different meanings, but it's sort of like a hack, arrived at despite limited resources. (So maybe that one has some relevance.)

Everything is so surreal right now. There are times I find myself tempted to administer one of those theatrical self-face-slaps you see people do in movies. (Omigod! In a way, I guess that means I almost have a Backpfeifengesicht!)

And now! A new segment I'd like call, ACTUAL CONVERSATIONS WITH BEN!

Me: You're such an asshole. (If I were German I'd have a cooler word than that.)
Him: I know.

Me: How long till things go back to normal? Or can they even?

Him: He'll kill us, Pri. Right now, I'm just trying not to get killed.

Me: You own a gun? Who on EARTH let you own a gun?
Him: Second Amendment, baby. I'm just kidding. Our nation's gun laws are a joke.

Me: Can you move your head? You're blocking the TV.
Him: Oh, sorry. Popcorn?

Sometimes I think of us careening across I-70, Ben checking his rearview mirror the day we moved. There was a moment when he lost control of the wheel and I had to reach across and take it. "We're in some deep shit, huh?" he said. And I said, "WE?!?"

It's funny how some things don't change. And how everything does. (Well, not funny, I guess.)

The memory won't leave me—the worst day of my life (and yes, it's still the worst, the worst by a mile). Yaz and Anushka took turns holding me. For hours until I fell asleep. Ben flew back on the first flight to New York. I remember the moment he walked into Yaz's room, at the foot of that enormous bed.

We were shattered, both of us, but we were also strangers.

I must have stayed at Yasmine's for a week, at least. No one pushed me. No one pushed him, either. I think they knew it was too much for us. I think they knew he was in over his head.

Somehow, we found routines. There were Girl Scout badges and dance classes, and drop-offs at the dry cleaners. But sometimes, when he would pour my cereal in the morning, or shut off my lamp at night, I'd catch these little flashes of terror in his eyes. So, I don't know. Maybe that's why I'm not scared right now. He's got that same look.

He's in way over his head.

(Priya Principle #304: Some faces could really use that punch.)

NINE

Monday, September 17

I look toward the window—neither at it nor through. When I break away, a husband and wife in matching visors and fanny packs are staring up at me from a booth. They may as well have TOURISTS stamped across their foreheads. "So you really don't have Reubens?" The man holds a menu at a distance from his squinting eyes.

"Sorry, sir," I say. "We really don't."

"What about a nice omelet?" asks the wife.

I take a second to close my eyes, drawing on swiftly draining reserves of patience. "Well, see, like I was saying, this is a vegan restaurant. So we don't have eggs. Or corned beef. Or anything else that comes from an animal." They look to one another, mystified, and the woman lifts a finger with a question at the ready.

"Why don't I give you two another minute?" I say, walking off before either can respond.

When I reach the kitchen, I check my phone. Priya's posts have dried up these past couple days. The most recent was something to do with study snacks—berries and nuts laid out with notebooks. And before that, there was a shot of city lights at night with the words *Stars can't shine without darkness.*

I don't know what it is I'm looking for. The wall I've hit hasn't exactly budged. But even if no else believes me, the more I think about it, the more sure I am that the *Saturday Selfie* with the birthday earrings could only be one of two things: some-body's slipup or a message. And what about that email? *HLEP? ZZ?*

I have to admit, every post since has felt sort of like non-sense. But if I've gone off the deep end, I don't think I care. I'm listening to the voice inside my head.

This morning I left for school at my usual time and sat on a stoop up the block until I saw Mom, Harrison, and Whit all climb into the Jeep and drive off. I dialed the school and excused my own absence, pretending to be Mom.

Then I dove.

One wall of my room now looks like an evidence board from *Law & Order*—all covered in sticky notes. The only prob-lem is I still can't seem to work out how to connect the clues with little tacks and strings. For a while I sat on my bed and stared at the calendar on my wall. I moved the month page back to June, where Priya had drawn a huge sad face in the box for the thirtieth—moving day.

I called Nick first. He sounded surprised to hear from me. "When was the last time you spoke to Priya?" I asked, getting right down to it. "Like really spoke to her. Not emails or texts or any of that."

He sighed. "Still on this, are we?"

"Please, Nick. Give me the date."

I could feel his reluctance. I could tell I was making him sad. Finally he said, "It would have been the day she moved, whenever that was. I was in London and we chatted while she packed. Must have been morning for her, late afternoon for me." After a pause, he said, "She seemed like she really didn't want to go."

When we hung up, I held the phone to my chest, an unnamed fear clawing up.

I called GRETA next. Anushka answered. "Well, hello! Finally got that fund-raising proposal ready for me?"

"Oh," I said. "Sorry. I'm a little behind on that, actually."

"Yes, well, you and everyone else," said Anushka. "There's a reason we set the deadline so early. Even Priya hasn't gotten anything to us."

"Huh." My heart beat faster. "Hey, when *was* the last time you spoke to Priya?"

Anushka paused. "God, it's been a while. She's emailed here and there."

"But what about talked, like on the phone? Not since your

birthday, right? When she sent bacon cupcakes?"

Anushka sounded vaguely alarmed. "You have quite the memory, Zan. Is everything all right?"

"Uh-huh," I said quickly, digging through my backpack until I found the documents I'd scooped up from Priya's house—sheets filled with dollar amounts and various emails about GRETA. I skimmed through until I landed on the one about the fire.

"Hey, Anushka? This is kind of random. But is Friends Elementary one of the places we'll be volunteering this summer?"

"Well, no, actually. Sadly it burned down a few months ago. They decided to redistribute the students rather than rebuild, so we lost a school."

"I see," I said. "I mean . . . That's awful." I shuffled through the papers some more. "What about the um . . . Priti School?"

"Priti, Priti," she said, clucking to herself. "Ah. They got a grant from a bigger charity, so they didn't end up needing us. It's been an unusual year. Lots of changes."

I lingered on the email from Ben to j.karim565.

Please take my call.

I swallowed. "Hey, this is weird, but um . . . Is there anyone named Karim involved with you guys by any chance?"

"Yes . . ." she said strangely. "He worked for us for a couple years. He was our quality control liaison on the ground. He actually quit not too long ago."

"Oh," I said. The paper trembled in my hand. "Um, what— what was his job?"

"He was sort of our bridge to the schools in Mumbai. He would check in. Make sure everyone was complying with our requirements to continue receiving funding. Ben was supposed to hire someone new soon, but he's been dragging his feet. At this rate, we'll have to start taking the trips ourselves again."

"Huh."

Anushka clucked into the phone. "Hey, Zan. I've got to run. But . . . is everything okay?"

"Yeah," I said. "Everything's great."

When we said goodbye, I went to Anushka's Facebook profile, hoping for a delivery date on those bacon cupcakes. Birthday: June 30.

Same as moving day.

I pulled up Priya's Instagram and scrolled until I landed on a sun-streaked photo of her vine-wrapped home here in Chicago. On June 30, she wrote:

I will miss my beautiful life here, and all the beautiful people in it. But I have to believe that this place, and these people, will stay with me wherever I go.

I was probably halfway to soccer camp by then.

She didn't post again for over a week.

It was hard to pull myself away from my Post-it notes and

go to work, but Mom and Harr were due back home by three thirty, and I didn't really want to bail on Arturo.

Before I left, I printed the email from the Northwestern day with Nick:

Sorry Zan. I can't. Maybe it's time to move on.

I printed all the photos, the statuses, the comments, since the move. I printed the ZZ email:

ZZWelcome way in/d.344itspdfiiiihauhlep.

I made a photocopy of the *Found you* note and added all the GRETA emails and documents. I three-hole-punched everything and replaced the contents of a binder meant for school.

I brought the binder with me to the restaurant and stashed it with the rest of my things in the corner by the salad bar. Now that I'm here, I realize I should have bailed. I'm flailing. I can't seem to come out of this fog.

"Hey." Logan comes by with a tall stack of salad bins from the fridge. "You okay?"

I'm just standing in the center of the kitchen. "Not really," I say, floating over to my bag. I pull out the book of clues. Maybe if I stare some more, something will appear.

Logan slides bins of olives and chickpeas into their slots before brushing his hands on his apron. He leans into the counter beside me and nods to the binder. "Let me see?"

I hand it over and he rifles through, stopping on the ZZ email. "Why 'welcome,' I wonder." He keeps flipping through as I begin to space out. I'm only half listening. I want my binder back. "And what's up with Priya and blueberries?"

I look at him, his words hitting on a delay. "What did you say?"

"I was noticing it earlier," says Logan. "They keep coming up." He leafs through the printed posts. "A blueberry tart at the beach . . . Blueberries as a diet tip . . . And then—yeah." He points. "They're here in the shot where she's talking about her favorite study snacks. It's kinda weird. Girl really likes blueberries." My heart lurches and he tilts his head. "What?"

"Holy . . ." I take the binder and look, my mouth gaping open.

"What is it?"

"Uh . . ." I'm struggling to form words. "'Blueberry' was sort of our . . ." How to put this? "Safe word? When we were younger? We used it whenever we needed rescuing from an uncomfortable situation." I can almost hear the echo of Priya's voice from the night of the bar mitzvah kiss with Eddy Hays. *We need a system moving forward. Like a code word for Get me the heck out of this!* My pulse has begun to race. "I can't believe I didn't notice that."

"So . . ." Logan blinks, confused. "What would that mean? The posts are coming from her, but they're like, coded?"

I look at the ceiling and groan. "What would the point of that be?" I straighten up. "She doesn't mention rhinoceroses, does she?"

"Huh?"

"Never mind." I take a few deep breaths as Logan goes to the dishwasher to grab clean ladles for all the salad dressings. "Tell me something good, Logan. I swear to God I'm about to have a panic attack right here."

"Hey." He comes over, drying his hands on his apron before placing them on my shoulders. "You're okay."

"Something good," I say. "Now."

He thinks a moment. "Oh, well, actually I do have one thing. I was going to surprise you after school with a ride to work, but then you skipped. I should clarify," he says, smiling. "A ride with four wheels and an engine, as you once put it."

I perk up. "Wait, seriously? No more lady bike?"

He nods, triumphant. "My aunt got herself an upgrade over the weekend and gave me her old car. For good behavior." He teeters one hand. "Ish. I'm still happy to have this job, though. The paycheck can go toward gas. Or school, hopefully." My stomach drops. "What?"

"Paycheck," I mutter. "Why didn't I—" I call out, "Hey, Sam?" She's studying in one corner of the kitchen. "Mind if I interrupt for a second?"

"Sure," she says, slamming a giant book shut and walking

over. "I think I've had enough with fucking torts for a little while."

Logan grins. "You really do spread sunshine wherever you go."

Sam shoots him a reluctant smirk. "What's up?"

I take a breath. "Do you know if Arturo ever got Priya's last paycheck to her?"

"Uh . . ." I see a familiar gleam of pity in her eyes. It's sad. Everyone here loved Priya. Now they never bring her up because of me. "Actually, no. He gave up. Honestly, it's on her at this point."

Arturo pops in through the double doors then. "Zan, you've got tables."

"Sorry," I say, my thoughts swirling. Why hadn't I followed up with Arturo? Or checked the address myself? Suddenly I'm wondering. Did Priya and Ben change apartments? Did they not make it? Did Priya lie?

My heart is racing, but the second I walk out, I feel something lift up inside me. Because Reggie is at his usual booth, and for a moment I'm positive he's come to help. I am *this close* to running back for my binder.

Then I see his face.

He gets up as I approach him, his body stiff, and I slow my step. I've never seen Reggie look like this before. "You've put me in a bad spot," he says, skipping hellos—but not in our normal, fun way. His voice is soft, contained, and possibly furious. He hooks his fingers through his belt loops, looking somehow more official in his uniform than usual.

"Reggie. What are you talking about? What's wrong?"

"I just found out a neighbor reported a break-in at Ben and Priya's the other night."

I step back. "Seriously?"

"Why didn't you tell me someone was with you?"

Oh shit. Logan. As in *still on parole* Logan.

The tourist couple from before is eyeing me. "Uh, miss? Miss! We still haven't ordered." I pretend not to hear them. "Miss!"

Arturo steps out through the double doors and I catch his eye. *Please?* He gets the message. "Hi there. Sorry to keep you waiting. . . ."

I return my focus to Reggie, gesturing to the booth, and we sit. "Okay, back up," I say, keeping my voice low.

"It was dark out," says Reggie, "but the neighbor was sure she saw a male. I don't get it, Zan. What were you thinking—trashing the place like that?"

"Okay, slow down," I say. "You mean the broken phone?"

Reggie frowns. "What phone?"

I shut my eyes. "I'm so confused. Reggie, I swear, I didn't trash anything."

"There was a desk on its side in the office. The file cabinet had been turned over. There was a big old dent in the wall.

What the hell were you doing in there?"

I stare at him. "Reggie! I . . . I didn't do any of that!" I shake my head. "Wait, the neighbor lady said it was dark out?"

"Yes," says Reggie. "And she was positive it was a male she saw climbing through the window. Who was with you, Zan?"

I lean across the table. "Okay, I'm telling you, you've got this all wrong. We—I mean I! *I* broke in during the day. And I just walked in through the back door. No window climbing necessary. I swear."

"So, what." He leans back into the booth. "You're telling me these were two unrelated break-ins? Total coincidence?"

For a moment I picture the man outside the gate, with the dark eyes behind glasses.

"Maybe," I say. Or maybe not.

When our shifts end, Logan and I head to my place. Reggie and I left things okay. He didn't have me arrested, at least, so that was positive.

We find Mom and Whit curled up watching TV, and I tell them we have to study.

Upstairs, I shut the door behind us and wake my laptop from its sleep. A quick search yields the property report for 418 Bellevue, Priya's failed California address. I exhale for what feels like the first time in hours. "Found it."

Logan walks around the room, studying the sticky notes on the wall. There are key phrases written out in big letters, strung together like an equation without symbols. *Found you, Stalker guy, Broken Phone, HLEP, Blueberries.*

"You should add the second break-in," says Logan.

"Yeah," I say. "Good idea. There are Post-its there on the desk." He walks over and scribbles down the words.

"We're definitely thinking the same thing, right? It has to mean something."

"Yeah," says Logan over his shoulder. "Whoever it was, he wasn't a genius. At least we were smart enough to check the back door."

"Well, actually, I locked it. Sort of absentmindedly, after you left." Huh. I'd forgotten about that. "Hey, I've been thinking about something," I say, the thought still working itself out. I set my computer aside and sit up on the edge of the bed. "What if we've been thinking too much about Priya? What if the real person in trouble is Ben?"

Logan turns around. "What makes you say that?"

"Okay. Well, for one thing, the note in his desk. *Found you.* It could read as threatening, right? I can't place how it fits together, but . . . I mean, all those unpaid bills in the mailbox? And his office getting broken into—all torn up like that? And then there was that guy who followed me last week. When I first met him, it was outside the house. He wanted to know if they still lived there."

"Huh," says Logan. "But you've talked to Ben recently. He didn't say anything, right?"

I shrug. "Maybe he couldn't."

Logan turns back to the wall of sticky notes, scratching at his jaw. For a second, I just watch him, the reality of the moment—of this whole absurd situation—washing over me. Logan has Instagrammed and crank-called and now here he is, regarding my wall of Post-it notes like we really are on *Law & Order*. At every turn, he's been here with me.

He's believed me.

I sit up a little taller as he traces an ink-stained finger along the edge of a bright pink square. "Hey, Logan?"

"Hm?" he says, still looking at the wall.

I feel a swell of abrupt, puzzled affection for him. "Why are you helping me?"

"Why does anyone help anyone?" he says, like a reflex. But after a minute, he walks over and sits down next to me on the bed, the mattress dipping. He's so close I can feel the rhythm of his breath, our arms and legs just barely touching. I'm so distracted by the smell of soap and the warmth of his skin that I almost forget to listen.

"At first . . ." He frowns, like he's really thinking about it. "I guess it was curiosity mostly. With the way things were going in my own life, maybe, I don't know. Maybe I wanted to throw myself into something. To get swept up. And . . ." A tiny smirk. "It didn't hurt that it meant I got to hang out with this really cute, ferocious girl in the process."

I smile into my lap, my face heating up.

"But now . . . It's more than that. Priya's important to you."
He shrugs. "Which means she's important to me."

When I raise my eyes to his, he's looking at me with a quiet
intensity I'm not sure I've ever seen before. "You're . . ." I swallow, my heart pounding. I can hardly catch my breath. "You're
such a surprise, Logan."

"Most good things are," he says, raising a mock dashing eyebrow.

"Shut up," I say, giving him a look. "I'm trying to be real
here for a min—"

He ducks down and kisses me, lightly, and I feel a jolt pass
through me, from his mouth to every part of me.

He pulls back and I touch my lips, a little stunned. I think
I may have just gotten my first clue as to why people willingly
go and *lose themselves*, and I am decidedly more amenable to
the idea.

He looks at me, his eyes like a question, and before I can
think, I close the space between us, kissing him again. I touch
his cheek, and his fingers trace the freckles up my arm. I catch
a glimpse of his crinkling eyes and it strikes me that I want to
make his face keep on doing that. Again and again.

We break apart, only to come back to each other. Our lips
are locked and smiling, like we're sharing a perfect secret. I
climb into his lap and wrap my arms around his neck. His hands
graze my waist and a shiver runs through me.

A rap on the door makes us spring apart.

"Jesus!" Logan works to catch his breath and I begin to snicker.

Whit calls from the other side, "Hey, uh . . . You guys alive in there? We're prepping dinner. Is Logan sticking around?"

"Oh, um . . ." I meet his eyes, still a little light-headed. "Yeah. I think he is."

We listen as she walks away, the energy between us quiet but not awkward, tinged with something like happy relief.

"Can I ask you something?" I say after a moment.

"Anything."

I straighten up, emboldened. "Would you like to go on a date with me, Logan Hart?"

"What'd you have in mind?" he asks. "Tracking down Priya's social security number at some government archive, perhaps?"

I glare. "I was thinking the Art Institute, *actually*. The museum. You can show me your natural habitat."

"I'd like that." We're both grinning like fools.

He glances at the clock by my bed. It's nearly eight here, so six in California. "Crap," I say.

Logan ticks his chin up toward the Post-it wall, and if it's possible, I like him even more. "Where were we?"

"The California address," I say, already reaching for my laptop. I scan the Bellevue property report until I land on the number for the management company. Logan hands me my phone, settling in next to me. "Okay, here goes," I say, suddenly anxious again. "Let's hope they're still open."

"ABC Management, this is Kimberly."

I exhale, smiling. *Thank you, Kimberly. You overzealous worker, you.*

"Hello," I say. "I uh . . . I'm trying to get something to one of your tenants, but it keeps returning to sender. Ben Grissom, 418 Bellevue, apartment C?"

The woman makes a smacking sound and Logan leans in to listen. "Apartment C, apartment C . . ." I hear typing. "Okay, ma'am, well, mystery solved! Mr. Grissom broke the lease back in July."

"Oh?" Logan's eyes meet mine. "Did uh . . . Did he say why?"

"I wouldn't have that information, ma'am. Plans changed last minute, I would guess. It happens."

I squeeze Logan's arm. "But . . . So he never moved in?"

"No, ma'am." A pause. "Who did you say you were again?"

"A friend."

She laughs. "Well then, silly. Sounds like he's the one you should be talking to!"

"Yeah," I say. "Thanks, Kimberly. I think you might be right."

Back again. And, ugh . . .

I don't know.

I think I'm running out of silver lining. What's the word for restless, furious, and sad all at once?

No. (NEIN!) Enough with the wallowing.

Always have a plan. PLANNING IS LIFE! There have been hiccups, yes, but I have to remind myself: there were successes on that To-Do list of mine.

Firstly: Um, what? Dial-up internet is a thing. I should have documented the glory sooner. It was a good moment. Doing recon in the basement, finding those forgotten boxes in the closet marked "office." When I swiped the dust from that massive monitor I thought, "Checkmate, fucker!" Then I remembered I knew nothing of comput-ers. (Despite everything TV would have us believe, my

South Asian heritage did not bestow upon me any innate tech-wizardry. But fortunately it turned out to be more a matter of plugging things in.)

I think I misjudged Amanda. She only sings when he's gone. Before I thought he just didn't like her voice, but now I wonder if it's actually a signal. Either way, she helped me find my moment. She was singing "Over the Rainbow" when the screen lit up. The DONG-GEE-DONG noises howled for what felt like an hour, and then . . . voilà! For a brief window, the world opened. I saw the icon: MAIL. I was so excited I didn't notice the singing stop. He walked in, shouting as my fingers raced across the keyboard. I thought of the only email address I knew by heart, and thrashed toward the SEND button before he yanked me away.

Dang.

I'm not sure if my plan to get him out into the world really worked. The hope was that he'd get himself spot-ted, or caught. But even if I did hit a wall with this one, at least all the taunting had the added benefit of making me extremely happy.

Me: That can't feel great. Knowing there's evidence out there, waiting to be found. The broken phone probably won't look great, either.

Him: Shut up.

Me: Aw. Don't get down. I always say, Gotta get through rain before the rainbow.

I almost wonder if I did it on purpose—letting those papers fly from my grasp so that some landed behind the desk. I've been mentally thanking myself for being cognizant enough to print them in that moment. I sometimes wonder what would have happened if I hadn't found out. If my phone hadn't run out of battery while we were packing up. If I hadn't been compelled by that bit of random musing and opened up his laptop.

The random musing that changed the course of my life? It's so dumb I almost can't bear to write it down. *Clears throat* Does excessive carrot ingestion really turn people orange? And if so, does it only occur in white people? The worst part is I never got an answer. (Okay, no, not the worst part.)

HOLD UP.
I have to admit something here. . . .
A small part of me is beginning to fear that this journal is, in fact, for posterity.

What kills me is that I could have gotten away. I was blowing it all up—dialing Anushka as we yelled. He ripped the phone from my hands and it shattered, the papers flying everywhere. And then—JUST THEN—the doorbell rang. He peeked out of the office, stealing a quick glance at the windows that overlooked the porch. I didn't see what he saw. When I spoke, he shushed me, and something in his face made me keep quiet.

I let him pull me to the garage, where his voice was so low it was barely a whisper.

Him: We're not safe here. That man out there? He's here for me.

Me: WHAT?

Him: Shh! I had help, okay? And when I shut it all down because of, well—you—my partner wasn't happy. He has guys . . . That work for him. And they're willing to travel. He warned that without a sizable payout, which I do not have, one of them would be . . . sent after me. After both of us.

Nothing in my life had quite prepared me for a moment like that. So you know what I did? I stood there, just like he told me to. When he tiptoed back inside, I didn't run. After a minute, he came back with the stack of papers and a laptop. We drove off together, before the man could get inside.

In the car, I stewed. He looked miserable. And pale. And I'll admit it—he looked sorry.

Me: Is there even a job in California?

Him: No. But I got us an apartment. You'll like it.

Me: He'll find it.

Him: Huh?

Me: If he goes through our house. You left the lease out on the kitchen table.

Him: I did?

Me: God. Did you even love her?

Him: Of course I—

Me: You have a funny way of showing it.

Him: She left you a college fund.

Me: That was before she'd even met you. And she only set aside enough for my education. She wanted me to work. To make something of myself. Not that you would understand. And anyway, you were already rich!

Him: I was, and then I wasn't. Money is a fickle thing.

Me: Just so we're clear. I'm not on your side.

Him: I know.

Ugggggghhh. I hate this. Okay, FINE. I shall call this next installment . . .

A Brief Reluctant Breakdown for Posterity:

Week One. We stayed in motels. Argued. Tried to make a plan. We bought clothes and supplies at Target and watched our backs. Paid for things in cash.

Week Two. He fired the nurse over the phone. I felt
bad. We showed up hours later. He wouldn't let me call
people. Knowing could put them in danger. We ate popcorn
and watched Jeopardy! Amanda seemed vaguely pleased
with the company.

Week Three. I got restless. Walks were too risky. But
at least I had the yard. He started spending time in the
basement. I noticed Amanda's landline phones go missing
from the walls.

Me: Aren't people going to notice all this silence? At
least let me tell Zan and Nick.
Him: Absolutely not. And anyway, I took care of that.
All your passwords are the same, Pri. Bacon? Really? But
don't worry. You've been getting lots of likes.

For a second I saw red, but breathed through it.

Me: People will know it's not me.
Him: We'll see.

Week Four. I woke in a clean, white room.

Me: . . . ?

Him: There may have been some Ambien in your smoothie this morning.

I was on a couch. The junk that was here when we arrived had been cleared out. He left the TV and the minifridge. There was a bathroom off to one side, and a closet. I noted the window—briefly hopeful, before I remembered Amanda and her home safety infomercials. I never noticed the door down here had a dead bolt. Maybe he'd installed it.

He was holding that ridiculous gun.

Me: Dude. This is a mistake.

Him: I wish we could trust each other, but I don't see how. You're too angry with me.

Me: Of course I am, but—

Him: It won't be that bad. I'll pick up whatever you want. Books? Snacks? You name it.

When I looked up, the man I knew had gone somewhere else.

So I steadied myself. I took a breath.

And then I asked for blueberries.

(Priya Principle #305: Always have a plan.)

TEN

Friday, September 21

At the front of the room, Señora O'Connell holds up a DVD. "Everyone! Today we're watching Almodóvar's *Mujeres al borde de un ataque de nervios,* aka *Women on the Verge of a Nervous Breakdown,* aka the story of my life."

Despite my mood, I catch her eye across the classroom and crack a smile. She found me the other day and apologized again for what she said about Logan. She referred to herself as a "work in progress." Said she's learning to trust the good instincts. To not always assume the worst.

I've been somewhere else all day. Exhausted. Sleepless. I keep feeling like I should be doing something.

I wish I knew what.

I'm already lost with this movie. An old guy is narrating

into a vintage microphone in black and white. A chicken flaps its wings.

I've seen an Almodóvar film once, when we chose movies to review for Spanish sophomore year. I remember picking it because it had a bullfighter in it. In the end it confused the hell out of me and was also pretty gross. Priya watched it with me in my living room, frowning for long stretches. Afterward she declared that anyone claiming to understand-slash-enjoy a scene where a tiny man jumps inside a woman's vagina was lying to sound smart. At the time, this seemed too specific to be a principle, but now I wonder if I should have put it down.

God, she was funny. Is.

Ugh.

All I want is to talk to her. Because I'm worried. Because I miss her. Because new things are happening. Good things, even. I know I have to have a life, and it doesn't mean I'm giving up. But there's so much I want to tell her.

Like how Logan stayed up late on Tuesday, drawing portraits of me in his room, an extension of our date at the museum—when he broke down everything from Degas's dancers to massive modern canvases splashed in single nonsensical colors. When he talked, he had this light in his eyes that filled my entire heart. I want to tell her how my whole house is scattered with Whit's things now, and Mom is always humming. How Arturo is making strides in winning over the Yun family, and Lacey is a surprisingly good lunch buddy. I want to tell her that Nick is *so* not over her, if she wants him back. Oh—and that I punched a guy! That Dad and I had another good, meaty dinner after we played soccer last night. That Harr still asks about her.

I want to find her. If she wants to be found.

But the thoughts always seem to devolve into the same old soupy mess. One fact in particular keeps changing shape inside my head—flipping backward and forward, mirrored and upside down. Ben is lying. Or Priya is. Both, maybe. Ben and/or Priya are lying.

I could call Ben again. I keep coming close. I'll hold the phone in my hand with his number on the screen and stare and stare. But something keeps telling me not to.

Señora O'Connell walks through the aisles, returning a quiz I must have missed on Monday. She stops at Logan's desk and I see his paper.

94

"Hey," she whispers to him as she passes. "Good job."

A yawn engulfs my face as I attempt to focus in the dark room. Even when the days are good, it's still so hard to sleep. I was Googling Ben's name when the sun came up this morning. He has no real online presence anymore. Just an old, out-of-date LinkedIn account. Some articles came up about his role at GRETA. *Money begets money,* he said in an interview a few years ago. *My late wife understood that. And she put that simple concept to good use.*

I searched *Ben Grissom* plus every bank. Plus *finance* and *hedge fund*. Plus *mergers and acquisitions*. I searched until I ran out of bank words. There was no trace of a job in California or anywhere else. Nothing since Chicago.

When I finally gave in and closed my computer this morning, I got up and passed Mom's open door. She was upright against a pillow in bed, cloaked in sunlight, reading while Whit slept. For a minute I watched her, kneading her bottom lip the way she does when something fascinates her. I almost wanted to try again, to make her see what I could. But I knew she'd only try to talk me down. I wouldn't make any sense. And the whole thing would go round and round.

Everywhere I go, Priya seems to pop up. A sound, a smell, a memory. Like she's getting through. I feel her in the walls, in my pulse, peering back at me when I close my eyes. I can feel it—her. Like she's reaching through the universe.

"Alejandra?" I jolt at my desk, one cheek pressed to my knuckles. The backs of my hands are wet from tears. The lights are on, and everyone is getting up.

Even Eddy looks worried. "Hey," he says, disconcertingly genuine. "Are you okay, Zan?"

"Yeah." I wipe my eyes and sniff, straightening up at my desk. "I'm fine. Thanks, Eddy." He looks unconvinced as he walks off, while Logan and Señora O'Connell stay standing over me.

"Sorry," I say, looking up at them. I try to smile, but my eyes spill over again.

Logan offers a hand and I get up.

"Can I help?" asks la Señora, but I shake my head. I take a big breath and let Logan lead me out the door. "Hey," she says. I turn around. "Whatever it is. You'll figure it out."

When the last bell rings, I head for my tree.

I drop my stuff and sit, the muggy air sticking to me. The school day is finally over. I should be relieved. And yet, I have nowhere to go.

You'll figure it out, la Señora said. And people say that, sure. Because what else is there to say? But sometimes—no. You don't figure it out! You only get more nothing.

I press back into the bark. No. No wallowing. No *quitting*! Priya wouldn't flail like this. Priya would have a mother-flipping plan! Even if it was a flimsy one, she'd commit. She would ATTACK!

I just need something, anything, to latch on to. Maybe I can retrace my steps. . . .

I get up. Brush myself off. And soon I'm walking, running, *sprinting* down the path. "Hey . . . *Hey!*" It's Logan's voice calling at my back. I stop, panting, and he runs to catch up. "I was looking for you. Where are you rushing off to?"

"Priya's house," I tell him through a gasp. "I want to see it. Reggie said the phone was gone. The office was wrecked.

Whoever broke in was looking for something. Or, I don't know. Hiding something? I need to see it for myself."

A cloud covers the sun, turning the sky an ominous purple in what feels like seconds. "Okay." Logan squints up. "So, should we go now or . . . ?"

I smile. "Uh-uh. You need to stay here."

He takes a step closer, a wiry eyebrow raised. "And why would I do that?"

"Hmm . . ." I stare back at him, reaching up to brush the hair out of his face. "Because you have a parole officer?"

He shrugs. "I'm not letting you do this without someone watching your back."

"I'll be fine," I say. "Really. You're very cute, and gallant and all that, but I can't let you—"

He kisses me. "I'm coming with you." So that's that.

It thunders before the rain.

The air is warm and full of static, the raindrops fat and far between. Even in the storm, Priya's tree-lined street remains a perfect, cozy picture. But there's a feeling here—like something in this place has gone horribly wrong. It's as stark as the water drenching me. We sneak around back and find the garage door open. The door to the house is open, too—which, I remember, is not how I left it. I suppose Reggie warned me of this, but it's still creepy: I wasn't the last person here.

We tiptoe in, and Logan jumps as a burst of lightning cracks, brightening the living room. I touch his arm. "You don't have to stay." But he ignores me and plows ahead, dripping all over the place.

I head for the office and see the phone has been cleaned up. At my feet, the desk is on its side. All the files from the cabinet are gone. I slide the closet door open along a track. No stacks of paperwork. Empty.

"Jesus," says Logan, peeking in through the doorway at the mess.

"Yeah," I say. He squeezes my shoulder—tight. I look up and Logan shakes his head, ever so slightly.

Somewhere in the house, a door opens, then closes.

And there are footsteps.

Neither of us moves at first, until the steps grow closer, and I point to the closet behind us. We tiptoe inside and I slide the door shut. In the dark, we stand pressed together, lungs filling up with the same air. In the quiet, our breathing is hot and audible. I can see out through the little downturned slats. The room is still, but my heart sinks at the thought of our wet footprints all around the house.

Someone walks in and I feel Logan tense up beside me.

The desk screeches against the floor. Then the file cabinet. A drawer slams open and shut. Another drawer. A crash.

"Christ!" says a familiar voice.

For a moment I see his face, and my body goes stiff. I wonder if he can see my eyes staring back at his in the dark.

The doorbell rings then, and Logan and I both relax a little as the footsteps trail off. After a moment, I hear a voice. *"Shit!"* The sound of running. Back door closing. The doorbell again. Once more. Again. And then it stops.

We're silent for another minute. Until we're sure.

Tentatively, I open the closet door and look around the room. The shock slowly wanes. Logan nudges me. "You okay?"

"That was Ben," I say.

"Whoa," says Logan. "So . . . Whoa."

I gape down at the overturned desk. "What was he looking for? And why'd he flip out and leave like that?" I walk out of the office to the living room and peer out the window.

Logan lingers behind. "Maybe he—"

"Wait," I say. Across the street, a man is getting in his car. I can't be sure but I think it's him. It's the man from Priya's house—from the zoo, and the show.

Just then, Ben's white Prius goes racing by and the man pulls out from his spot, driving off in the same direction.

"Yoo-hoo," says Logan, waving a hand over my eyes.

"Holy shit," I say, pointing toward the cars as they drive out of sight. "That was . . ." I turn around to face him. "The man who followed me—I think he's who rang the doorbell."

Logan looks worried. "Wait, the guy was *here*?" I nod. "So . . . what? The man is tracking Ben now?"

"I don't know," I say. "Maybe."

"Why?" I shake my head. Shrug. "That's a long drive from

California," he says after a moment.

"Yeah, well . . ." I sigh out. "The lady told us they never moved in. Maybe they didn't make it far at all."

Logan frowns. "Is there any other place they'd be likely to stay? Somewhere driving distance from here? . . . An investment property? Or . . . a vacation home the family uses to get together?"

"There is no family," I say. "Just them. Well, except . . ."

My mind jumps to the ZZ email. The sender was *The Grissoms*. As in more than one Grissom. As in a wife, maybe, and a late husband. My mouth falls open, my ears ringing, and all at once, a tidal wave of stupid fucking posts comes rushing to the forefront of my brain.

Stars can't shine without darkness. . . .

Look through rain to see the rainbow. . . .

Everything happens for a reason. . . .

They're Bed Bath & Beyond words. Pseudo-Buddhist language.

The kind that comes in whimsical fonts.

"Indiana," I murmur.

"What?" says Logan.

"Oh my God." I run a hand through my wet hair, pacing. "Oh my *God*. In the ZZ email. It was sent from the Grissoms! Plural. And, and . . ." Logan seems lost but I can't explain it any better yet. A thought is bubbling to the surface. "Logan . . ." I stop and stare at him. "Think about it. In the message, it said

'Welcome way in,' right? What if it was an address? As in Welcome Way, Indiana?"

Frowning, Logan pulls out his phone and types quickly. My heart pounds against my ribs. His eyes meet mine, a little stunned. "There's a Welcome Way in Green Plains, Indiana."

He holds out the screen and an image of the neighborhood pops up with the map. The houses all look the same, but I'm certain I've been in one of them. "Holy shit," I breathe. "I know where she is."

The ride takes an eternity, though Google says an hour. I don't speak the whole way there, eyes glazed, cars weaving all around us. Logan doesn't speak either, just drives. Our clothes are still damp. Once in a while, he covers my hand with his own in the space between us.

The gliding treetops start to slow as we pull up to the open gates, the words *Green Plains* chiseled into vine-covered stone. In a sea of garages, there's no way our car will go unnoticed, so we park along the low brick wall that separates the village from the road.

Logan turns off the ignition, a quiet coming over us. "The grandma's house," he says. "You're sure."

"Stepgrandma," I say. "I only visited once, but the street looked exactly like what came up on Google."

"A lot of streets look like this."

"I'm telling you. It can't be a coincidence. And all those Bed

Bath and Beyond inspirational quotes? It's a long-standing joke. She was telling me the whole time."

"Telling you what?"

"Well . . ." I waver. "That I don't know. To come here, at least. I think."

Birds chirp above us as we walk, shrill against the low rumble of a distant roadway. There aren't even sidewalks here. Just curbs. I jump when my phone rings. But it's only Mom, wondering when I'm coming home. I text that I'm hanging at Logan's for a while and switch the ringer off.

"So what do you think of the babe magnet?"

I come up from my thoughts. "The what?"

Logan smiles. "The car."

"If you're referring to the taupe Volvo station wagon with the *Eat More Kale* bumper sticker on it, you may want to reassess your terminology."

"Hey," he says. "You were sitting in it, weren't you?"

I think he's trying to ease my stress, but it isn't working. He pulls my hand from my mouth. I'm doing it again. My nails are practically gone.

"You remember which one it is?" he asks as we come upon the street sign for Welcome Way. There are maybe thirty houses on the little bend before it ends, without explanation, and turns into burnt grass. There's no storm here. No signs there ever was. It's somehow fitting for this tidy place.

"Not really," I say. "They're like . . . identical." The houses are spaced far apart with yards of grass or gravel, with only slight variations here and there. Most of the garages are closed, and I can't see how we'll tell the difference without Ben's Prius.

A woman drives by with a neighborly wave, so I do the same. The sun has begun to set, the sky unfurling into brilliant sheets of gold and grapefruit pink.

Logan gives me a look like, *So . . .*

"Stay there," I say, crunching across the gravel to sneak into a side yard. Through a first-floor window, I see a little girl sitting cross-legged while chatting with a teddy bear. Her eyes go wide when she sees me, but I shake my head—*shhh*—and duck out of view before she can say a word.

"Okay, nope, not that one," I say when I come back.

"So one at a time," says Logan. "That's the plan?"

"Do you have another suggestion?"

He thinks a moment. "It's getting dark. You take this side. I'll do the other. We'll be faster that way."

I nod, the depths of my gratitude plunging deeper. Before he runs off, I grab his wrist, pulling him back to me, and I tilt my face up to catch his lips. "Thank you," I say as we pull apart.

"Don't sweat it," he says, walking backward with a grin.

"Now go!" I hiss. "Look for pseudo-Buddhist wisdom!" He crosses the street and disappears behind a cluster of trees.

From a side yard, I stand on tiptoes to peek into a big kitchen. I hear a garage door creak open, and soon a man is walking in and setting down a briefcase. I move before I'm seen. A bunch of homes have lights out. No movement I can see. Another has a Rottweiler that growls and sends me jumping back from an open window.

In the street, I look around for watchful neighbors. No one.

At another house, I peer in through the glass pane in the front door. A bunch of boys are playing video games over rowdy conversation, passing bags of chips and cookies back and forth. I catch sight of Logan across the street, crouching down beneath a first-floor window. I watch his lanky body pop up. After a moment he looks back at me with a thumbs-down and juts up his chin to me as if to say, *Anything?*

I shake my head no, and he hurries away.

The next house has the very same glass-paned door as the one before it. I see an empty, firelit living room. And I hear singing. I squint into the glass and make out a smattering of needlepoint pillows, covered in decorative words.

Dream

BELIEVE

Whimsical fonts, you might say. I strain to read more.

When life gives you lemons . . .

Dance like no one is . . .

YOU ARE A STRANGER HERE BUT ONCE.

An eerie feeling comes over me, like a drop of water slid-ing backward up my spine. I look behind me. Logan has disappeared—must have slipped into another yard. I move slowly, along the side of the house, toward the sound. There's a window overlooking the backyard. It has no curtain, but it's high up on a slope. From tiptoes, I pull myself up and find myself peering in at an empty pantry filled with paper towels, boxed pasta, and canned food, gently lit by a far-off hallway light.

"Damn," I say, my face pressed to the glass.

I drop down into the yard, a little shiver running through me as I return to myself. I'm not sure what I was expecting.

It feels like night has fallen all at once. The golds and pinks have turned to blue.

A light turns on above me, one floor up.

A window opens, letting out the sound. The voice is grav-elly but pretty, one word lazing into the next. It's like a call. Pulling me. I scan the yard and land on a rusted ladder on its side. It's heavy and noisy as I hoist it up and rest it against the side of the house. I don't think as I draw closer to the music. I just climb—slowly, silently, until I'm up there hovering, look-ing straight at the back of the old woman's head.

Amanda.

She sings into a mirror, a lamp illuminating her face. On the windowsill before me sits a pillbox, marked with the days of the week. A pair of plush slippers rests beside an ornate dresser. A silky robe drapes on a hook, below a huge banner that reads *HOME IS WHERE THE HEART IS!*

The woman's eyes lock with mine in the mirror as she sings, more curious than startled.

> *A heart full of joy and gladness*
> *Will always banish sadness and strife.*
> *So always look for the silver lining*
> *And try to find the sunny side of life.*

I scramble down the ladder. *What was that?* The windows along the side of the house are all above eye level. I pull myself up, one after the other. A dim kitchen light is on. There's a cluster of bananas on the counter. A curtain blocks most of my view at the next window, but I can see in through a small slit. The dining room looks scarcely used. There's china in a cabinet.

I hop down and peek out at the street. No Logan.

I look up, to the second floor, and run back for the ladder, wincing with each tinny sound as I clutch the cool metal and start to climb. The light in the other bedroom is off, but I can see in faintly. Target bags in one corner, with products lined up on the dresser, and a pair of dressy men's shoes against one wall.

Back down, I scan the street again. No Logan. We must keep missing each other. I should stay still. I should wait. I kick at the dirt and a loose pebble bounces away. I hear a *plink,* and I realize it's hit glass. There's a little slit at the base of the house—a sad excuse for a window that looks onto the basement.

I see flashes from a TV. Plush cream carpet. A blanket over legs. Feet up. A profile on a big white couch. She's eating popcorn, a flowery little journal discarded off to one side. It's her.

Priya. Just . . . there. Just sitting there, her face lit by the shifting light. She looks absorbed in the story, eating kernels one by one. She looks . . . fine.

"What?" I say out loud. I lower myself to sit and watch her through the glass. I feel abruptly numb, but tears prickle behind my eyes, the thought crashing down like a heavy weight: It was in my head. She let me feel this way. Let me live in the dark. She wasn't reaching. Didn't feel me reaching back.

Sitting there, crossed legged in the gravel, I let it out: the doubt, the fear, the worrying. I expel a baffled breath—or maybe it's a sigh of relief. Because I meant what I said. If she's okay, then I am. Or will be.

For a minute I just cry, letting myself grow puffy and splotchy and sniffly. Because I'm hurt, and drained, and probably foolish by any reasonable measure. But as I watch her there, it strikes me—I'm not ashamed of caring this much. Because I'd rather live my life trusting in people. Even if once in a while, I'm dead wrong.

As I get up, I think Priya glances over, but I don't wait to find out. I wipe my tears and take a breath. I need to find

Logan. To get out of here. My feet drag against gravel as I work to calm myself.

Behind me, I hear a shuffle—a few sharp taps against the glass. With a heavy sigh, I turn around and walk back. I'm not sure I'm ready to face her, but I crouch down anyway, jolted by the moment her eyes meet mine.

I'm still crying, and I realize so is she. I throw my hands up and let her see me. *What the hell?* She says something I can't quite hear and runs off.

"Priya, wait!"

I watch her at the couch. She comes back a second later with the journal, opens it to a middle page, and scribbles something quickly before slapping it against the glass.

HELP

My ears begin to ring.

She holds my gaze, waiting. I don't understand.

And then slowly, slowly, I think I do. The singing stops, and her expression shifts.

I keep my eyes on her. Try to smile. Try to say, *It's okay.* My hands tremble, tears on the screen as I start to punch in 911. *It's okay now,* I tell her, my shaking finger over the button.

The song comes back and Priya's eyes go wide.

What?

She shouts something I can't make out. A slap to my hand sends the phone flying. No time to look up.

Sharp pain.

A blow to my skull.

I see black.

HELP

Shit. Okay. Evidence. This is evidence!

If anyone finds this, my name is Priya Patel.

Ben Grissom stole funds from my mother's charity, the GRETA Fund.

His partner in Mumbai, Karim, sent someone after us because of a financial dispute and Ben has become increasingly paranoid.

He's been holding me against my will for several weeks in his mother's suburban home.

I just witnessed him strike my best friend, Alexandra Martini, from the basement window.

I hope she's okay.

I hope this journal was not, after all, for posterity.
Shit, I think he's coming downstai

ELEVEN

Friday still? . . . I think?

Time had passed.

How much, I'm not sure. The ground beneath me is firm but soft. Carpet, feels like. I've kept my eyes shut. Heard bits and pieces, in and out.

It was Priya's voice that came first.

"What did you do?"

"What did I do? What did *you* . . ." There was a pause. "The email. But I checked. It was just garbled letters."

"I'm sure it was the email among other things. You weren't exactly a criminal mastermind through all of this."

It went on like this for some time, as my heart threatened to leap out from my chest. But I stayed as I was, collecting strength, the pain raging at the back of my head.

Now, though, I feel hovering.

Warm breath on my face.

"I didn't mean to hit her that hard."

"You need to call 911. Leave before the ambulance comes, I don't care. But all this? It's going to come out. And you don't want a dead girl on your hands."

A few tense moments pulse by and I work to quiet my racing mind. I have to listen. To understand.

"I know what you're trying to do."

"Look around you, Ben." Priya's voice is strangely calm. Delicate, even. "Use that Harvard brain of yours. You keep digging deeper every day. I'm not even messing with you right now. I swear. For your sake and everyone else's, you need to end this before you bury yourself entirely."

"Stop," he says.

"Ben—"

"I said stop!"

All I want to do is open my eyes. But I stay frozen.

"What's your plan here?" she says after a moment. "What are we thinking? Double homicide? In your mom's basement? Huh." I can actually feel her smiling. "You'd be like the ulti-mate loser of murderers."

I have to work to keep my lips from curling up. I've missed that wit of hers. I know I shouldn't, but I peek—just for a second—and see a jolt of recognition pass through her before I return myself to darkness. "I have a gun," says Ben, making my insides clench. "Now might be a good time to show some respect."

"Please. Maybe no one else was looking for me. But Zan's family will notice she's gone soon enough. The cops will find this place. All this carpet down here is basically a giant evidence sponge. And I highly doubt anyone's going to be pointing fingers at the sweet old lady upstairs." A lingering silence swallows up the room. "You've backed yourself into one hell of a corner, Ben." A pause. "Get some cold washcloths. Maybe we can wake her up."

He scoffs. "Why would I want to do that?"

"Alive girl, dead girl. Those are your choices." After a moment, I feel him get up. "Not there," she says. "You took all my towels for the laundry. Go upstairs."

"Priya—"

"Go, Ben! She's hurt!"

Over grumbling I hear a door close and the click of the dead bolt. I open my eyes and Priya remains frozen, listening for footsteps.

I sit up, mouth gaping, and she pulls me in for the tightest hug of my life. "He got your phone?" she whispers as we break apart. I nod, still frozen and stunned. I feel myself prickling awake as I take in the room. Everything soft and white and cozy. It's oddly terrifying. My eyes spill over, hot tears streaming down my cheeks.

"Hey." She grips my chin. "We can't freak out right now."

I look to the narrow window up by the ceiling. "Should we try to break the glass?"

"Can't," she says. "Shatterproof. Amanda had it installed after some infomercial on home invasions." She sighs up at the ceiling. I can hear Ben talking, but there's no other voice. "Must be on the phone."

I look toward the murmuring above us. "Ben did this? Wha . . . Why?"

"A while ago, Ben got himself buried. Money stuff," she whispers. "He was spending more than he made. I should have seen it. But uh, basically he started scamming GRETA." I stare at her, taking this in. It oddly fits. "And . . ." She leans in close and keeps her voice low. "There was a guy in Mumbai. Helping him."

A lightbulb. "Karim?"

She nods. "It fell apart when the volunteer program got the green light."

"The fire at Friends Elementary," I whisper, beginning to understand. "And the Priti School grant . . ."

"Yeah," she says. "Ben had to shut it all down before we showed up to schools that didn't exist." She pauses. "How do you know all this?"

"I have my ways."

She smiles, impressed. "Well, it went sour when Ben cut out the other guy. He said he was going to send someone after us to collect his money." I think of the note in the office—*Found you*—and the man I met outside their house. The "family friend." Jesus.

I shake my head, still confused. "Okay, but why are you down here?"

She thinks a moment. Shrugs. "Despite everything, for a little while there we were weirdly . . . in this together? And then . . . we weren't." She freezes. A door opens upstairs. Footsteps rushing down.

I find my position on the ground and close my eyes.

The dead bolt clicks open. "What took so long?" says Priya at once, convincingly angry. "This is serious."

"I had to take a call," he says, his voice strained.

"Cops again?" she asks, a hint of pleasure in her voice. "More updates on the break-in you committed at your own house? Here's a pro tip for you. Bring keys next time." The words click in my head. I did that. I locked Ben out! I feel a wet cloth against my cheek. "Don't you see what's happening? It's all catching up with you. Just let me get Zan to a hospital."

"Stop it."

"It could work. I won't say a word till you've fled the country."

"You know I can't leave," he says. "That man is still after me. I could have been killed today. Is that what you want?"

"Ben," she says, "you know I didn't want any of this. But Zan's not waking up."

I feel something hard nudging me—a shoe, maybe. "God. She's really out."

"Just run, Ben. Grab your passport and head to Canada, or Mexico. Like we've talked about a million times before. As long as Zan makes it, no one's gonna look that hard. And even if someone is chasing you, is that scarier than prison?" I wish I could see his face. I can't be sure, but I think it's working. "Leave me your phone," says Priya, "and I swear on my life—on *Zan's life*—I will give you a head start."

The room is still. Three sets of filling lungs. I hold my breath and hope my racing heart won't somehow give me away. I swear I can feel Priya's heart racing too. "Yeah," he says. "Yeah, maybe you're right."

I relax, just for a moment, before I sense a sudden shift. He's closer to me now. I can feel it. "Her arm," he says. "It wasn't stretched out to the side like that before."

"What? Yes it was."

He laughs. "Wait. Are you listening to this, Zan?"

"Ben . . ."

"Get up," he says. I realize he's talking to me. *"I said get up!"*

"Ben. You're imagining things."

"Okay. If she's really unconscious, then this won't scare her." I hear a click and can't help it. I open my eyes.

A gun is pointed right at me.

For a moment, the world seems to slow as Priya leaps to

stand, and I shout, "No!" I watch her hand connect with metal before the gun flies from Ben's grip. It feels as though the whole room freezes, until I whisper, "Fuck," the moment the gun hits the carpet.

Unfreeze.

Ben lunges for the gun, but Priya kicks it away. *"Ben, stop it!"* They're on the ground in seconds, Priya clawing at his arm as he strains to reach. When his hand gets too close, she pulls his hair, and he shouts. They roll over, once, twice, but he wriggles free.

Ben stands and I'm jolted awake. I leap to my feet and try to throw a jab, which he dodges. From the corner of my eye, I see Priya bend down to pick up the gun.

I charge at him again, but his wrist makes contact with my throat.

I clutch my neck—can't breathe—and realize Reggie taught him that. *Goddammit, Reggie!* I jump back the moment he heaves an elbow toward my middle. I know the sequence. Windpipe, solar plexus, groin.

Ben smiles at me, abruptly wicked, and I scream as I attack again—provoking his response. I duck before he can make his move, and when he whips around to face me, I throw a body punch. He clutches his gut, coughing, and before he can straighten up, I sling a hook to the face that makes him cry out.

Blood gushes from his nose as he stumbles back. My first

two knuckles seethe with pain, but I shake it off. "Zan!" calls Priya. "Run!"

She's ahead of me, flinging herself up the stairs. I'm right behind her, almost to the top, when I collapse forward, my chin slamming into wood. I twist back to see his arms wrapped around my legs, pinning me there.

"Ben." Priya looms above us at the top of the steps, framed by an open door, the gun pointed down. It's a bizarre sight, to say the least. "You need to let her go now. Don't make me use this. Please," she says with quiet terror in her eyes. "I'm a *fucking pacifist,* but I'll do it."

After a moment, his arms go slack. Then I kick behind me, and he lets out a wail as I scramble up the steps. When I reach the light, Priya slams the door, flicking the lock.

We stand there a moment, heaving in the cozy living room. She peers down at the gun in her hands. I catch my breath, meeting her wide-eyed stare. And then, I shit you not, she *laughs.* "Holy guacamole," she says, shaking her head.

She opens the gun's chamber and lets the bullets slide into her palm.

I glance toward the foyer, suddenly aware of the banging sound coming from outside. Logan's face peers in through a glass panel. "Zan? *Zan!*"

I run to open the door and Logan's face falls as he touches my chin. I can already feel it swelling where it hit the stair.

"I'm fine." He looks past me, still in shock, and Priya studies us quizzically. "Oh, sorry," I say. "Priya, Logan; Logan, Priya."

"Hi," she says, with a slight, curious smile. "We better go. Can you call 911, Logan?" He nods quickly and gets out his phone. We've only made it a few steps when a rattling hum starts above us.

"Aw, crap," says Priya.

I follow her gaze. It's Amanda, cruising steadily down the banister on the seat of an electronic stair lift. "Priya dear? Is that you?" We wait for a good thirty seconds. The chair is quite slow. At the bottom, she unbuckles herself, takes hold of her walker, and frowns. "What's going on? Who are these people?"

"We have to go," says Priya.

"Hmm . . . No thank you," she says, shuffling past without further discussion.

"Mom," Ben calls from the other side of the basement door. He starts pounding. "Mom, I'm in here!" Logan walks out onto the front porch, plugging his ear to concentrate on the phone.

Amanda eyes the basement door, pondering a moment, before addressing Priya once more. "I think I'll . . . go make some tea."

"Mom!" Ben shouts as she shuffles away. A gas stove clicks in the other room and the doorknob to the basement jiggles. Priya and I both watch as something thwacks the wood from the other side, like Ben is throwing his body weight against it. The door doesn't budge. *"Goddammit, Mom!"*

I nod toward the kitchen, incredulous. "So . . . She was here for all of this? Thanks a lot, Grandma."

Priya sort of wavers. "Ben took all the phones from the house. And she wouldn't have been able to get down the basement stairs. There were days I got the sense she was on my side. Hard to say, though. Amanda has dementia."

"I most certainly do not," Amanda calls from the kitchen.

Priya smiles. "Kind of goes in and out."

"Police should be here any minute," says Logan, returning inside.

Ben bangs on the door again. "Hey. Okay, hold on. Maybe we can work out a deal here."

Priya shoots me a deadpan glance.

"So," says Logan. "Should we . . . wait outside?"

Priya looks past him through the open door, and the gun falls from her hands, shooting a loud blank that makes me jump up with a shriek. My heart pounds as I follow Priya's stare.

On the street, a man is hurrying out of his car, his dark eyes set on Priya. My pulse skyrockets. It's him. The "family friend." I rush to close the door, but Priya stops me.

"Zan!" she says, prying my fingers from the handle. "Hey! What are you doing?"

"It's him!" I cry. "He's after you!"

The man is standing over us now, his expression oddly gentle. I swallow.

"Priya," he says softly. "Is that you?"

I feel my body go slack as she nods, with a weird glassy-eyed smile.

I search Priya's face. I don't understand.

"Um, Zan?" She bites her lip. "This . . . is my dad . . ."

The words take a moment to sink in. "Wait," I say. *"What?"*

The man's eyes land on the gun at our feet. "Um, is everything okay?"

Priya takes a long breath. "You know what? I think so."

In the living room, we sit by the fire, police lights flashing through the windows. The cops have been pulling us aside, taking statements one by one. The EMTs examined Priya in the back of an ambulance and cleaned a few cuts from her scuffle with Ben. They gave me ice for my chin and want me to watch for signs of concussion.

Ben's probably halfway to the station by now, his hands cuffed behind his back. They let Amanda ride along. Someone will have to set her up with a nurse again when all of this is done. Priya says she'll visit. She's a better person than I am. Though I don't know. Maybe she's right. Maybe Amanda did the best she could.

Priya seems okay, but dazed. I think everyone is. At the moment, she's reclining against a needlepoint pillow in my lap, with her legs outstretched on the couch, an arm slung over her head. She's been explaining bits and pieces of the whole sordid ordeal, between long, exhausted silences.

We all sat, frozen, as she told us about the weeks she and Ben spent on the run, before she wound up in the basement.

I couldn't help but grin as she explained the other stuff. Like how once she knew Ben was keeping up her social media, she decided to feed him inspiration. "I must have asked for twenty crates of blueberries, just to make sure it got through."

"And the selfie by the lake?" I asked.

"That I just suggested," she said, shrugging. "Honestly, it felt too easy. I told him people would get suspicious if I never showed myself in front of all those beaches I was supposedly going to. I knew that picture would be backed up on the cloud. I hoped you might recognize the earrings I left behind."

"What about all the cheesy sayings?"

Priya sighed happily. "Your girl was a walking Bed Bath and Beyond for a while there. I guess it wasn't a great sign for Ben's mental state that he didn't catch on. It's not like I was subtle. I wanted those phrases to stick in his head, but do you know how hard it is to fit *Dance like no one is watching* naturally into a sentence?"

"Well, I hate to break it to you," I told her, "but that one never came up."

"Really," she said, sounding vaguely disappointed. "Well, what did make it?"

"Oh, you know. Stuff about seeing rainbows after rain and stars through the darkness."

"Ah," she said with a serious nod.

"Oh, and everything happens for a reason."

She sighed. "Right. I'd like whoever coined that one to

please explain what just happened to me."

"I am *so sorry* it took me this long."

"Are you kidding?" She scoffed. "I'm just glad you got the message."

Logan is on the phone with his aunt now. I can see him through the open door, pacing the porch with police lights at his back. He's cute when he's serious. Well, cute all the time. He said he'd call my parents, too. I want to stay with Priya. As long as she wants me to.

"So, Julian," I say to the man seated across from me.

"So," he says, appearing generally (understandably) overwhelmed by the past hour. "We meet again." He laughs, sort of, and no one quite knows what to say. Priya still hasn't explained this piece of the puzzle. And I don't want to press, but . . .

"I was going to tell you," she says after a minute, sitting up to face me.

You'd think I'd be hurt, but I'm not. Definitely curious, though. I want to understand. "When did this all . . . ?"

"Last spring," she says. "Something was nagging at me. More and more, I felt . . . lost. Like I didn't fit anywhere. Or . . . come from anywhere. I barely knew my mom's side. I went with her to India for that one visit when I was little, and everyone was really nice, but I felt so completely foreign."

"Is that why you wanted to get involved with GRETA? To connect?"

"Maybe," she says. "A little bit. And at the same time, I had this whole other half, you know? I would talk to your mom about it. On nights I stayed over, if I couldn't sleep. After a while, I started to get the feeling there was something she was holding back. So I did some digging. Turned out I was right."

I hesitate. "What do you mean?"

"You know the girls' trip story?"

"I do."

She grabs a stray pillow and fiddles with its tassels. "Well, there were a few omitted details. Like Julian wasn't a random guy. Their friend Tasha knew him from MIT. My mom could have called him up anytime. She *chose* not to tell him. Not to let him in my life. I guess she wanted to be free. No strings attached."

"Huh." I take this in. "So. How did you . . ."

She draws a long breath. "I had this huge box of cards and other stuff my mom had saved over the years. One day I started combing through it, and I came across this picture. It was a group shot of our moms and some other people. There was a note from their friend Tasha on the back. It said something like, *Julian crashing girls' night.* There was a guy off to the side, wearing an MIT sweatshirt. I recognized the periodic table menu in the background."

For a minute I just stare at her, the realization landing like a thud. "So my mom knew?"

"Yep," says Priya. "I confronted her about it right around my birthday and she caved. Told me everything. I made her swear not to bring it up to anyone until I figured out where he was or . . . if he even wanted to know me. And then I just sort of . . . kept on keeping it to myself." She holds my gaze. "Zan. It wasn't . . . personal. I just needed to work it out on my own. I hope you're not mad."

"I'm not," I say. The words come automatically, but it strikes me how much I mean them. "Priya. We can have our own lives sometimes. Really. We don't have to . . . share every little piece of ourselves."

"But I want to," she says. "Usually. You're my Zanita! My Mrs. Zantastic! And I'm finding I really hate secrets. But this one was just . . ." She shakes her head, like it still blows her mind.

"I get it," I tell her. "Really."

She eyes me warily. "When did you get so reasonable? And what parts of your life are you not telling me about? I'm suddenly feeling very jealous."

I laugh. "There's nothing . . . Well." I glance toward Logan on the porch. "We have a little catching up to do."

Julian smiles at us—I assume because we're adorable—and Priya seems to relax a bit. "Well. I'm impressed your mom didn't tell you, to be honest."

"Yeah," I say, thinking it over. "She kept hinting that she

thought you were, like, I don't know. *Finding yourself.* So that sort of makes more sense now."

"I guess it comes with the job," says Priya. "She's good at keeping people's secrets. My mom's too."

"Were you mad?"

She pauses a moment. "At first, yeah. But she was in a tough spot. I think she was afraid it would change how I saw things. Knowing my mom lied all those years. Alice was the only person who knew. Even Ben didn't get the whole story. And she was right to worry. For a little while, I *was* mad at my mom." The crack in Priya's voice makes me want to cry. "And I hated that."

She sniffs and shakes it off. "We found that Tasha had gone off the grid so I couldn't go through her. But there was a 'Class of' year on Julian's MIT sweatshirt. I used an old student directory to find him. It was weird at first, but we started talking on the phone. I was really excited when he got a job offer from U Chicago. We'd not only be able to meet, but actually get to know each other. Then moving threw a wrench in everything." Julian shoots her a sad smile.

"He's the one you were calling," I say. She catches my eye, curious, and I shrug. "There were a couple times. Little moments when I knew you weren't telling me something. Nick too."

"Oh," she says. "I'm sorry."

"Don't be."

"How is Nick?"

"Misses you," I say. "But don't worry. He'll take you back in a hot second. Just watch."

She laughs, then frowns suddenly, turning to Julian. "Wait a minute. I don't understand. How did you get here, exactly?"

"Oh," he says, shrinking into himself a little. He's definitely peculiar. But in a nice, nonstalkerish way, I realize now. "I worked it out that I could get to Chicago a few days early back in June. It was last minute, so I decided to surprise you. But then no one came to the door. I figured you'd already left."

For a moment, Priya looks stricken. "You were the one who rang the doorbell that day. Ben must have thought you were part of that group after him." She clenches her fists. "*Ugh!* You don't even look Indian!" She forces a calm breath and turns to me. "That reminds me. I'm half Armenian. Isn't that cool?"

"I mean, I'm from Jersey," says Julian. "So don't get too excited."

Priya chuckles softly, then tilts her head. "So . . . *How* did you end up here?"

Julian sits up in his chair, scratching at his stubble. "It was . . . a feeling, I guess. When you didn't come to the door or take my calls, I got worried. I almost asked you, Zan, that first day we met. Priya had told me so much about you, and I figured if anyone knew what was going on, it would be you. But when you said Ben and Priya were still living at the house, it sort of threw me off and I didn't know what to say. Seeing you at the zoo felt like a sign, but then you bolted. I tried to catch up with you, but you kept running away." He pauses. "In retrospect, I realize how creepy that probably was."

"Definitely creepy," I tell him. "But . . . it's all good." When he laughs, I see a little Priya in there. "Sorry I lied," I say. "I didn't want anyone to know I was snooping around."

"No, no," he says. "I'm glad you did. I was just confused enough to come back again today. I peeked in and rang the doorbell. The next thing I knew, Ben was staring at me through the window. Suddenly he's running out from the side of the house way down the block to his car. It seemed awfully strange, so I followed. I tailed him for a few errands and started to wonder if I was being paranoid. But I was sort of committed at that point. I lost him at a light by the entrance to the neighborhood. Drove around for a while . . ." He shrugs. "And then I spotted the Prius."

Logan walks into the living room, his phone in hand. "Literally every adult in our lives is driving to Indiana right now. Also, Zan's mom just texted," he says, reading something on the screen. "Apparently Anushka and Yasmine are hopping on the first flight to Chicago."

Beside me on the couch, Priya lets out a sigh, her eyes wet but fiercely bright. "Thanks for calling everyone, Logan."

He nods—"'Course"—and to me, Priya mouths *I like him*.

I smile, hit with another rush of emotion. Every time I look at Priya, my heart swells a little. It's almost like the world has returned to its axis. The ground is solid. *I'm* solid.

I'm sure there will be other heartaches—the kind the come out of nowhere, and knock me straight on my ass. I've lived enough to know there's not always a rainbow after the rain, and plenty of things happen for no reason at all. But maybe that's all the more reason to fucking *LIVE LAUGH LOVE!* or whatever. Because when you do, once in a while, you find a bright spot. The kind of love that just is. And that's something I never want to stop believing in.

Logan joins us on the couch, kissing the top of my head as he sits. A smile spreads across my face. We still have a lot to learn about each other, but something tells me he might be a bright spot, too.

"I think I need a minute outside," Priya says, standing. She turns to Julian. "Hey, um, don't feel like you have to stick around if you've got plans."

"Priya." He smirks. "Pretty sure I can clear my schedule tonight."

She nods, her face brightening, and I stack a few inspirational pillows to lean back into on the couch.

I look across the room, to where Priya has stopped at the threshold. She squares her shoulders and takes a breath before slipping out into the night. As I watch her go, relief settles over me, slowly, like a bedsheet floating down from the air. Through the open door, I hear crickets chirping steadily against the stillness. And when I look closely, even in the flashing lights, the fireflies still glow.

From: Priya Patel <priyawouldntwannabeya514@gmail.com>

To: Zan Martini <martiniweenybikini12@gmail.com>

Date: Fri, Aug 30, 8:32 am

Subject: I JOINED A CULT!!!!!!!!

I didn't join a cult. But where are you?? You'd think you were in some rural village in the middle of nowhere right now. Oh wait, you are! But no excuses. I was told you would have internet.

I heard you're running soccer practices with the girls? And teaching boxing? Maybe we should tweak our name a bit. GRETA: Girls Reaching Equality Through Ass-kicking. I guess that's kind of GRETAK, but I can run it by the board. I'm still a bit miffed with Anushka and Yasmine for letting you work out there FOR A YEAR. I appreciate you sticking around for the summer, but did you have to leave so early? In my time of need? I'm not sure you've fully grasped the irony of my being a high school super senior after all those college courses. For two core classes and a FREAKING GYM CREDIT!!!

Deeeep breaths All in all, I'm being very zen, Zan. Sleeping most nights, though sometimes I recruit Harr for a cuddle. Sean the Shrink seems to think I'm making progress anyway. I'm not sure I'll ever get used to the idea of sitting on a couch for a predetermined hour and deliberately talking about the worst parts of my life. I have to fight the urge to make jokes. Sean does not seem to know what to do with my jokes. But a lot of the time it feels really good. Healthy. Maybe even a little brave.

I've kept your room the same. Cleaner, though. I hope that's okay. Your mom and Whit keep telling me to make my own touches, but I like it the way it is. Makes me think of you. I can tell they're both missing you, like empty-nesters now. Well, except for me and Harr, and Bee, who Logan's brought over a few times (she's really taken to your brother, by the way— you're going to have to watch that boy).

I went by the SAIC dorms to visit Logan the other day. He's seriously going to love it there. He'll probably tell you this himself when you guys talk, AFTER you talk to me (I am a lady after all, and he a mere matey). You have to make him show you his new stuff. The one of you? There are no words. Speaking of words, have you said it yet? Just spit it out, woman. New Principle! #3-twenty-wherever we left off: Freaking tell people when you love them. It'll be the final step in the full eradication of your chronic boylessness.

What else? Harr says your dad has been playing bass again. This week he has a gig. :) And I know he's getting excited to come visit you. (I'm next!)

When I'm not busy missing you endlessly, I've been occupying my time with college application stuff. I think after this year, I'll be ready for a clean slate.

Nick is talking Yale Law after graduation, which would certainly sweeten the deal (at the moment Yale is back to number 1 on my list, but it changes daily). My dad says he'll visit wherever I go. And Yaz and Anushka are a short train ride from most of the schools I'm applying to, which will be nice—lots of slumber parties in my future.

Yasmine has been so amazing lately, helping with all the legal stuff. As for Anushka, I'm starting to think this year has kind of popped her whole People Are Mostly Good bubble. But she'll come around. I know I have. I was going through photos this morning and came across one from when they visited in May for my birthday. You and I took the picture of ourselves—making silly faces with tongues out. But behind us, you can just make out Yaz, Nush, your mom, and Whit all talking in your backyard. Something about that picture made me think of my mom. She would have loved to be there. She would be so glad to know I've got these women behind me.

So, Zans Christian Andersen (am I losing my nickname game?). If you're still figuring out this whole What Should I Do with My Life thing this time next year, think you could be figuring it out on the East Coast?

I'll probably pester you with a few more of these before I log off for the night. But for now, miss you absurd, stupid amounts, O Zanny Boy.

From: Priya Patel <priyawouldntwannabeya514@gmail.com>

To: Zan Martini <martiniweenybikini12@gmail.com>

Date: Fri, Aug 30, 8:34 am

Subject: CONSIDERING BUTT IMPLANTS!!!

Eh? Did that one hook ya? No?

From: Priya Patel <priyawouldntwannabeya514@gmail.com>

To: Zan Martini <martiniweenybikini12@gmail.com>

Date: Fri, Aug 30, 8:37 am

Subject: I REALLY COULD COOK METH YOU KNOW!

I might! You'll remember, I was very good in AP chem. C'EST POSSIBLE! You don't know! . . . Anything?

From: Priya Patel <priyawouldntwannabeya514@gmail.com>

To: Zan Martini <martiniweenybikini12@gmail.com>

Date: Fri, Aug 30, 8:40 am

Subject: THAT'S IT. I'M DONE WITH BACON!

Well, that one I'm sure you knew was a lie.

From: Zan Martini <martiniweenybikini12@gmail.com>

To: Priya Patel <priyawouldntwannabeya514@gmail.com>

Subject: Re: THAT'S IT. I'M DONE WITH BACON!

Ahaha I'm here! I'm not gonna to read all that yet because I need to see your face—DO NOT LOG OFF! Long story but we JUST got power back. The kids may fight me for this computer but so help me GOD I'm Skyping you now. Stand by!

From: Zan Martini <martiniweenybikini12@gmail.com>

To: Priya Patel <priyawouldntwannabeya514@gmail.com>

Date: Fri, Aug 30, 9:02 am

Subject: Re: THAT'S IT. I'M DONE WITH BACON!

Damn you, internet. Work! Trying again. Also, where'd you go? I would feel better with confirmation that you are still there. Are you still there???

From: Zan Martini <martiniweenybikini12@gmail.com>

To: Priya Patel <priyawouldntwannabeya514@gmail.com>

Date: Fri, Aug 30, 9:04 am

Subject: Re: THAT'S IT. I'M DONE WITH BACON!

YESSSS! It's ringing!!!!!! God we have so much to talk about. Are you there? Well? Are you???

From: Priya Patel <priyawouldntwannabeya514@gmail.com>

To: Zan Martini <martiniweenybikini12@gmail.com>

Date: Fri, Aug 30, 9:04 am

Subject: Re: THAT IS IT! I'M DONE WITH BACON!

Yeah, ZanaBanana.

I'm here.

Acknowledgments

I am an emotional person with the very best people and there aren't enough pages to express my thanks, but I will try.

Jennifer Mattson, my agent, thank you for believing in me, and this book, and for being generally lovely and hilarious. I can't imagine having a better person in my corner. What a journey it has been!

Donna Bray, you brilliant mind, you! Never have I had so much fun writing as I have going back and forth with you. I am in awe of your brain, and so grateful for the fact that you somehow managed to make this book feel even more "me" than I thought possible. Thank you for everything.

To the many publishing masterminds who helped make this thing a book, I am forever in your debt. Bethany Reis, Laura Harshberger, Michelle Taormina, Alison Donalty, Bess Braswell, Aubrey Churchward, Patty Rosati, Alessandra Balzer,

Tiara Kittrell, and the rest of the Harper team, thank you thank you thank you! The same goes for Taryn Fagerness, my foreign rights agent, and Philip Pascuzzo, for giving me the cover art of my dreams.

Huge weepy thanks to my amazing friends, from Cambridge to Bowdoin, Chicago to Brooklyn, who I thought of so much while writing this book. You are the people who grew alongside me at all different stages of life, and who always seem to click in no matter how long it's been or how far apart we may be. I am especially grateful to the very gentle friends who read early drafts (Alex, Rebecca, Sara, Abby, and Julia), and to the many more who were therapists and cheerleaders through this process. I'm so lucky to have you guys.

To Nicole Panteleakos, who I met, by some miracle, just weeks after moving to New York, both of us nannies on a playground in the right place at the right time. All I can say is, where on earth would I be without you? You taught me how to Twitter, and what a query was, and sat beside me in cafes across Brooklyn while we both scrapped old projects and tried again. I'm so happy to have gone down this road with you. I still can't believe we got offers on the same day.

To my whole extended family, thank you for your love, encouragement, and support. You are the best, and I have no doubt that the Loutzenhiser/Catt/Christo/Addisons will have significant influence over the sales of this book. (Also, Gram, I still use my LOL mug from you every day at my desk, and consider it to be my writing good luck charm.)

Little Peter, my much-cooler-than-me teenage brother, thank you for being such a great kid, and for putting up with the never-ending book discussions. I hope we never stop watching movies and playing board games, and I fully expect you to continue keeping me relevant as I get older.

Big Peter, thank you for being a friend and for all those trips to the Inn.

To my dad, who is the weirdest and the funniest, thank you for letting me treat you like a human dictionary growing up. Your opinion means more to me than just about anyone's, and though I was too embarrassed to tell you back then, your belief in this book was enough to make me cry.

To my mom, exuberant co-mermaid and Louise to my Thelma, thank you for always being the voice in my head, cheering me on and propelling me forward. I try so hard to be like you. Most people see all the ways something might not work. You always see how it could.

To my husband, Bobby, who has long since accepted seeing himself in my work (because how could I resist? He is just too damn charming and wonderful): there is no thank you big enough. During all those years nannying and working odd jobs, you called me your "lottery ticket." It would be my greatest honor to one day make you my trophy husband.

And of course, thank you, dear reader! Without you, all of this would just be ink on a page.